W9-BTD-126

GRANDGHOST

A Selection of Recent Titles by Nancy Springer

GRANDGHOST

Nancy Springer

This first world edition published 2018
in Great Britain and the USA by
SEVERN HOUSE PUBLISHERS LTD of
Eardley House, 4 Uxbridge Street, London W8 7SY.
Trade paperback edition first published
in Great Britain and the USA 2018 by
SEVERN HOUSE PUBLISHERS LTD.

British Library Cataloguing in Publication Data
A CIP catalogue record for this title is available from the British Library.

ISBN-13: 978-0-7278-8792-4 (cased)
ISBN-13: 978-1-84751-914-6 (trade paper)
ISBN-13: 978-1-78010-970-1 (e-book)

All Severn House titles are printed on acid-free paper.

Severn House Publishers support the Forest Stewardship Council™ [FSC™],
the leading international forest certification organisation.
All our titles that are printed on FSC certified paper carry the FSC logo.

Typeset by Palimpsest Book Production Ltd.,
Falkirk, Stirlingshire, Scotland.
Printed and bound in Great Britain by
TJ International, Padstow, Cornwall.

ONE

I answered the phone on the third ring. 'Hello?'

'Beverly, it's Kim.'

My Big Apple agent. At once, my heart rate doubled. Inanely, I asked, 'How are you?'

'Fine. Beverly, we need to talk.'

This meant *she* did the talking, in her rapid-fire New York voice. Listening made my eyes feel old and weak and watery behind my trifocals, because she was talking about my last-ditch effort, my rather desperate very best try, and she was saying it wasn't good enough. She was rejecting it. Not that I couldn't handle rejection, but by my own agent? So much worse than being rejected by an editor.

My heartbeat slowed to grow sluggish with despair. Leaning more and more heavily against the countertop while wishing for a chair, I stood in the kitchen (necessarily, as I still have a telephone that is fastened to the wall), but peering through the Florida room into the studio, past the easel, I could see outside via the picture window. I could see the sunshine, the green mimosa fronds and some Gulf fritillaries, long-winged subtropical butterflies, hovering orange over yellow-and-lavender lantana blossoms. That glimpse of my teeming, subtropical backyard helped me clear my throat and speak.

'So you don't think it's marketable.'

'Beverly, yet another rehashing of a rather grim Grimms' fairy tale? No, I don't think so, no matter how beautifully you illustrated it.'

So much for a year's work. Hanging on, I managed to protest, 'But I don't think anyone else has done *The Six Swans* lately.'

'For good reason. The princess burning at the stake while she hands out jackets she wove from nettles? It's brutal and too hard to understand.'

As a child, I had loved brutal stories that were hard to understand, but it was no use saying so. 'Would you send it along to

Benson anyway?' The one remaining editor with whom I had established a working relationship.

'Not unless you can get it to me in digital format. Benson's art director is not going to deal with a stack of paper. None of them will anymore.'

'All righty, I'll see what I can do, Kim.' Thus, mendaciously, I ended the one-sided conversation with all the gung-ho I could muster, but *without* asking whether anyone from any publisher's art department had put out feelers in my direction. I didn't ask because I already knew the answer. It was a big fat hairy NO.

Not that anyone would spell it out to me, but each day more and more I was reading the writing on the wall: publishers didn't want me to illustrate their picture books anymore. Throughout my adult life I had assumed I would keep doing what I did best until I died, but I was wrong. Starkly put, I had gone out of style, no matter how versatile my touch with my acrylics, my ability to render anything from watercolor effects to impasto. My expert impressionistic realism was out. Phthalo was in. Two-dimensional bling was in. Slick, quick stuff extruded from a computer like plastic from a manufacturing machine was in.

'Goddamn everything,' I told my kitchen fiercely to prevent my hot eyes from leaking tears. 'Goddamn technology.' I focused on the venerable black Bakelite rotary phone for sympathy; with its circular dial, it seemed to have a face of sorts, or at least a big nose. 'It's not like my social security is going to cover fancy software or a scanner, much less, whatchamacallit . . .' I knew exactly what I meant by whatchamacallit, which I would need to replace my dial-up modem if I were ever to send digital images at the speed New York required, but I couldn't think of the damn name, and when I have brain blips like that I get really scared I'm going to be like my mother, who had Alzheimer's all the way for her last couple of decades. I mean, I had already lost enough without losing my mind. I'd lost my waistline, my self-esteem, my eyebrows, my sense of well-being, my best friend aka my husband . . .

I felt my eyes go from hot to scalding, but it had been two years since Jim had died – throat cancer misdiagnosed until it was too late – and dammit, I had cried enough. Rather than accrue any more weepy time, I opted for hard labor, turning to slam out of the kitchen into the heat of the summer day, grab a shovel from the garage and go dig up some more bricks, which for some curious but baffling reason were almost as plentiful in the ground around my place as armadillo holes.

Even in my post-rejection depression, with heavy canvas work gloves on my hands as I pushed a wheelbarrow across my jungle of a yard, I loved this place, gift of Jim's life insurance money. I loved the fresh flower-scented air, the wide sky, the towering longleaf pines and the soaring cumulus clouds and, small in the midst of it all, the little concrete-block bunker of a house that was now my refuge from ever having to survive blizzards and Seasonal Affective Disorder again. My Florida home's picture windows and terrazzo floors, all the rage back in the fifties, combined with excellent natural light, made the best studio space I'd ever had. Too bad my career seemed to be over.

Spotting the burnt-ochre corner of a brick sticking up from the sandy yard, I stopped to dig it out and heft it into the wheelbarrow, my idea being that someday, with less interruption from bricks and fire ant hills, invasive privet and wisteria determined to conquer the world, I might have a lawn of sorts. The bricks scattered everywhere had gifted me with hours of pleasant, ghoulish speculation about the previous occupants of the house. What the heck had they been doing – throwing the things at each other?

I noticed a chalky white oyster shell, detritus of some long-ago cookout, and I picked it up and pocketed it. If it cleaned up nicely, I would put it in a shoebox with other found objects I was collecting for no reason.

A bit farther on, attracted by a scattering of doll daisies, I saw an area fairly bristling with bricks, and I welcomed the discovery. Grunt work was just what I needed right now. I attacked with the spade, dislodging whole bricks and broken bricks, heaving them into the wheelbarrow, never mind sweat and dirt . . .

'Neighbor,' a voice twanged like a banjo from behind me, 'what the Sam Hill y'all doing out here in the heat of the day?' By 'y'all' she meant 'you.' The ubiquitous Southern 'you-all' had encroached from second person plural to include, quite illogically, second person singular.

As I needed to roll my eyes, I did so before I showed my face, before I stood up and turned around to answer the speaker.

'Hi, Wilma Lou. It's only about ninety.' Same as her age. A skinny, hunched and peering wrinkly person, my nearest and, indeed, my only neighbor, she spotted movement in her yard or mine like a chicken hawk. I avoided her when I could, because she sold religion and Avon products with great and equal fervor.

But today she was carrying neither a tract nor an Avon catalog; she lifted a knobby forefinger in admonition. 'Y'all's just asking for heatstroke!'

'You're out here with me, and you're not falling over yet.' However, my hands felt even hotter than the rest of me, so I pulled off my work gloves and tossed them into the wheelbarrow.

'Well, ain't y'all afraid of snakes hiding in them bricks?'

Everyone I met in this area seemed to be innately terrified of snakes. The answer was no; I trusted snakes to scoot when I came klunking around, but Wilma Lou didn't give me a chance to answer. 'Ain't y'all got no kin can do that kind of work for you? I need chores done around my house, my children or my grand-children take care of it.' She wore a spotless print shirtwaist dress as always, and she gave my grubby shorts and T-shirt an accusa-tory glance. 'Ain't y'all got no family?'

'Not here.' My two hard-working daughters, ages forty-three and thirty-nine, lived in New York and New Jersey respectively.

'Your grandchildren ain't nearby?'

'My grandchildren are non-existent.'

To my own surprise, I sounded astringent, almost acid, and I felt a veritable alligator of bitterness bite down on my heart. All right, I was in a funk because of *The Six Swans*, but something deeper and more fiery in my chest demanded my attention.

Apparently, Wilma Lou noticed nothing sharper than usual in my Yankee accent. Instead of bristling, she merely blinked, uncom-prehending. 'What for kind of grandchildren y'all got?'

'I don't have any. But when I phone my friends, they tell me all about theirs.'

'Well, ain't that nice.'

I did not find it nice, not at all, and it kept me from staying in contact with those friends the way I should, but a lucky brain spasm saved me from retorting. I exclaimed, 'HughesNet!'

'Say what?'

'HughesNet. That's the stupid word I couldn't think of. Excuse me, Wilma Lou, I think I hear my phone ringing.' This was a spontaneous fabrication allowing me to flee to the house, jogging.

'Grandchildren,' I muttered along the way, feeling an odd pang still stinging my heart. 'Oh, what the hell. In another ten years I wouldn't be able to remember their names anyhow, if my mind is slip-sliding away as it seems to be.'

I washed sweat off my face at the kitchen sink, had a drink of water and then, feeling a need for comfort, I ambled into the studio. The best thing about my life was the way my job gave me relief from Wilma Lou or almost any other kind of bad news, personal or global. My best personal gift was the way I could rest in my own art. Not that professional-quality painting wasn't hard work; it most certainly was. Sometimes it felt impossibly difficult. Yet the joy and challenge of painting made everything else seem dismissible, even when I was just visiting my vocation, as now.

I relaxed in my favorite multicolored, overstuffed chair to spend some time with my latest baby, the unfinished portrait on the easel. I had started it practically the moment I had come home from the post office after mailing *The Six Swans* to Kim. Hoping for a final success yet anticipating the rejection that would be one too many, I had begun my rebellion ahead of time: a life-sized depiction of the head and shoulders of a child. An imaginary child, approximately age five, she would be a lovely, idealized, wide-eyed little girl such as Jessie Willcox Smith used to portray, and I fully intended to give her blond hair, violet eyes like Elizabeth Taylor's, and clothe her in the prettiest ruffled, lacy, lavender dress I could imagine.

During the past forty-some years, I had illustrated picture books with lop-eared bunnies wearing jackets, chipmunks living in houses, skunks going to school and badgers sick in bed, and parakeets, caterpillars, bumblebees . . . I had anthropomorphized just about every conceivable kind of animal, and enjoyed it. But for the most part publishers and art directors had not allowed me to depict actual human beings. Political correctness intervened: supposedly, children could deal with talking alpacas more readily than they could with cultural diversity.

Screw all that. To hell with politics and profit margins, and if publishers didn't want me anymore, fine. In my dotage I would paint whatever I pleased.

I leaned back where I sat, contemplating the translucent underpainting of thin sepia, the extent of what I had done so far on my little girl. With her vestigial eyes she contemplated me in return. I smiled at her, and my mind toggle-switched into its default mode for the studio, starting to drift like a heart-shaped pointer on the Ouija board of my psyche, processing data and making surprise connections. Kim, my agent, thumbs down, no sale. No more career. It would be all loss and no gain from here on, except maybe in regard to my weight. The kind of apron I had, nobody wanted. My belly felt like a baby on my lap when I sat down. It felt that way right now. It felt good. Screw skinny people, especially shallow skinny people like Jim's sister, Gayle, my socialite-in-law, who wouldn't believe this place where I lived now – no shopping malls, no theaters, no bookstores/coffee shops, no art galleries. For me, no . . . future?

'What are people my age supposed to do?' I whispered rhetorically.

Devote themselves to their grandchildren, that was what.

But I had none. Damn everything, what was I myself supposed to do?

The little girl on the easel, inchoate in thin raw sepia but already quite defined and alive to me, gazed back at me fondly; as the creation dearest to my heart right now, she *was* me because of the way she had issued out of me. And, a sudden blush of my heart told me sweetly, she was also my daughter Maurie when she was about five, and Cassie – yes, she was both of my children as I remembered them from decades ago.

'You're my kin,' I told her, and then my Ouija-board heart and mind glided like the two wings of a butterfly slantwise into artist's prerogative. 'You're my first grandchild,' I told her. 'My very first. And after you, I can have as many as I want, and we can all live together.'

There. I'd get along financially with Social plus increasingly pitiful royalties plus rent money from the house I'd left behind in Montclair, New Jersey, and I knew what I'd be doing with myself: painting imaginary grandchildren. I'd take care of my future in my own kooky way.

Feeling centered and content, I stood up to go explore the kitchen for something by way of supper. 'You can help me think of a name for you,' I told the little girl as I passed her. 'OK? We'll work on you in the morning.' Without feeling the least bit silly, I blew her a kiss as I left.

After supper, the tilted golden light of sunset lured me back outside. Seen between the tall, balletic bare trunks of the longleaf pines, sunset's slow-waltzing horizontal display seemed more glorious every day, as if it were growing closer. At such times I feel a sense of deity, not as creator, but as the sunset itself, and the skein of ibis crossing it, and the trees it gilded, and the grass, and I suppose the entire universe.

I guess I am a pantheist of sorts, which feels better than being the uncomfortable agnostic I was for many years. My parents had made half-hearted efforts to raise me Christian, but I wasn't having it. Crucifixes – those with carved figures of Jesus in agony on them – made me physically ill, as did the Sunday School descriptions of what he went through, and I could not get past my horror. Since when did torture signify love? Besides, the more I thought about life after death, the less it made any logical sense. I gave up on organized religion, but throughout my teenage years and beyond, spiritual feelings wouldn't let me alone. Now, at age sixty-seven, I still could not believe in my terrifying childhood God, but I definitely believed in something that swelled my heart when I saw the sunset.

As the bright clouds lingered, I walked down the backyard to get my shovel and wheelbarrow and put them away in the garage. But the old-gold afterglow on the bricks seduced me to pull a few more out of the ground. With sundown, the day had cooled to eighty-ish, a breeze had sprung up from thunderheads moving in from the Gulf and altogether I felt motivated to continue digging bricks for as long as daylight lasted.

As I pulled brick after brick out of the sandy ground, I realized that this time something was different. These were not just a few bricks scattered on my yard's surface. There seemed to be layers of them and, during the next half hour or so, I dug quite a hole.

Dusk deepened, fireflies started their little light show and a mosquito homed in on my sweaty arm; I swatted it. I straightened up to stretch my aching back and take a look around me, thinking of quitting for the night. It was getting pretty dark, almost too dark to see. But not quite. I noticed something: a curve of chalky white, deep in my excavation.

Curious, I pulled off my work gloves to explore it with my fingers. It felt like bone, interestingly curved. Maybe I could use it as the matrix for a mobile or something. Careful not to break it, I rooted around it until it loosened, then drew it out and held it up. In art school I'd had a lot of anatomy classes . . .

My eyes widened and I muttered, 'No way.'

It was getting too dark to really see, I told myself. I couldn't be sure. Bone in hand, I headed back toward the house. Just outside the kitchen door, I turned on the porch light to have a better look.

'No *way*,' I exclaimed, this time in protest. But nothing I could say was going to change what I held up to the light in both hands.

Gracefully tapered and shaped in a way that is unlike any other bone in any vertebrate I knew of, it was a human collarbone.

Yet it was too small.

Instantly, I rejected the thought that came to mind; instantly, I doubted myself. Who did I think I was? Some kind of expert? It had been a long time since college, and I had to be mistaken, the way my brain had been burping and farting lately. The bone was nothing, just part of a raccoon or something.

But what if it wasn't?

I made up my mind. In the kitchen on top of the refrigerator was a large flashlight. Casketing the bone in the tin breadbox built into the old countertop, I grabbed the light and headed back out to the darkest place in my backyard.

I managed to illuminate my excavation by angling the flashlight at a downward slant on a stand I shimmed out of the inevitable bricks. Then I got down on my hands and elbows, my butt in the air and my head in the hole, to ease a few more bricks out of there, digging with my fingertips.

Near where the collarbone had been, I found what seemed to be lightweight print fabric, looking gray with dirt in the beam of the flashlight but perhaps formerly yellow or white, and blobbed or dotted with what once might have been printed roses.

Lifting the scrap of fabric, I saw a skeletal rib.

I laid the fabric back down where it was, then let it alone. Didn't move it. Mosquitoes had gathered around me like clog dancers at a buffet, but I didn't make a move to drive them away. Let them suck my blood; that would be just fine and dandy under the circumstances. I felt shivery even in the heat, as if I were sunsick, and I wanted to run away someplace and hide, yet even more I wanted to stay and dig up – more. Just more. I could not allow my mind to get very specific about what I might find next.

I put the fabric back in place and started working in the opposite direction, above where the collarbone had been.

After removing a few more bricks, I found what I dreaded and expected.

I uncovered the forehead, the eye sockets and cheekbones. That was all. That was enough. In a way, it was too much. I couldn't go on. The small skull looked straight up at me like a pale, empty-eyed face from a very dark place, and I stared at it even as I pulled back, got to my feet and stood like a pillar of salt, my heartbeat drumming out the moments it took me to break away, grab the flashlight and run for the house to call 911.

TWO

Nicholas Crickens, at age twenty-three the youngest deputy in the Skink County Sheriff's Department, found himself the first to arrive at the scene and could not believe his good luck. It was not every day that a call went out for response to a 10-54d – a dead body.

The reporting party had requested 10-40 – no lights and sirens, but he slewed into the unpaved driveway at speed anyhow, throwing up sand and pine straw with his tires. Even if he hadn't seen the number plain as day on the mailbox, he would have figured he was in the right place, because it looked like every single light in the little ranch house was turned on, which was what people tended to do when there had been trouble in the night.

He parked his cruiser on the scraggly lawn and headed toward the house. The old woman came out to meet him under the porch light. Not *old* old – not like leaning on a walker or anything – but

old as in short and dumpy with jowls and the beginnings of a
turkey neck. She was wearing a red waterproof jacket in the ninety-
degree heat and she looked shook up – no, 10-22 that, disregard.
She wasn't too shook up to give him a good once-over. As he
strode up to her, he got the feeling she was patting him down with
her eyes and her mind. Intense eyes and intense mind, studying
him as if she were memorizing him.

'Ma'am, are y'all all right?' he called as he approached her.

Looking him straight in the face, she raised her eyebrows, or
at least she flexed the place on her forehead where eyebrows should
have been.

'Are y'all in danger of any kind?' Nicholas clarified. 'I'm
supposed to ask when I respond to a call about a dead body.'

'Oh, for goodness' sake.' Her voice was soft but not in a Southern
way. 'I told them and told them it's not a dead body as such. It's
a skeleton.'

The 'as such,' plus her Yankee accent, plus the fact that she
was wearing shoes and socks instead of flip-flops or cowboy boots,
all combined to inform Nicholas that she was not from Skink
County or anyplace close by. Therefore, he had no idea whether
she might be a Democrat or an Episcopalian or some other frightening sort of mutation. Through her picture window he could see
the front-room wall inside her house, and she had it covered with
silly pictures of loopy-faced caterpillars, foxes wearing tuxedos,
waltzing rabbits and such. Weirdest decor he'd ever seen. Handle
with care, he thought. Possible 10-96: mental person.

He said, 'I 'spect we ain't got a code for skeletons – least none
I can recall. Where's it at?'

'Around back. You have a flashlight?'

He did, of course, in his belt, and he held it in his fist beside
his head, proper cop-style, as he followed her down the yard to a
wheelbarrow piled full of bricks, beyond which he saw more bricks
and a shovel strewn around a sizeable hole in the ground.

'In there,' she said, pointing.

A person would think the replicas he had seen on twenty-three
Halloweens would prepare him to look at a skeleton, Nicholas
reasoned with himself, but apparently they did not. The white
sheen of the partially exposed skull gave him such a jolt that he
blurted, 'Is it real?'

'*She* seems to be distressingly real.'

'Y'all think that was a *girl*, ma'am?' Skeletons weren't supposed to be little girls. They were supposed to be big and scary, not small and terrifying.

'Yes, because she appears to be wearing a dress, although, of course, I could be mistaken.'

What now? Follow procedure. Doing that, automatically Nicholas started his report. 'Um, your name, please, ma'am?'

'Beverly Vernon.'

Getting out his notebook, Nicholas realized he was rattled, thinking he could write and hold a flashlight at the same time. He had to make a mental note: Beverly Vernon, as he put the notebook away again. Then he couldn't think what else to do. Get the yellow tape, secure the crime scene, but where exactly might that be? Just around the skeleton or the whole damn backyard? Nicholas had no idea; he was trained to deal with more recently deceased persons.

Headlight beams swept across him, and the Skink County Sheriff's cruiser, having driven down the yard, pulled to a stop a few feet away, headlights on. Nicholas felt illuminated and relieved. 'Looks like it was a little girl, Chief,' he said as the older man of far more girth stepped to the graveside – might as well call it a graveside – with his flashlight raised like a weapon.

The chief took one look at the bones and one look at Mrs Vernon and barked at her, 'How'd y'all know to dig here?'

'Who said I did? I merely wanted to remove these pertinacious bricks from my property.'

Nicholas saw that Mrs Vernon was giving the sheriff the visual pat-down same way she had done to him and figured the chief might not like it. 'Boss, howsabout if I take Mrs Vernon somewhere else to get her statement?'

'Y'all just go ahead and do that, Crickens,' grumbled the sheriff. 'We ain't even really identified that these here ain't animal bones, and I don't suppose y'all called for the coroner yet?'

'No, sir.' Damn, he should have thought of that. 'Please come with me, Mrs Vernon.' He led her away as two more vehicles pulled in, one state cop and one from the next county over, as was not unusual when there was nothing better for law enforcement to do. 'In your house would be best, if that's OK, ma'am. Next folks to arrive are likely to be reporters.'

She uttered a few expletives he wouldn't have expected from a lady her age. And when they got inside, he saw not only walls covered with those weird pictures – ducks in dresses, cats having their hair done, like that – but also 3D paper birds and stuff hanging on loops of yarn from the ceiling of the Florida room, and on its table, bowls full of plastic milk carton caps, Mardi Gras beads, pens and pencils, all sorts of inexplicable junk. So when Mrs Vernon sat down with him at the table, Nicholas decided to take it real easy with her. Just in case she really was a 10-96.

He requested and took careful notes of her full name, phone number and address, then ventured in a conversational way, 'Y'all lived here long, ma'am?' That was the last question he got to ask for a while; she talked him an earful. No, she'd only moved here a year ago, after her husband had died and she'd decided she wanted to live in Florida, but what she called the real Florida, not tourist-trap Florida. Being self-employed, she could work wherever, although she hadn't known then they might not *want* her to work anymore, which made no sense because she painted excellent illustrations, if she did say so herself, not goofy stuff that looked as if it was done with cat snot. Both of her daughters had followed her into the art field, at least at first. Maurie, who was forty-three and married to a lawyer, had started out teaching art at a prep school but now taught history at Cornell and was a published essayist as well. For some reason, Maurie and her husband did not have children, and Cassie, who would be turning forty in a few months, wasn't even married, except to her business. A true entrepreneur, she had opened an ambitious art gallery in upstate New Jersey, but had been not been able to make it financially, even though she lived over the store, until she turned it into a trendy Wi-Fi, coffee and gluten-free muffins cafe with the work of emergent artists displayed on the walls. The woman said she talked with her daughters once a week, on Sundays usually. She wondered what they would say when they heard about the skeleton in the backyard. It was an hour later where they lived, in the Eastern Time Zone, and she didn't think either of them would appreciate it if she called and woke them up now to tell them about it.

'No, I guess not,' Deputy Nicholas Crickens agreed, even though he didn't agree. A person should be able to call kin anytime, not just when convenient, and it didn't take a freaking genius to see that Mrs Vernon was either lonely or upset or half a bubble off plumb – maybe all three, what with that freaky-bright stare of hers plus the compulsive way she had been yakking, although she didn't seem to want attention from just anyone, especially not the media.

Which made Nick think. 'It's a wonder your phone ain't ringing off the hook by now. I mean, you got a landline?'

'I do. It's been here forever. But it's not listed in my name.'

'I hope them news buzzards don't manage to sniff it out anyway.'

Mrs Vernon shrugged, standing with her back to him, looking out a window at the ruckus in the backyard; Nicholas could hear from inside the house the drone of the generator powering several strong lamps lighting the scene bright as day.

'What a circus! They put a tent over her.' Mrs Vernon sounded surprised.

The skeleton, she meant. 'Yes, ma'am, in case it rains.' Which was a no-brainer; it rained practically every day. 'It's going to take a while to exhume her properly.' Nicholas had decided by now that this woman was nuttier than squirrel turds, but probably not dangerous. 'Mrs Vernon, would you please explain to me what for y'all were out there digging bricks on such a hot day like today was?'

Turning to face him, she sighed, peering into her empty coffee mug. 'That's simple. I was feeling a bit wrought.'

'A bit what?'

'Wrought. In a temper. In a state of high dudgeon. I needed to fling bricks around.'

'You were pissed off?'

She smiled, even laughed a little. 'Very well put, Deputy. Yes, I was quite pissed off.'

'How come?'

She sighed, although she still smiled at him wistfully, and she said, 'For personal reasons I'd rather keep to myself, Deputy. Now, are you sure you won't have a cup of coffee?'

It looked like it was going to be a long night, so he said yes, he would.

After the nice young policeman left, I locked all the doors, drew all the blinds and turned out all of the lights in the house as a deterrent to reporters. Deputy Crickens had told me that vans and cars full of them were lined up along the easement of the road in front of my house, and that one of his colleagues blocking my driveway was the only thing keeping them away from the crime scene and thus, indirectly, away from me. Once the cops were finished processing my yard, then I would be under siege.

However, it looked as if the cops still had plenty to do. After assessing the muddle of lights, vehicles and people in my backyard, I took a prescription sleeping pill, deployed my earplugs and went straight to bed. I'd had enough.

But despite earplugs and the pill, I woke up at sunrise. Becoming an early bird was apparently one of the many annoying side effects of getting older, along with undependable memory, thinning eyelashes, rosacea pimples on my nose, skin tabs on my neck and athlete's foot in my armpits, where it didn't belong, like the hair on my upper lip.

I made a face at myself in the bathroom mirror, got dressed in a fresh T-shirt, green polyester slacks, matching froggy-print socks – I love novelty socks – and my most comfortable Skechers. I managed to locate my glasses without too much difficulty. Then, with stiff, arthritic knees (another annoyance), I limped to the kitchen window to see whether the authorities still occupied my backyard.

Yes, although fewer in number, they did. But at least they were colorful about it, and geometric, working within a square of yellow crime-scene tape secured to T-posts, beneath a bright red pyramid of canvas, in the open space beneath which I could see the hole in the ground as a lozenge of darkness considerably longer than before.

Naturally, I had to check it out. I am, after all, an artist, meaning that my inner child lived on in my aging body, making me prone to depression but also to compulsive curiosity. Heading out into the relative coolness of early morning, I breathed deeply of air no warmer than eighty degrees as I strode down my yard toward the excavating strangers – one of whom stopped me at the yellow tape. 'Sorry, ma'am, you can't approach beyond this point.'

'What?' Just a bit slow in the morning, as usual, I recognized him as the no-neck sheriff who had taken over the night before.

I peered up at his pugnacious face. 'This is my land,' I reminded him. 'I could have you arrest yourself for trespassing.'

As too often happened, my sense of humor failed. The sheriff began to look heated, although not yet by the ambient temperature. 'You think I want to stand out here all night taking charge of your skeleton?'

My skeleton? That one was arguably still inside my body. But with a skittery lurch of my mind, I recognized that I did, indeed, feel a sense of ownership regarding the one buried in my yard. I demanded, 'Do you have any idea yet who she is?'

'Who she *was*? Can't comment on an investigation ain't barely begun yet.' He flapped a porky hand toward what he refused to let me see, apparently to point out two young men poking around between twine that had been strung to form a grid covering the grave. My backyard find was being handled like an archaeological dig.

Another person, a woman kneeling by the grave, called across to me, 'Ma'am, would you happen to know what year this house was built?'

'1957.' I peered at her much as I peer at everyone, I suppose, taking her in: brunette, tall, taupe skin not tanned but naturally tending toward olive; some Apalachee heritage, maybe. Her strong-boned face struck me as beautiful because of its faultless symmetry, but she was not young, merely younger than I was.

The sheriff turned around, not to look at her but to glare. She didn't seem to mind or even notice, continuing her conversation with me.

'They used bricks for filler back then,' she told me.

'No wonder the damn yard is full of bricks!'

'Yeah, well, they tend to work their way to the surface.' Her accent, while relaxed, was not drawling Southern. 'They could have been piled on this body any time since then, but the extent of decay—'

'Doctor Wengleman,' interrupted the sheriff with some force, 'we ain't discussing this case with Mrs Varner.'

'Mrs *Vernon*,' I corrected him. And then said to her, 'What about the design on the dress fabric? Can you date that?'

She lifted her eyebrows in approbation. 'Now, that's an idea! And the fabric itself—'

'Don't need no talking about right here and now!' interrupted the sheriff with some force, glowering at the woman, then turning on me. 'Mrs, um, Vernon, if you don't want me all over you like flies on a rump roast, I suggest you git back into your house and stay there, take your phone off the hook and don't talk to no reporters when they come knocking neither.'

And here I had been going to offer him a cup of freshly brewed coffee. Screw that. Rolling my eyes, I obeyed him only for reasons of my own. I wanted to write down the tall, tawny woman's name before I forgot it.

Back indoors, I scrawled it with a Sharpie on a scrap of origami paper. Dr Wengleman. There. But where could I put it so that it wouldn't get away from me in the mysterious way that my notes to self often did? After some thought, I placed it under one of my many fridge magnets: rainbows, butterflies, daisies – this one happened to be a hummingbird. Then I stoked my old four-cup coffee maker and fired it up, got myself a bowl of Special K for breakfast, and while I ate, I studied the rather slender phone book serving Skink County. Sure enough, Dr Wengleman turned out to be the county coroner. I planned to contact her the minute she got back to her office, where presumably the sheriff couldn't tell her what to do.

Meanwhile, a cup of coffee and my studio awaited me . . .

Or so I thought, before I heard the kitchen screen door squeak open. Even before she rapped and her reedy voice called, 'Beverly? It's Wilma Lou,' I knew who it was. The media lined up across a drainage ditch from my front yard couldn't get to me, not yet, but apparently the cops had neglected to station an officer to keep my nosy neighbor from intruding.

After arranging a smile on my face, I let her in. 'Coffee?' I offered without much enthusiasm. OK, I had moved to the Bible Belt of my own free will, and OK, I got along fine with most people here, and they didn't have to know I rolled my eyes at their bumper stickers. But for Wilma Lou I made an exception: I didn't want to get along, no thank you. Wilma Lou prayed aloud on every possible occasion; if she dropped a package of eggs, she stood and prayed that they would not be broken. Heck, she prayed over road kill. At Halloween she prayed over the children as she gave them lollipops wrapped in Bible verses. And I couldn't seem to keep her from sticking her long nose into my business. She just plain irritated me.

All hunched and earnest, ignoring my offer of coffee, she scuttled into my personal space and laid a twiggy hand on my arm, peering up at me. 'Beverly, is it true what I heared – they found a body in y'alls's backyard?'

Grabbing on to me worse than a wisteria vine, she brought out every bit of my innate perversity. I stiffened. 'How did you hear such a thing?'

'Well, it's true, ain't it?'

'Was it someone you knew?' I gave her a pretty hard counter-peer, but she didn't retreat. I should have known I couldn't faze her that easily. Wistfully, I imagined having someone else – maybe a nice, quiet drug dealer – as a neighbor. 'How long have you lived over there, Wilma Lou?'

'Since my wedding day in 1956, and my husband put the brick facing on it for me, unlike this house which Papa was building at the same time, and I ain't hardly never had nothing but good Christian neighbors over here.' Evidently, she meant this as an appeal to my better nature, for she grasped me with her other hand as well. 'Y'all *are* a Christian, ain't y'all?'

'No, not really.'

She gasped, let go of me and jumped back as if dropping a rattlesnake. I wasn't expecting such a reaction; I had answered her question gently enough.

'But . . . then . . .' she stammered, squeaking. 'But then what *are* y'all?' Her horrified gaze scanned the children's book art on the walls of my house wildly, as if she had just realized it conveyed some dread significance.

That did it. My perverse sense of humor took over. 'Zen Shinto,' I told her promptly. 'I worship animals. Are you sure you won't have some fresh coffee?'

'N–n–no, thank you, I better go.' She scuttled toward the door in reverse as if afraid to turn her back on me. Once outside, she blurted, 'I'll pray for y'all!'

'You go ahead and do that. No offense taken. Have a good day,' I called after her as she fled toward her property line. I imagined I wouldn't find her on my side of that line again anytime soon, and my mood improved immediately.

Smiling, I filled my favorite mug, then headed for my studio.

THREE

As I've tried to say before, I am one of those fortunate individuals for whom going to work gives more than it takes away, completes me more than it depletes me, builds me up more than it wears me down. I go to work for recreation, to create again, to restore myself.

So I walked into my studio to look at the portrait awaiting me on the easel, the one I had just started. But when I saw it, such a shock gobsmacked me that the earth seemed to quake. I backed off, set my mug of coffee down on the table so I wouldn't drop it, and plopped on to a chair so I wouldn't fall over.

What I observed was impossible. The painting was mine. As uniquely my own as my handwriting. Every brushstroke testified that it was mine, yet I didn't remember having done it that way at all. My concept remained clear in my imagination, but the portrait . . . instead of being a classic oval, the face seemed pinched at the top and square at the bottom. The eyes I intended to be wide and innocent still greeted me with their vestigial gaze, but were now deep-set and shadowy under straight brows – no way had I made her eyebrows so straight! And I knew I had painted a soft mouth suggesting just a wisp of a smile, not a grim one as uncompromising as the brow line.

Yet it was not as if some vandal had broken into my studio and messed around with my work. Everything was just as I had left it. The portrait on my easel, all the brushstrokes ineluctably mine and not a single one added – the painting remained just as I had left it, but eerily different.

I stood up. 'You are supposed to be my *granddaughter*,' I whispered to the sepia face in protest, and the sound of my own voice broke me wide open. 'Please tell me I'm not losing my freaking *mind*!' I strode over to the easel and reached up to rip the painting off it, tear it to shreds, trash it and start over. But, just in time, wisdom of experience overruled me. This peculiar artist's wisdom is to be found, I'm sure, in painters, poets, songwriters, creative people of all sorts everywhere, and the wisdom is: when the work starts to push back, be humble. Submit. Let the unconscious mind take over. Sometimes it knows better than you do.

Evidently, my first grandchild was not going to be exactly what I expected. And wasn't that a rule of life? What could be more true of a real child?

My life-sized child was still a life-sized child.

Did I want my grandchild to be real or didn't I?

'Whoa,' I muttered. 'I'm crossing a big, fat, hairy line here.'

I hesitated a few moments longer. But finally, because my fingers itched to paint, I shrugged off my misgivings, sipped my coffee, then started to sort through my paints, mulling over my palette: a hint of pale carmine for the light areas of blond hair, a trio of indigo, violet and viridian for the scrumbled background, raw umber and cadmium yellow and cobalt blue . . .

I planned where my darkest darks and lightest lights had to go, then started, as always, with the deepest shadows, laying in broad strokes along the neck and one side of the face and nose, obediently following the mysteriously modified contours. I set off the head with the beginnings of background, going very gently around the hair, trying not to be sudden. I laid in the medium planes of the face and the buttery sheen of the hair, toning down the golden yellows with just a hint of blue. And I roughed in the eyes – a wisp of raw umber to outline, a touch of thinned violet for each iris, burnt umber mixed with indigo for the pupils, but nothing more; I needed to take care not to get lost in details at this stage. I needed to see the portrait as an organic whole, not as structural parts. Midtones, not lines, gave me the shape of the face and nose.

To an onlooker, this might have seemed like not much progress, but it took hours. When the light changed to gray in preparation for the standard Florida mid-afternoon thunderstorm, I was ready to quit. My straining eyes and my aching shoulders told me I had done enough for one day. I put the brushes I had used in a pan of soapy water in the kitchen sink, made sure the lids were tight on my paints, cleaned up the inevitable mess around and under the easel and the worktable that stood beside it, then turned away.

Stretching, I wandered over to the window to see what was going on in my backyard.

The wind was rising, agitating the crepe myrtle bushes and the hair of the four people who remained. Three of them – the tall, angular woman and the two men who had been helping her – were loading boxes into the back of a white van. And the other one – the no-neck sheriff – started to tear down the crime-scene tape.

Aha! I scooted out the door and trotted down there, invigorated by the smell of ozone and the sound of distant thunder, brushing past the sheriff to have a look at the hole in my yard. But that's all it was – a large, empty hole with a couple of beetles exploring it and a copious number of bricks piled around it.

'Where is she?' I demanded.

'The skeleton?' Dr Wengleman turned to me, holding down her flailing hair with both hands, her smile worn-out but friendly. 'All boxed up to go to the morgue.'

'Then what?'

'Then we lay her out on a table and try to figure out who she is and what happened to her.'

'Murder is what happened to her,' said a sour growl behind me – the sheriff. 'People don't just plant young'uns for fun. And whoever done it, they been getting away with it fifty, sixty years.' The large man looked grim and very sweaty. 'Somebody help me take down this so-called canopy?'

'What am I supposed to do with this hole in my yard?' I asked. I really wanted to know; should I leave it alone for evidence or what?

But the sheriff grumped, 'Whatever you want. Use it for a duck pond. In a couple minutes it's gonna look like one.'

'Yikes.' Feeling the first big drops starting to spatter down, I ran for my house, waving. 'Nice to meet you all,' I called over my shoulder.

'You, too,' I heard the coroner respond.

Once I stepped into the kitchen, I felt as if I ought to eat something, so I chomped on an apple as I watched the coroner's van trundle up my yard and out my driveway – aka the part of my yard that had been naturally paved by pine straw – followed by the sheriff's cruiser, followed by a similar cruiser that had apparently been parked out by my mailbox to keep the reporters at bay.

Crap. Here they came. Three vehicles. Local newspaper, local TV, local radio.

But also here came the rain, pouring, sheeting in the wind,

bright as steel needles in the lightning. And here also came thunder, loud and scary as a Howser at close range.

Those reporters wouldn't stand in the storm knocking on my door for long. But just so they wouldn't see me, I ducked into the back room, the studio.

Lightning flared, and in its explosive light I saw the glare of dark, angry eyes meeting mine. From the easel.

Just for half a second, while the lightning strobed.

I stood in the gloom, my heart pounding. No. I hadn't seen what I had just seen; it must have been an illusion.

The people at the front door started yelling, 'Mrs Vernon!' and pounding, but the thunder volleyed louder – that and the rain drumming on the roof. By comparison, mere pesky reporters at the door seemed puny. I ignored them.

Lightning crackled again, and again I saw . . . no, it simply couldn't be. Forgetting all about concealment from reporters, I flipped on the studio's overhead light so I could take a good look at the painting.

My portrait of a sweet little girl – but, inexplicably, her eyes were no longer violet and serene the way I had made them. The brushstrokes were mine, but they depicted a narrow glare. The child on my easel was a sullen stranger. Her hair – I remembered painting smooth, long blond hair, but . . . how could I be so mistaken? Her hair looked rough, shaggy and the color of a dirt road.

A thin whimper reeled out of my throat like fishing line, and I started sweating even though the central air conditioning was doing its job. My art – even in artificial light, how could I be so mistaken about my own art? I remembered what hues I had used, or thought I did, but I had no proof, because I had cleaned up and rinsed out the rag and made sure all my acrylics had their lids on tight so they wouldn't dry out.

Just the same, I rushed over to my worktable to check the paints I *thought* I had used – but I found no telltale drips to differentiate what I thought were my palette colors from the others.

Thought? I should *know*.

I didn't remember painting my precious portrait, my pretend grandchild, this way at all, yet there she stood, unmistakably my handiwork, scowling at me.

There was something wrong with me, my memory, my mind. Had to be. I whimpered again, then fled, ignoring the voices now shouting at my front door. I locked myself in the bathroom with the lights off and took a shower in the dark, trying to calm down.

Berthe, call me ASAP. Mom alert level orange, Cassie texted her sister. She always called Maurie 'Berthe' to annoy her; Maurie's legal name was Berthe Morisot Vernon. Cassie's was Mary Cassatt Vernon. Right from the very beginning, their eccentric mother had made nothing simple for them.

Eccentric maybe going on cuckoo?

She was texting Berthe from upstairs. It was a phone call from Mom that had driven Cassie to take refuge in her home above her cafe, Creative Java. Few understood the derivation of the name. When she had first refurbished the tall old fieldstone mill along the Passaic River as an art gallery, she had dubbed it Creative Juices, My Foot! after her mother's habitual response to that cliché about the artistic process. When the gallery had tanked, Cassie had kept the price-tagged paintings on the walls but retrofitted the place to serve espresso, calling it Creative Juices and Java, meaning fine art and fine coffee. But people, not understanding, kept asking for fruit-based beverages she didn't serve, so she had been stuck with Creative Java. Well, many forms of pressed coffee were indeed creative. She hoped her teenage employees didn't get too damn creative – espresso macchiato with frowny faces, with swastikas, with phallic symbols – while she left them unsupervised for what she hoped would be a short time.

She was doing so, sequestered in her loft-like, secondhand-store-furnished apartment upstairs, because, right from the first hellos, something shadowy behind Mom's bright voice had alarmed her. 'I just came out of the shower, where I nearly scalded myself, the water is so hot, but at least some of the reporters have gone away now,' Mom had chirped.

'Reporters? What do you mean, reporters?'

'News reporters, because yesterday I found a skeleton in the backyard, sweetie. They just took it away, and now I don't want to turn any lights on. I'm standing here in the dark in case there might still be some lurking in the bushes.'

'*Skeletons?*'

'Damn nuisance reporters, silly.' Mom's laugh had sounded friable, as if it might crumble along with her facade of normalcy. 'And, oh, just by the way, I seem to have become an old gray mare turned out to pasture. How are *you* doing?'

Long accustomed to hit-and-run conversations with her mother, Cassie blew straight past that. 'What do you mean, you found a skeleton?'

'I mean I found a skeleton under some bricks I was digging because Kim turned down my *Six Swans* book.'

'Kim turned down your new book?'

'That doesn't matter now, honey.' Mom's voice downshifted, geared for rough terrain. 'Unfortunately, it was the skeleton of a child.'

Still uncertain whether the skeleton was a skeleton or a metaphor for the rejected picture book, Cassie replied neutrally. 'No wonder you sound upset.'

'I'm not upset, not really. I'm just calling for something to do while I wait for the rest of the reporters to go away for sure.'

'Uh-huh.' Reporters again. Media meant something must have actually happened. 'So there was a skeleton in your backyard. And it was the remains of a child.'

'Yes.'

'So does anybody have any clue who he was or how he got there?'

'She.'

'She?'

'Yes, it's a she skeleton. There were remnants of a dress. As to how she got there, not a clue, but it sure doesn't look good.'

'Because?'

'Abuse? Neglect? Murder? How did the poor little thing get there? We might never know.'

Cassie took a long, contemplative breath before she said, 'So, is that what's "not really" upsetting you, or is it the reporters, or Kim and the new book?'

In a very, very low voice, Mom said, 'None of the above.'

Cassie felt the hair on the back of her neck prickle. 'Mom? What—'

'Nothing.' Mom sounded brittle. 'Never mind. I really ought to get going, honey.'

'Going where?'

'Crazy. No ha ha never mind it must be my imagination I love you bye.' With scant punctuation, Mom hung up.

Cassie listened to ghosts tittering in disconnected cyberspace for a moment before she put her iPhone back into the pocket of her jeans. Then, rather than returning immediately to what might well be chaos in her cafe, she stood, thinking. Going crazy, ha ha? And if a picture book rejection was not the foremost of Mom's problems, then what in the world of Mom could possibly be going on?

Rolling her eyes, Cassie had then pulled her phone out again to text Maurie. She knew Mom would not phone Maurie because, in Mom's thinking, Maurie was not to be interrupted. Maurie might be teaching a class, writing something important and academic, or attending some sort of professional lawyer-and-wife function with her husband instead of merely (like Cassie) living over the little business she ran, being single and dependably available. Damn it all anyway, why did older sisters have to be so frigging superior?

But Cassie thrust that immature sentiment aside at once. Mom didn't need a pair of bickering siblings; Mom needed a team of grown daughters – or at least Cassie thought she might. She had never before heard her mother's chipper voice ring so hollow. Mom had sounded almost frightened.

From somewhere in the woods and weeds behind my house, a whippoorwill called at irregular midnight intervals. From one of the tall longleaf pines off to the side, beyond the open grave in my backyard, an owl offered occasional spectral remarks. Then the coyotes started their eerie chorus of atonal wails. Lying on my bed in the dark, listening when I should have been sleeping, I wondered what else was out there. My brain, always a bit skewed by bedtime, offered an odd thought: how did I know the coyotes were coyotes? Every night I heard them, but I had never actually seen one. Same with the whippoorwill; how did I know it was a brownish bird with a mustache that nested on the ground? I had never seen one of those either, only pictures in books. I *had* seen owls, but how did I know it was owls making those shiversome sounds? It would have made just as much sense for me to think that something else entirely . . .

No way. I was not going there, not paying attention to darkness within my mind or otherwise, and nothing I heard in the dark was paying the slightest attention to me or my problems. The world was a random, chaotic place.

'Why don't you give poor Will a break?' I muttered in response to the whippoorwill. Very probably someone had whipped, beaten or otherwise abused to death the skeletal child I had found, but almost certainly I would never know who, who, who, as the owl said. Was I lying awake because I felt a bit haunted?

Or was that thought just another proof that my mind was slipping into random chaos of its own? I didn't believe in ghosts. Did I?

'Paintings don't change all by themselves,' I mumbled.

Or did they? Late at night, when I played solitaire on my computer, always the same solitaire on the same computer, sometimes the cards looked slim and elegant, sometimes fat and clownish, sometimes like friendly cartoons but sometimes cloak-and-dagger sinister. Moreover, the black was sometimes more black than usual, and the hearts and diamonds varied from a scarlet color, almost orange, to deep crimson. Weird? Not to me. I not only accepted those variations in my perception, I barely noticed them. Implicit trust in the unconscious mind was fundamental to my being an artist. Any good artist would say the same. And the uncanny way disparate artworks by different artists seemed to emanate the same symbolism . . .

Did I believe in the *collective* unconscious?

'Oh, God,' I groaned, turning over in bed, trying to flounce away from the questions in my arguably senile head.

Oh, God? I couldn't possibly believe in God in any literal way; too much didn't make sense. Yet I had just called on God to *please* let me get some sleep, now that the reporters had finally gone away after I had spent the entire evening hiding from them in the dark.

I felt in the dark both literally and metaphorically – really in the dark – and there was no use trying to be logical about anything that was taking place. In the morning, I would go back to my painting, and whatever wanted to happen would happen.

'Whip poor Will!' called a night bird.

'Who? Who? Who?' called another.

FOUR

Once I finally got to sleep, I woke up later than usual, which should have felt luxuriously good but didn't. Lovely light, perfect for painting, streamed in between the window curtains, but the thought of painting – specifically, of the painting in process right now – made me feel as if staying in bed might be a better option. In my mind, the night-time shadows seemed to have carried over into the morning. Lonesome howls. Whip poor Will. Who? Who?

What unspeakable things had someone done to that child?

And why did I feel as if I, of all people, had to find out?

Eventually, my stomach and bladder issued a joint ultimatum that got me out of bed. I moved slowly, but it didn't take me long to get ready now that I was old enough not to bother with makeup, a hairdo or even underwear. Within a few minutes after brushing my teeth, I had put on a T-shirt, knit slacks and matching kitty-cat-print socks in an effort to cheer myself up; I had slipped into my oldest pair of Skechers, found my glasses and headed toward the studio.

I made it as far as the Florida-room end of the studio, where what I saw on and around the dinner table stopped me short. I stood dumbfounded and gawking, trying to make sense of one thing at a time. Bowls overturned. Bright-colored bottle caps ranked in lines on the floor like little round rainbow soldiers. Mardi Gras beads laid out to form a rectangle around them. A dozen of my precious origami cranes and swans and butterflies pulled down along with the bright-colored yarn that suspended them from the ceiling, scattered on top of the table.

I hadn't done that, had I? I would remember, wouldn't I?

Of course I would remember. And I would never get down on the floor with my bottle caps when it was such a struggle to get back up.

Unless maybe I had been sleepwalking?

But I hadn't walked in my sleep since I was a child.

Still, who else would have played with my toys?

Or was I just scared to say there had been an intruder in my house?

Yes. Yes, I was definitely spooked by the idea of who that intruder might have been. I was so frightened that I tried to pretend it was a perfectly ordinary petty thief, about which I should call the police. Checking for stolen items, I grabbed my wallet, which was sitting on the table surrounded by origami flittercritters. But all my cash was in the wallet, along with my credit cards. And I had nothing else worth stealing. Except . . .

I gasped. 'Oh my God! The portrait! Please not the portrait—' Three breathless steps took me farther into the studio, and no, thank God – in whom I did not rationally believe – I saw no damage, no sign that anything had been disturbed. On the easel, the half-finished face of a ragamuffin girl regarded me with apparent distrust.

Who else would play with my toys? I felt my guts slosh, my insides flip over. 'It was you, wasn't it?' I whispered. I must have stood there for a minute, staring at her.

She stared back.

And I blinked first. 'But it couldn't have been. I am so not ready to deal with anything kookier than an imaginary granddaughter.' I took a deep breath and shrugged away everything I'd been thinking. 'I'll get to you, contrary grandchild of mine, as soon as I eat some breakfast,' I told that strange face which, I reassured myself, had formed out of my unconscious mind.

This scruffy, scowling urchin was not at all the 'granddaughter' I had envisioned for myself. She was better; she was real instead of idealized. I felt my heart smiling because the painting promised to be good, very good indeed, maybe even masterly.

I made coffee, and instead of my usual cereal I had an English muffin; for some reason, I didn't feel very hungry. Leaving the dishes in the sink, I went straight to my easel; the Mardi Gras beads et cetera could stay where they were a while longer. Maybe I didn't want to take the time to pick them up. Or maybe I didn't want to upset the child – and whether I meant the child within me or something else, I refused to contemplate. It was time for my brushes to do the thinking.

I selected a favorite fake-sable filbert brush from the handmade (by me) pottery jug where they all stood at attention, and I started with something easy – the scrumbled background comprised of wriggly dabs of violet, indigo and viridian green. Once I felt warmed up, I then sneaked some indigo into the shadow under the jaw, coaxed strokes of shaggy hair down around the neck and shoulders, roughed in the umber shadows forming the nostrils and mixed a muted pink for the mouth. The child incarnating under my touch refused to smile even slightly; it was as if someone other than me had taken charge, but I was used to this and considered it a sign that the painting was going well. My hands, brushes, eyes and arms all partnered to paint in a way that sometimes seemed barely to consult my brain at all. As if in a kind of trance, I worked the entire picture, placing lights and highlights, smoothing transitions between tones, shaping curves, allowing myself hints of detail to complete the mouth and eyes.

I painted all morning and through lunchtime, reluctant to stop when things were progressing so well, except that I had not yet touched the little girl's dress, which was nonsensical; I should have roughed it in along with everything else. Something was blocking me when it came to the dress, and it would be unprofessional of me not to push through the block.

I had planned to give my 'granddaughter' the prettiest dress I could imagine, but throughout this project plans had changed – OK, that was an understatement – but anyway, regarding the dress I had to compromise. For my stubborn subject, smocking or ruffles or lace seemed out of the question, but surely I could still use lavender, I decided. Surely the contrary child could put up with a nice, fresh, simple dress in such a yummy color.

With a sense of being back in control, and with a large brush, I laid down a round-collared lavender dress with a hint of shirring below a yoke top. I shaded the deepest darks in the folds of the fabric violet, then bolstered the midtones with pale cerise, and at the height of the lights I dared a bold, thin glimmer of yellow, then hints of yellow rimming the face and the sandy-brown hair, tying the portrait together.

Painting the final touches – stray strands of hair catching the light against the background – I felt good, very good, about this particular work of art. But by then it was mid-afternoon, my shoulders and arms ached and my stomach was grumbling.

Moreover, the minute I stopped painting I felt as restless as a monkey in a cage because I hadn't been out of the house in three days.

Not to worry; I could rectify that.

I capped the paints, washed my brushes quickly but thoroughly with both hand soap and dishwashing detergent, cleaned up the usual mess, then grabbed my wallet and my car keys to take myself out for dinner.

Without even needing to decide where I was going, I drove my ancient Volvo, which my daughters affectionately called the Vo, to Waffle House. Cooter Spring, the small town nearest where I live, was pretty much defined by a Waffle House at one end and a Piggly Wiggly at the other. In between, widely spaced in the usual Florida panhandle way, strayed a hardware store, a pharmacy, two churches, two thrift shops, three hairdressers, some modest pastel houses, and – incongruously central to so much banality – the eponymous spring, with cypress knees surrounding cypress trees, anhingas posing cruciform on cypress branches to dry their wings, all sorts of egrets, herons, other water birds, a jungle of wildflowers, the entire subtropical enchilada This glimpse of Eden was surrounded by a chain-link fence to protect the foolish from the bottomless water and the cooters from the foolish. The cooters were yellow-bellied turtles that had been there since Spanish times, some of them the size of laundry baskets. Occasional tourists gawked at them through the fence, but natives hardly noticed them anymore.

'How y'all doing, Shuug?' greeted a woman in a Waffle House apron and baseball cap as I came in. Not that she knew me – very few people in Skink County did – but Southern hospitality, in the form of 'Honey pie,' 'Darlin',' 'Ladybug' and the like, extended to all, even to people with Yankee accents. 'Shuug,' apparently an abbreviation of 'Sugar,' didn't faze me, but 'y'all' bothered me a little, as I was only one person. Like, how was all of me doing?

'OK, except the head, maybe,' I replied, sliding into a booth.

She gave me a genuine laugh, as I'd hoped; I like to make people laugh. 'Something wrong in the head?'

'Got to be. I came in here for dinner.' Waffle House steaks and pork chops were notoriously dreadful.

She played along. 'Uh-oh.'

'No, not really. I'll have a waffle and scrambled eggs and bacon.'

My suppertime breakfast came with grits, of course – a Southern anomaly I did not touch, only eyed suspiciously. And it came with yet more redundant calories in the form of buttered toast, with which I made a bacon sandwich. Damn the carbohydrates – full speed ahead! Afterwards, I headed home contented in tummy and mood, driving slowly under the panhandle's big sky to admire the usual spectacular sunset, trying to think of exact names for the lambent colors in the sky but never quite succeeding.

I met hardly any traffic, one of the many things I liked about living here. So I was singing as I walked into my house, although not as well as I used to. Another of the insults of age, on top of hair relocation and bad breath and rosacea and yeast infections and everything, is an awful quaver in the singing voice, especially on high notes, but that didn't keep me from trying. Warbling some half-forgotten folk song from my college years, I opened the kitchen door and, as if to shut me up, the phone rang. Being a telephone of the old black Bakelite circular-dial school, it rang with a bell and clapper and with great authority. I jumped to answer it.

Maurie considered that Cassie was probably overreacting as usual, but she had promised her kid sister she would give their mother a call, and so she was. This was the first chance she'd had, the first free moment while she was walking across Cornell campus to attend a symposium on 'Unwritten History: The Losers' Viewpoint.' Neither her sister nor her mother seemed to understand how much her career demanded of her. Even now, in the summertime, when she was not teaching classes and correcting piles of papers, she still had academic obligations: graduate students to mentor, faculty meetings to attend, the necessity of putting together curriculum syllabi for the fall, plus struggling with applications for grants, plus her own personal research, and, perhaps most stressful, scholarly essays to write in the spirit of 'publish or perish.' This had been one of those days when she was scheduled up to her ears. But now she finally had maybe five minutes . . . and, millennial damnation, Mom's answering machine picked up. Considering that only *her* mother would still use such an outdated device as an answering machine, Maurie left no message, but tried again with the same result. Rolling her eyes behind their black-rimmed glasses, she thumbed redial one last time.

'Hello?' Mom sounded out of breath.

'Were you outside?' Maurie complained without introduction; she knew her mother would recognize her voice.

'I went out for dinner.'

'Mom, if you would get a cell phone like a normal and rational person, you could pick up wherever, or I could just text you!'

'Since when have I ever been a normal or rational person? I suppose Cassie told you I found a skeleton in my backyard?'

Indeed, Cassie had, and Maurie had accessed the *Skink County Observer* online to verify:

Florida State Police investigators confirm that unidentified skeletal human remains have been discovered near Pinestraw Pillow Road, approximately eight miles north of Cooter Spring.

A deputy with the Skink County Sheriff's Office responded to a report from a homeowner a few minutes after eight p.m. Wednesday. Upon arriving on scene, he observed that the homeowner had been digging in her backyard and had uncovered some bones that appeared human. Sheriff Bronson Pudknucker arrived shortly thereafter and verified probable cause to call in state investigators and the Mid-Panhandle Medical Examiner's office.

The homeowner declined to be interviewed for this article.

'Only thing we're sure of yet is it ain't just animal bones,' Sheriff Pudknucker advised. 'Could be homicide, suicide, secret burial by folks couldn't afford an undertaker, old bones left over from Civil War times or even earlier. We don't know nothing and we ain't disclosing no further information.'

The Skink County Coroner, Dr Marcia Wengleman, however, confirmed that the remains are being investigated as a suspicious death. She said she could not identify the gender or age of the victim until after forensic examination. At press time, the remains had not yet been removed from the unmarked grave where they had been found. Anyone with

information about the possible identity of the remains is
asked to call the Skink County Sheriff's Office or Cooter
Spring Crime Fighters.

Maurie considered that being so tight-lipped was unnecessary
posturing on the part of the authorities. Probably half of Cooter
Spring knew, as Mom did, that the skeleton had belonged to a
little girl. Maurie didn't care; she just wanted to find out how her
mother was doing.

She said, 'Yes, Cassie told me. That must have felt a bit
Kafkaesque, finding bones in your backyard.'

'Oh, the bones are the least of the surrealism that has
been going on around here.'

'Surrealism?'

'Inexplicable weirdness. Somebody or something has been
moving my playtoys around.'

'What? Somebody broke in? Did you call the police?'

'No, nobody broke down any doors, and no, I didn't call the
cops because there's really nothing to report except frivolous
objects moving from one place to another. Don't fuss, honey, I'm
fine.'

Maurie heard something a bit fake in Mom's too-bright voice,
just as Cassie had described. 'Was it maybe your neighbor, the
one with the down-home name, the Avon slash religious fanatic?'

'Wilma Lou?' Mom laughed in a way that seemed inappropriate.
'She's not coming near me. No, I don't think it was Wilma Lou.
Maybe I just have poltergeists.'

Or maybe, Maurie thought, Mom was experiencing mental decline
the way Grandma had done. When Grandma was in the first stages
of Alzheimer's, she had frequently said with genuine consternation,
'People are moving my things around!' because she didn't remember
having moved them herself. Short-term memory loss manifested
first.

Halted under the portico of a Cornell classroom building,
Maurie bit her lip. She didn't have time to deal with a putatively
senile mother right now; she would be late to the symposium. She
promised herself she would call Cassie right afterward.

'Mom, since when do you believe in poltergeists?' she asked
in a teasing tone. 'Are you OK?'

'Of course, sweetie,' Mom said with too much emphasis. 'I'm *fine.*'

After talking with Maurie, I felt exhausted by the weight of all the things I wasn't telling her, all the things I didn't want to think about; I needed passive entertainment. So I headed back to my bedroom, which is where I keep the only TV in the house, not for pornographic purposes but simply because I think a TV looks ugly in a living room, and there's so much violence on TV that most of the time I would rather read.

Not that night. I actually fell asleep with the TV on.

The next morning, awakening, I felt recovered. Actually, I felt pretty damn good. Weirdness or no weirdness, evidently I had reconnected with the familiar blissful vibe of being in the middle of an art project that has become challenging, or has taken a puzzling turn, or has otherwise proved interesting.

Silly me.

I headed into the Florida room, squinting and yawning, a mug of coffee in one hand and a bowl of Special K in the other, and what I saw hit me so much like the punch of a furious fist that I dropped both the cereal and the coffee, adding their mess to the wreckage that made me flinch: origami birds crumpled, flung to the floor or torn into confetti. Bright bottle-cap circles of plastic smashed, shattered, scattered. Strings of Mardi Gras beads snapped and strewn. Bowls broken. All sorts of silent hurt things bearing screaming witness to anger.

At first I gawked, stunned, breath and reason both knocked out of me. Then I gasped, and in a kind of sick replay of the day before, I cried, 'The studio! Oh, God, no!' Headlong, heedless of whatever I might crunch underfoot, I ran through the mess, darting toward the easel.

I saw the life-sized portrait, gave a choked cry, felt my knees weaken and my whole body go watery with shock. Not that the child's defiant face had changed – it glared back at me with a sort of dark and sullen beauty I had never before achieved in paint – but her hair had reverted to being short and shaggy, and her dress . . .

It was the dress – no longer lavender – that nearly made me faint, because I recognized it. Torn and grimy, the dress painted on the portrait in my own distinctive style was dirty yellow, the color of urine, printed with flowers – little brick-red roses.

There was no mistaking my own brushstrokes. And there was no mistaking that fabric, that print, either. I had seen scraps of it hugging the child, the skeleton, secreted in my backyard.

FIVE

Never mind the next several hours. I spent them not quite literally gibbering but definitely non-functioning; forget breakfast, not even able to clean up the mess I'd left on top of the other mess on the floor. I was, as folks say, walking around in circles and bumping into walls. I really thought I was losing my mind, and no wonder, considering my options.

If I chose to think a spirit from the backyard skeleton had somehow infiltrated my home, thrown a temper tantrum in my Florida room and morphed my art into its own image, then I was obviously losing it, because believing any of that meant believing in ghosts, and nobody with any common sense believes in ghosts.

However, if I chose to think I had tattered my own precious origami and repainted the dress myself without remembering, in my sleep or in a schizophrenic state or whatever, then evidently I was so bonkers I needed to be institutionalized.

Ghost or gonzo? I wasn't sure which scared me worse.

I never should have called my daughters, of course, but I was so upset I needed to talk with *someone*. So I tried Maurie, but got her voicemail, on which I left a one-word message: 'Gadzooks!' Then I called Cassie, and she picked up.

Trying to joke, I said, '*Why* do things always have to break down over weekends?'

'Like what, Mom? The fridge again?'

'No, like me. A breakdown of the nervous sort. Either that or I need to change my mind about ghosts.'

'*Ghosts?*'

'Her dress matches the one that was on the skeleton, and I was sure I painted it lavender.'

'Her?'

'The little girl . . .' But I must not say anything to either of my daughters about grandchildren, much less about yearning for them and deciding to paint a fantasy family of them! To avoid that subject, I blurted, 'Somebody or something came in here and put my collection of found circles on the floor and pulled down my flying origami, and then the same bump in the night came back and destroyed everything.' Ghosties and ghoulies and long-legged beasties, plus other things, went bump in the night, according to Robert Burns. I hadn't heard the phantom of the Florida room go bump, but I had seen the damage.

'Wait, Mom, slow down. Somebody broke in and did what?'

'There's no need for her to break in. She *is* in somehow, not just in the painting but in the house. Or at least in the Florida room. Making a fool of me. Making me think I've lost my marbles.' Again, I tried to joke. 'I suppose she wants me to find them so she can play with them.'

'Mom.' Cassie's voice sounded cautious and a bit too calm. 'Have you talked with Maurie about this?'

'No, she didn't pick up.' All on its own, my body let out a shaky sigh, meaning I was finished fussing. 'It's just as well I didn't talk with her; she's gotten so teacherish,' I told my other daughter, hearing my own voice back to normal, perky and wry. 'Listen, Cassie, sweetie, don't worry about me. I'm all right now. I just have a major mess to deal with, and after that I need to decide what I'm doing today.'

'Mom, if you really have a home invasion, you need to call the police.'

'No, I just need to clean up the spilled cereal and broken coffee mug and ruined origami and stuff. What about you? Any weekend plans?'

For some reason she laughed, but then she couldn't seem to explain what was funny. She said she had to go.

Still in a bit of a state, I didn't get any painting done that day. Instead, I took my time sweeping up and picking up and throwing broken things in the trash; I even mopped the Florida room's floor. But then I didn't want to stay in the house and eat there, no matter how clean the place was now. I went to Waffle House again and had a hamburger; they make very good burgers. With hash browns, scattered, smothered, diced and capped, which means loose, with onion, tomatoes and mushrooms. I love the jargon. And the carbohydrates. Comfort food.

'Are you going to the Two-Toed Tom Festival?' the friendly waitress asked me.

'The *what*?'

'The grilled gator festival up in Esto.'

I was beginning to understand that, in Skink County and adjoining areas, the national holidays were almost meaningless compared with the Boiled Peanut Festival, the Possum Queen Competition, the Watermelon Festival, the Down Home Rodeo and, above all, the Chicken Purlieu Memorial, dedicated to the memory of the confederacy; 'chicken Purlieu' was the mainstay ration of Robert E. Lee's troops, and having eaten the slop once, I considered it no wonder the South had lost. But a grilled gator festival?

'Two-Toed Tom?'

'Biggest, meanest gator ever was. Twenty-four foot long, red eyes like a devil, all but two toes missing off one foot from a steel trap. He roamed them swamps around Esto eatin' off cattle and horses back in the eighties.'

'*What?*' I'd expected a legendary gator from much longer ago. 'Come on!'

The short order cook was listening in. 'Even ate some people,' he volunteered.

'You're messing with me!'

'No, we're not!' The waitress spoke with earnest haste. 'Folks was terrorized, went after him with guns and traps, and one guy even tried dynamite. He was so pissed off because Two-Toed Tom ate his mule, he blew up a whole swamp and everything in it. Then he heard a ruckus from the next swamp over. Two-Toed Tom was eating his wife.' She pronounced the word 'wahf' to go with 'Waffle House.'

I badly wanted to roll my eyes. A wahf-eating gator, my hind foot. But I said, 'I hope the guy killed him.'

The cook trumped that. 'Nope, nobody never killed him nohow. He's still out there.'

'No way! How old is he supposed to be?'

'Well, if it ain't Tom still leaving two-toed tracks, then it's his ghost.' The waitress grinned, thrilled at the idea of a gator ghost.

'And Esto has a *festival* for him?'

'Sure! Two-Toed Tom is Esto's claim to fame. Do you like gator meat?'

'I don't know. Do you have it on the menu?'

'Damn shame we don't.'

I ate my burger and my hash browns, and the waitress brought my check, and as I drove home I tried not to think about Two-Toed Tom. Not that I had anything against a tall-tale gator, but I didn't feel comfortable with the idea of a gator ghost.

Or any sort of ghost.

Back home, I went into the studio as if drawn there by a gravitational force, sat down in my Joseph (upholstery of many colors) chair and gazed at the artwork gazing back at me from the easel. Even though it was finished, it would remain on the easel for the time being, because it was not finished with me.

I had not signed it. I wouldn't dare.

Instead of the happy, golden, idyllic fantasy granddaughter I had meant to create for myself, I faced a child so terribly real I could barely meet the gaze of her dark eyes. They pierced me with rage – it was hard not to look away from such blistering rage – and pain. Always, I knew from having lived a fairly typical life, burning pain follows just beneath raw anger like a shadow. But in the portrait I saw a haunting, fire-eyed, huge, monstrous alligator of pain, anger and hurt too vast for a child to carry.

Impulsively, I whispered, 'What did they *do* to you?'

My heart squeezed. To my astonishment, I realized that I could learn to love her, this hostile young granddaughter, so beautiful in her own unlikely way, with her square, stubborn chin, her scowling brow, her hacked-off hair. Something terrible had happened that had left her buried in my backyard, and half a century later she was here, now, in my studio because she needed . . .

No. I didn't want to go there; Esto could have its ghost but I most certainly did not want one of my own; my body clenched and I very nearly chickened out. But the sentence in my mind completed itself just in time.

She needed a grandma.

The word, the concept, my obsession compelled me. I couldn't run away.

Yet I couldn't seem to move forward, either, mentally speaking. The terrain was far too strange.

So I sidestepped. I smiled at the portrait's intense young face and said conversationally, 'Dear, howsabout if I go get my origami paper, then come sit here and keep you company and make some more flittercritters to replace the ones you pulled down?' I needed to fetch the paper from the back room where I segregated playtime craft materials from my art. 'I'll be right back.'

For the most part, folding origami was what I did for the rest of the day: I sat in my Joseph chair folding swans and swallows, hummingbirds and butterflies with their bright paper wings lifted to soar, while the nameless, fey child on my easel silently watched me.

Sunday morning, I sidestepped my situation in another way, by sleeping late. In a sense this was not procrastination, because I had assigned the matter of the changeling portrait to my unconscious mind for processing, so the longer I dozed, the more time I gave myself to arrive at some kind of insight. I finally got up with remnants of dreams trailing like smoke in my mind, quickly gone, although on the way to the bathroom for some reason I mumbled 'spitting image' to myself.

During my shower (my scorching hot shower; I really needed to set the water heater's temperature gauge lower) I mused on this phrase. Spitting image, expectorating image – why would anyone think that was a compliment? After I got dressed but before breakfast, I looked it up online, arguably a mistake; beyond agreeing that the proper phrase was 'spit *and* image,' most of what I found was opinion, confusion or folk etymology having to do with God creating humankind from spit and mud, or children being the spit (euphemism for ejaculate) and image (lookalike) of their parents, or maybe it should have been *splitting* image. Oh, come on. But reading one reference from a British source, I felt hair prickling on the back of my neck: *Spit and image: spit is an ancient synonym for, or corruption of, the word 'spirit.' In referring to 'spit and image,' one bespeaks both inward spirit and outward appearance.*

I researched no farther, but mulled over spirit and image as I dawdled with my toasted bagel at breakfast, or perhaps I should say brunch. It was afternoon when I finally set foot in the studio.

Perish the thought that I could have gone somewhere else instead. My art is my life. Only serious illness and death held priority over it. Specifically, Jim's death. Also, years ago, I had taken a few days off for Maurie's wedding, and I supposed if a grandchild were ever to be born . . . silly thought. The point is, for me to turn my back on my art for any lesser reason would have changed me into a frightening stranger to myself.

I found the portrait of a child still frowning at me and still on my easel, although some other things had been moved around. Somehow, my origami flittercritters had flown down from the table where I had left them. I saw them arranged in circular clusters on the floor: butterflies both large and small in one, swans in another, hummingbirds with hummingbirds, swallows with swallows, all facing inward.

'What are they doing?' I asked the shaggy-haired girl on my easel. 'Having committee meetings?' Because, of course, she knew; she, or her spirit, had put them that way. Even an unhappy child can play.

'None of my business, of course,' I added, backing off a bit to sit in my Joseph chair, my thoughts circling and circling, like Two-Toed Tom chasing his reptilian tail, as I contemplated her.

'Once upon a time,' I told that life-sized young face, 'an artist named Magritte made a very realistic oil painting of a pipe – for smoking, you know; briarwood with kind of a curvy stem. And he titled it, "This is not a pipe," which made him famous.'

I sat there with an imaginary calabash in my real mouth, trying to reason like Sherlock Holmes, and I came to a most unreasonable, indeed reckless, conclusion.

I said, 'According to Magritte, you are not a child. You are the image of a child. But you and I know better. Your spirit helped me help you to create yourself in your own image – the image of a very specific child who was buried in my backyard.'

There. I'd done it, I'd said it aloud, I'd committed myself to the cause of craziness, and it was a good thing I was sitting down, because I felt shaky and I knew damn well it wasn't due to low blood sugar; I'd just eaten.

'I'm scared,' I admitted to the child, 'but don't worry, I'll suck it up. I'd rather be crazy with integrity than sane and heartless.'

The portrait's steady gaze demanded more.

'I know it's not about me. It's about you.'

And that was as far as I could go, for the time being. The spirit from my backyard grave had taken me by the hand to manifest the image for some compelling reason, driven by some terrible need; that much I could see in the portrait's haunting eyes and taut mouth. I felt guiltily glad that mouth could not speak. The image's silent cry for help was harrowing enough. Someone had failed the child terribly, and she needed a grandma. I had set out to paint a grandchild. Well, then, I had to be that rescuer.

But how?

SIX

I was still sitting there, in what writers used to call a brown study – better than a purple funk, I suppose – when I heard a car pull into my driveway and stop. I stayed where I was, listening as the car doors slammed, because no one visited me except, occasionally, mail delivery. But this was Sunday, so it was probably tract pushers from whom I needed to hide. Even worse, it might be reporters again.

Somebody knocked on the front door. As if motionlessness were necessary for concealment, I froze like a bunny in my chair.

Someone knocked again, and then a voice I knew yelled, 'Mom!'

What? Cassie! My heart leaped, and so did my body in its arthritic way, heaving off the chair to galumph toward the door. Through the picture window I could see – knock me silly – both Cassie *and* Maurie, my wonderful daughters, looking tired and oh-so-beautiful. Thank the genetic luck of the draw they were tall, slender and dazzlingly dark like their father, not short, sandy and freckled like me.

I couldn't get the door open, or my arms around the pair of them, fast enough. Hellos and how-are-yous flew out of us like corn popping.

I let go of them long enough to shoo them into the house. 'Why didn't you tell me you were coming? I could have cooked something.'

'Spaghetti,' Cassie teased, referring to the limited extent of my culinary repertoire.

'Yes, by all means, I would have cooked spaghetti!'

Maurie said, 'We'll take you out to eat, Mom.'

'But what are you doing here? Both of you together?' Cassie in her generic blue jeans and high-topped sneakers, Maurie in her fashionable black shoes and slacks and blazer with red silk neck scarf; the two of them had always been irreconcilably different. Not hostile, but it was a surprise to see them together on what must have been quite a spontaneous vacation trip. 'How did you get here?'

'Delta Airlines, Mom.'

'Rental car, Mom.'

Blinking and owlish, the pair of them.

It delighted me so much to see them in some sort of conspiracy, even if it was at my expense, that I laughed aloud. 'Well, come in! Come in! Coffee? Milk and cookies?'

Joking about gluten-free cookies and agreeing on coffee, they followed me to the table in the Florida room but did not sit down; they stood looking with raised eyebrows at the mess of bowls, bottle caps, Mardi Gras beads and origami birds on the floor.

'You should have seen it before I cleaned up,' I said.

Maurie said, 'You really ought to have called the police if somebody came in and did this.'

'Nobody came in. No forced entry.'

'Are you sure? Has anybody else been victimized by vandals? Did you ask your two-named neighbor? She would know, wouldn't she?'

'If Wilma Lou knew a thing about any of this, she'd be sitting up on top of the house, praying. Please don't tell her. Don't tell anyone. Nobody's been in this house except me, but do you really think I did this myself?'

Shaking her head and looking bewildered, she faced me, trying to speak, but just then Cassie yawped, 'Oh my God!' She had strayed into the studio, only a few steps away, and was gawking at the portrait on my easel.

Maurie hurried over to join her, and they both stared. I followed and had a look for myself, just in case my painting had grown fangs or something while my back was turned, but it was still the same: a life-sized rendition of a shaggy-headed, rather grubby child with a hard-eyed, hurt gaze.

Or at least anger and pain were what I saw in her eyes. But I didn't say a word, waiting to hear how my daughters might react.

Very softly, Cassie said, 'Mom, your stuff has always been good, but this is *marvelous*. A masterpiece.'

Cautiously, I admitted, 'It's different.'

Maurie said, 'Gadzooks! This is what the *gadzooks* was about, isn't it, Mom? Where did it *come* from?'

Cassie had an eye for excellence in art, Maurie for deviance from the norm. I smiled, proud of both of them, but I told Maurie, 'You don't want to know.'

'Yes, I *do* want—'

I interrupted, but fondly. 'You two jetted down here to check on me, right? To see whether I'm slipping? Because my phone calls have been a bit bizarre lately?'

They didn't speak, but their very still faces answered me.

Nodding, I assured them, 'If that's the case, then believe me, you don't want to know all about this painting – not yet. Just stick around for a day or two, and you'll see. How long are you staying?'

Cassie looked at Maurie. Maurie said, 'We have a flight back on Wednesday morning.'

'Then we have Sunday, Monday and Tuesday!' Appreciating their busy lives, I told them quite sincerely, 'That's wonderful.'

Cassie and Maurie followed their mother down the yard to see the 'duck pond,' as she called the excavation in the backyard, before the customary afternoon thunderstorm moved in. Walking across more weeds than grass, behind their mom's back they exchanged glances, but it was too early to arrive at any consensus, not even a silent one. Cassie thought Mom seemed fine – maybe a bit too fine. Mom wore the air of one who has just received an advanced degree or found religion. There was no more dithering in her; she seemed to have become quite sure of something.

'I think they put her over here to keep her from contaminating the well water,' she remarked as they arrived at the raw wound in her yard.

Maurie looked around, anywhere except at the grave. 'Such a

superfluity of bricks,' she said, sounding so bored and scholarly that Cassie knew at once her sister felt as uneasy as she did.

'Enough to hold her down,' Mom said, freakily matter-of-fact.

Silence threatened; Cassie hastened to speak as banally as she could. 'What are you going to do about filling this up, Mom?'

'I'm going to plant a tree here.' Mom made this a pronouncement, but then her voice softened. 'I haven't decided what kind yet. Something indigenous, like a magnolia maybe. Let's get back inside the house before we get rained on.'

During the rainstorm they sat at the table – sure, there was a living room, the front room, with a comfortable sofa and chairs, but their family has always sat at the kitchen table to talk – and they caught up about Maurie's professional honors and her husband's promotions within his law firm, Cassie's business frustrations, the logistics of Mom's skeleton. It wasn't long before Maurie, while still chatting, started cleaning away this and that, slipping off her chair to pick up bottle caps and Mardi Gras beads. Cassie watched her with amusement, and so did Mom, who observed, 'Maurie, you certainly take after your father.'

'Well, why did you leave this catastrophe lying around?'

'I was busy with the painting. Anyway, this is the South, baby. Relax.'

'The South would drive Dad crazy,' Cassie put in. 'He would want to trim the jungle around your house into rectangles.' Her father had been a mechanical engineer with a nearly religious commitment to the straight line as the shortest distance between two points.

Mom laughed. 'Wisteria doesn't rectangulate very well.'

'What about those jigger-jagger monstrosities?'

'Spanish daggers? Jim would have hated them.'

Her voice issuing from beneath the table in an oracular way, Maurie said, 'You're free to go your own sweet solitary way, Mom, now that he's gone.'

'Honey pie, I always did what I wanted. Most of what I wanted when Jim was alive was to give him—' Mom's voice suddenly lost momentum.

'We know, Mom,' said Cassie. Give Dad happiness, support, indulgence and just plain love was what Mom had always done but couldn't bring herself to say. She communicated better in paint than in words.

Finished with the detritus on the floor, Maurie popped her head up above the edge of the table like something from *The Muppet Show*. 'Mom, would you like me to hang these origami birds from the ceiling for you?'

'Yes, by all means! You're tall enough so you won't have to climb on top of the table.'

Before Cassie could ask whether her mother had actually risked her aging bones in such a reckless way, Mom disappeared toward the bedroom end of the house. Immediately, Cassie consulted her sister with her eyes. Maurie shook her head.

'But she seems OK,' Cassie murmured.

Maurie shook her head harder. 'That painting,' she whispered, but then she heard Mom approaching, and grew still and hushed. Mom reappeared bearing scissors, an ancient glass mayonnaise jar full of paper clips and several balls of rug yarn in different bright colors. She had always kept her craft things segregated from her art things, as if fearing some sort of cross-contamination. Back in her office, so called because her computer lived there, most likely she also had crayons, markers, rubber stamps, beads, potholder looms, flowers made out of Styrofoam egg cartons, who knew what.

'I don't have a stepstool,' she chirped.

'You've never in your life had a stepstool, Mom. We should get you one. And a cell phone, for God's sake.'

'I have a cell phone, dear, in the Volvo's glove box, just in case of emergencies.'

Probably an ancient flip-open cell phone with a dead battery, Cassie thought.

'But I'm in the house most of the time, and there's no signal out here.'

Rolling her eyes, Maurie climbed on to a chair, Cassie handed her a yellow origami swan and a paper clip, and Mom passed along a length of red rug yarn and offered instructions. So they continued until all the 'flittercritters,' as Mom called them, were colorfully hanging from the ceiling where she wanted them. Then Mom exiled the yarn, paper clips and scissors to the office again, and the rain had stopped, and it was time to go out for supper.

They went to a Chinese buffet, as Maurie flatly refused to eat at Waffle House. As if Southern-style Chinese food – meaning peas, carrots and gravy – was better, Cassie thought, picking at her sweet-and-sour chicken while listening to Mom venting about Kim and the rejected book and how she felt as if her career was over without warning, how she had expected to keep on keeping on indefinitely and what was she supposed to do now – get herself a pair of cowboy boots and go line dancing? Maurie appeared bored by Mom's monologue, but Cassie felt a pang of loss; what had happened to the mom who had always taken care of her? Who was this disappointed and needy little old woman?

'Mom,' Cassie told her, 'that portrait you just finished, please send it to me. I'll display it in the cafe, and I guarantee you'll have the New York galleries wooing you in no time. They trawl my place for talent, you know.'

'Really?'

'Yes, really. Mom, you're not too old to start over as a mainstream artist.'

'Gadzooks,' added Maurie.

Mom became thoughtfully silent. Maurie signaled the waiter and asked for the check.

When they got back to Mom's house, Cassie got her suitcase out of the rental car and lugged it inside to the guest room; Maurie did the same. Both of them dumped their luggage on the floor because there was nowhere else to set it; the guest room also served as a junk room for abandoned exercise equipment. The handlebars of the stationary cycle, or similar portions of the treadmill, would perhaps be useful to hang clothes from. Meanwhile, both of them stared at the double bed they had to share.

Cassie broke silence. 'Just don't go grabbing me in the middle of the night thinking I'm your husband.'

Maurie snorted. 'I'm more likely to grab you thinking you're *not* my husband. Would you prefer to sleep on the couch?'

'I'd rather sleep in the bed and *you* sleep on the couch, indiscriminate grabber. I bet you snore, too.'

'Don't you?'

'How would I know? I've never slept with anybody in my life.'

'Why do I not believe that?'

Tired from travel, they wrangled merely pro forma, as siblings, meanwhile ambling to the front end of the house to see what their mother, who had strangely become elderly, maundering and short, was doing.

When they saw, they forgot to bicker anymore, but stood like brunette meerkats, watching as their mother tenderly removed the portrait of a child from her easel and slipped it into a cardboard portfolio. Then Mom seemingly set up the easel for another artwork, but not in her usual way. She placed a large sheet of cheap sketch paper on the easel, and left more of the paper scattered around the easel on the terrazzo floor. Then she took her ugly old jug full of cherished brushes and disappeared toward the back of the house.

Cassie and Maurie looked question marks at each other. Cassie spoke first. 'She's up to something.'

Maurie said, 'She's dangerously close to the edge of gaga.'

Their mother reappeared with a clump of plastic-handled craft brushes, a big box of crayons and a margarine tub full of markers. Cassie asked, 'Mom, what are you doing?'

Without answering, she put the chintzy brushes where the other ones had been, then set the crayons and the markers on the smooth concrete floor in a haphazard way along with the randomly placed sheets of paper.

'Mom,' said Maurie in the tone of one taking over, 'does the worm in your brain have a name?'

'Not yet.' She shooed her offspring toward the living room with her plump old paws. 'Never mind. We'll see what's what in the morning.'

SEVEN

As usual, I woke up at the butt crack of dawn that Monday, but instead of feeling annoyed, I felt wide awake and ready for action. It took me only two or three blinks to realize why I was so unusually alert: I had set up an experiment of sorts, leaving those blank sheets of paper in the studio, and I wanted to see whether anything had happened.

But, confound it, I couldn't go look, not if I wanted to prove anything to my daughters about what had been going on in my house. The results (if any) needed to be found by them first.

So, wide awake and wryly aware of the irony that I was wide awake, I made myself stay in bed until I heard the sounds of bare feet in the hallway, the toilet flushing and water running in the bathroom sink. Twice. I wanted both Maurie and Cassie to witness that I was not up before them. Just in case.

When it sounded to me as if they were finished in the bathroom, I all but levitated out of bed, covered my sleep shirt with a caftan and toddled out of my room, all my arthritic joints creaking. 'Good morning,' I told my daughters through the doorway of their room.

'Coffee,' Maurie responded, still in fashionable fishy-print pajamas, brushing past me and heading toward the kitchen. Cassie zipped up her jeans, blinked a smile at me and trailed after her sister.

I, of course, needed to go to the bathroom. But a couple of minutes later, as I was brushing my teeth, I heard what I kind of expected: one of my daughters screamed, and then they both yelled, 'Mom!'

I rinsed my mouth before I put on my slippers and shuffled out to the kitchen, where I could smell coffee starting to brew. Through the Florida room, I could see Maurie and Cassie at the threshold of the studio, standing abnormally close together and looking spring-loaded, eyes wide, hands to their mouths as they stared toward the sheets of paper I had put out for bait the night before.

I took a look myself, then joined my daughters, squeezing between them, an arm around each waist. 'Dang,' I remarked, 'I knew it. She had to go and use my paints; forget the crayons and markers. But at least she didn't throw a fit and trash the studio.'

'Who?' gasped Maurie.

'Now, that is the question.' Although I myself had few doubts anymore. Unmistakably, the paintings had been done by a child, because kids nearly always painted that way, grabbing the paintbrushes in a ham-fisted grip and scrubbing colors on to the paper, making laborious outlines with paint rather than filling in forms, and wreaking utter ruin upon the bristles of the paintbrushes, which was why I had put my good brushes away.

All of the sheets of paper had been used. On the easel, the

paper had been turned sideways to accommodate four rudimentary people in a row, stick figures with balloon heads and flaring skirts: baby girl, small girl, not-quite-so-small girl and a towering woman with a wide-open mouth, looming over the three children. The gesture was unmistakable: she was yelling at them, arms raised; from one hand dangled something brown and snaky.

As for the pictures that lay overlapping on the floor, I wanted a closer look at them, but as I stepped forward, my daughters cried out and grabbed me to hold me back. I stopped and turned around to calm them down. 'Shhhh. Chill, you two. Now you know why I was so freaked out when I phoned you, but I've gotten used to it, and I'm pretty sure she's harmless.'

'Who?' Cassie whispered, wide-eyed.

'Well, it has to be the little girl from the backyard, don't you think? It started the night I found her.'

Cassie stared. Maurie's hands flew up as she cried, 'Mom, that's crazy!'

'What exactly started?' Cassie asked in the same stunned whisper.

I gestured at the evidence *du jour.* 'This sort of thing.'

Maurie burst out, 'It's just somebody playing tricks! It's got to be.'

'Honey, think whatever you want to think; it is what it is.'

Staring at the painting on the easel, Cassie breathed, 'The children have no hands.'

'Huh?' I turned to take another look.

'The children have no hands. That means they have no power.'

That was a lightbulb moment for me. 'The child feels helpless! That explains—'

Maurie interrupted, giving every indication of feeling helpless herself. 'You are both being gullible imbeciles!' She stamped her foot, gesticulated wildly, then took off running. A moment later, I heard the guest-room door slam.

'Explains what, Mom?' Cassie asked.

'Explains why she is so angry.'

'My pissy sister?'

'No, the . . . you know . . . the *child.* She stomped my beads, ripped up my origami – and look at these.' Maurie's outburst hung around me like a cloud, but I knew from long experience that she needed to be let alone for at least ten minutes before I tried to talk to her. So I allowed myself a mental shrug, then bent to study the other pictures the child – or whatever – had done, the ones on the floor. I picked them up one by one. Crudely painted – or drawn in paint – point blank and without perspective, they were somewhat ambiguous to interpret. One appeared to be a rounded sort of white rectangular object with jagged, ferocious flames shooting up from it. Another looked like a squat H . . . no, with a stick figure reclining on the crossbar, it had to be a bed, and above it hung a purple cloud dripping torrents of cobalt rain. The other pictures all showed the same object in various colors – at least it seemed to be the same object or nearly so, but it was hard to tell because each time it was nearly obliterated by a large, heavy black X.

Cassie had continued staring at the easel. 'They don't have any mouths, either,' she said, her tone still stunned. 'Not even sad mouths. The only one with a mouth is the mother, and she's yelling.'

So she, too, felt that the large figure was the mother. Oddly, my own daughter's intuition set my mental boat to rocking more than the latest manifestations of the inexplicable did. Beckoning for Cassie to follow, I fled to the kitchen. Coffee. I needed coffee and could tell it was ready; it had stopped dripping. Blundering to find three clean mugs, I figured out why Cassie's reaction had put me off balance; it resonated with my own far more than I had expected. She was supposed to be my pragmatic child, not the brilliant, insightful one. Maurie, not Cassie, was a scholar.

As if she heard me thinking, Cassie remarked, 'I've been studying graphology for years, Mom. I just never told you.'

'Why not?'

'Because half the time I was analyzing your work.'

My eyes opened wide and my mouth likewise, to spew questions, but Cassie headed me off. 'Not now, Mom. We need to figure out what to do about, you know, your nocturnal visitor.'

'Please, one crisis at a time.' I poured coffee, thus taking care of the first crisis. 'I was just waiting for Monday; I have a plan. Right after breakfast.'

Even before she slammed the guest-room door, Maurie had made up her mind: there was no point in her staying here, at Mom's

house, a minute longer, not when Mom had tricked her into this
visit with puerile stunts, seeking attention like a spoiled child –
because, of course, this morning's paintings were Mom's goofy
idea of a prank; there was no other rational explanation. To think
otherwise was just plain insane, frighteningly so, and fright made
Maurie angry. That, and the thought of her important academic
time wasted due to other people's stupidity, and having been made
a fool of, however briefly, determined her to withdraw from any
further involvement forthwith. Mouth clamped, Maurie rationalized
that, were she to stay, she might say or do something hurtful to
her mother. She had gotten her clothes on and was packing quite
rapidly but not in a panic – no, not at all – when her sister yelled
from outside the door, 'Berthe! Breakfast!'

Maurie unclenched her teeth to speak with what she considered
admirable calm. 'I'm not hungry.'

'OK! Don't kill the messenger!' Cassie's footsteps retreated.

Moments later, rental car keys in hand and luggage trundling
at her heels, Maurie reported to the breakfast table – but not to
eat. 'I'm out of here.'

Over their cereal bowls, Mom and Cassie stared at her like a
pair of clueless first-year students from the same sorority.

'See ya. Bye.' Maurie turned and headed toward the front door,
but she couldn't get away that easily, of course. Her sister inter-
cepted her.

'Are you taking the rental car?' Cassie demanded.

'Of course I'm taking the rental car! How else would I get to
the airport? Move.' Cassie stood in her way.

Cassie stepped aside, probably only because Mom elbowed her
to take her place. On Mom's face was that infuriatingly martyred
look mothers get when they are hurt, disappointed, stricken, but being
ever so calm about it. 'Maurie, honey, please don't go. We can talk—'

'No, we can't talk! I am going to *lose it* if I have to stay here
a moment longer!' Every muscle clenched, Maurie felt herself
starting to sweat.

'Sweetie, that's how I felt at first.' Mom reached toward her to
give an understanding pat.

Maurie jerked back. 'Don't touch me!'

For once speechless, Mom let her hand drop, and almost let her
mask of maturity drop as well. Her face struggled.

Cassie cried out in protest, 'Sis!'

'Never mind, honey.' Mom transferred the calming touch to Cassie and stepped aside, taking Cassie with her, as she gave Maurie a smile, the dreaded strong-mommy smile, fit to break a daughter's heart. 'You go ahead then, sweetie pie. Consider yourself hugged and kissed.'

Not trusting herself to reply, Maurie rammed out. She knew she looked and acted raving mad, and she hated that, yet felt she had no choice. She *was* angry. The alternative to angry departure was unthinkable.

Of course it hurt when Maurie left that way. It would have hurt no matter what way she left; the going away of a child, even a grown child, leaves a painful absence, not to say abscess, in the parent. But her going away in a snit made it worse.

Cassie and I stood there. Then she said, 'If you need to cry, Mom, for gosh sake, cry.' She hugged me.

Hugging her back, I allowed myself a few sniffles, then said, 'Howsabout if we both go back to bed for an hour, then start the day over?'

'Nah. I'm hungry.' Cassie let go of me and returned to her cereal.

I bleated, 'How long do you think she's going to stay mad at me?'

'Come on, Mom. It's not *you* she's pissed at, not really. Give her a few days, she'll deal.'

Comforted by Cassie's pragmatism, I sat sipping my coffee and thinking. After a while, I said to Cassie, 'Your sister has always been so logical about everything that what she saw here this morning scared her right out of her stringently academic mind.'

'Yeah, well, what about *my* mind?' Cassie stopped eating. With her spoon, she poked at her cereal as if it had turned against her.

'Are you feeling a bit spooked?'

'Well, yeah. Aren't you?'

'I was, the first few days.'

'And then?'

I shrugged. 'Then something in my head either clicked or snapped – it's hard to tell the difference – and I got over myself.'

'Clicked together or snapped apart, huh?'

'The jury remains out.'

Cassie leaned back, giving up on her cereal but not, apparently, on me. I saw a faint smile. 'You said you had a plan.'

'Yes, I do.' Then I shut my mouth quite decidedly.

'But you're not going to elaborate.'

This was correct, as I indicated with a shrug. I did not care to talk about my plan, which was to get a good look at the skeleton found in my backyard in order to see whether the shape of its skull actually did match that of my weirdly begotten portrait of a child. What would I do if my eerie inklings were confirmed? I would worry about that later. First, just to get started, I needed the name of the nice woman who was the coroner. I got up from the breakfast table to peer around for it.

'What are you looking for, Mom?'

'Something I wrote down and put somewhere.'

Cassie rolled her lovely amber eyes. 'Could you be a bit less specific?' She knew I could have scrawled information on anything from a Sudoku book to a clothes dryer sheet, and she started turning things over accordingly. Eventually, it was she who found the origami paper under the hummingbird magnet. 'Is this it? Dr Marcia Wengleman?'

'Yes!' I pounced. 'Now we need the phone book.'

'Oh, Lord.'

'It should be right by the phone.' I found the book.

'And the phone is right where it belongs, attached to the wall,' said my daughter in sar-Cassie-tic approval.

Ignoring her, I flipped pages, found what I wanted, then dialed Dr Wengleman's office in the Skink County Courthouse. A secretary picked up. I was pleased but not surprised when Dr Wengleman accepted my call; I had thought she was my kind of person. Her voice sounded friendly. 'Good morning, Mrs Vernon.'

'Please, call me Beverly.'

'Beverly, what can I do for you?'

'I need access to my skeleton, please. Or not *my* skeleton, exactly, but you know what I mean.'

She knew, and sounded distressed not to be able to oblige. 'I'm sorry, but unless there's some compelling reason—'

'I need to give her collarbone back.'

Marcia Wengleman's voice skidded upwards. 'You have the missing collarbone?'

'Yes, but in all the commotion, I'd forgotten about it until now.' This was true.

'Could you please bring it to my office? Immediately? The medical examiner is transporting the remains to Tallahassee later today.'

Aaak. I was just barely in time to see that skull. I took it upon myself to be stubborn, dense and eccentric. 'I want to return it directly to the little girl herself, Doctor Wengleman. That child means a lot to me, and unless I can see her and explain to her, I prefer to keep the collarbone as a memento.'

Sheriff Pudknucker, I'm sure, would have come after me with a warrant, and certainly the coroner could have threatened the same, but she only said plaintively, 'You can't do that!'

'Then let me see the girl, please.'

I imagine she rationalized capitulation as an acceptable shortcut through what could have become a major legal hassle. 'All right. Meet me at the morgue in an hour.'

After getting directions, I thanked her, hung up and turned around to find Cassie staring at me. 'You have the collarbone? In the *house*?'

'In the breadbox, to be exact.' It felt nice to know where something was for a change. I crossed the kitchen to lift the lid, peered and once again lost my faith in my own sanity.

I was staring at an empty tin box.

I said a few bad words, then, 'I put it here, dammit! Collarbones don't just walk off by themselves!'

Cassie muttered something to the effect that in my world they might. Ignoring her, I yanked open a kitchen cupboard and started rooting. 'Cassie, help me find it!'

She did that for a while, climbing on a chair to inspect the high shelves and the top of the refrigerator for me. But when we had tossed practically everything in the kitchen on to the floor, she became impatient. 'Mom, this is hopeless. I'm going to take a shower.' She stalked off, and perhaps did not intend me to hear when she mumbled, 'I should have bailed with Maurie.'

Maybe she didn't believe there had ever been a collarbone. But

I knew there was, dammit! Lunging into the front room, I started pulling cushions off the sofa.

From the back of the house, Cassie screamed, 'Mom!'

If anybody had asked me, I would have said I couldn't run anymore, not at my age, and I would have been mistaken. When my baby girl called me like that, I dashed to her.

She was standing beside the bathroom with a towel wrapped around her, staring at something in the bathtub – maybe a scorpion, I thought. They had been known to intrude.

'I pulled the shower curtain back,' Cassie said not very steadily, pointing, 'and there it was.'

I looked. No, it wasn't a scorpion. In the middle of the empty bathtub lay the missing collarbone.

Cassie didn't mind that her mother took the collarbone and left to meet the coroner without her. She had thought she wanted to go along, but when push came to shove, she felt as if she could do without any more weirdness for the next few hours. In fact, trying to calm down and relax, she prolonged her shower until her skin began to prune.

And no matter how much she tried to space out, she couldn't help thinking. How had the collarbone gotten into the bathtub? It certainly had not been there yesterday evening, when Maurie had showered. Cassie thought about maybe phoning Maurie – or, no, texting her to call back when she got off the plane – but decided against it. Maurie would almost certainly think Mom had put the collarbone in the bathtub herself. For the time being, until she'd had a chance to unbend a bit, Maurie was Cleopatra, the Queen of Denial. Maurie thought Mom was playing games. But whatever was going on at Mom's place wasn't Mom's idea of fun, Cassie felt sure of that. She could tell this was not a laughing matter to her mother. Mom was dealing with it because she had no other choice.

How the hell had the skeleton's collarbone put itself in the bathtub?

For that matter, how the hell were any of the weird things going on in this house happening?

Cassie had no answer and doubted she ever would.

Maybe she was asking the wrong question. Maybe a better question would be: Why?

Why had the collarbone ended up in the bathroom?

No reasonable answer came to mind for that, either.

Sighing, Cassie turned off the shower and got out. While she had been in there, the only thing she had decided for certain was that the water was ridiculously hot; the water heater had to be set way too high. Toweling herself dry, she made a mental note to help Mom correct that.

Helping Mom. That was what this trip was supposed to be all about. Cassie could kind of understand why Maurie had bailed, but she was not going to. Not. She was staying until . . . until something made sense.

Damn, she had to figure this thing out. Why had that bone been in the bathtub?

After getting dressed, Cassie wandered into the studio and looked at the childish drawings again. Especially the one on the easel. Three girls, no hands, no mouths, and their powerful mother . . .

Cassie had never been 'whupped' in her life, but just the same, it hit her like a whupping: the brown, snaky thing dangling from the mother's hand was a belt.

EIGHT

Marcia Wengleman stood leaning against her official van, waiting for me as I pulled around the small local hospital into its back parking lot. Apparently, she was used to the heat; she made no effort to shade or fan herself. She was wearing a tank top, shorts and flip-flops; in other words, she was professionally attired by Cooter Spring standards.

I grabbed my portfolio (in the bottom of which I had placed the bone of contention) as I got out of my boxy old Volvo. No purse; I detested dragging a purse around, and had ceased decades ago. I carried my wallet and keys in my pockets. In fact, I no longer would buy any clothing without pockets.

Dr Wengleman met me with a smile. 'Collarbone?' Just asking, her tone said.

'Not until I've seen the skeleton.'

'Okey dokey. This way.' She led me to the building, unlocked a featureless steel door, ushered me in, then escorted me downstairs into what must have been the hospital's basement, where she unlocked another heavy-looking steel door. I stepped into a large room that felt refrigerated.

'Not that our kiddo needs to be on ice,' she remarked.

The overhead lighting was bright enough to make me wince. And despite being chilly and looking spotless, the place reeked. 'You need Febreze,' I said.

'Maintenance scrubs the place daily with Clorox and Lysol, and we've hung so many air fresheners it looks like Christmas, but it's no use. Nothing puts a dent in the smell of death.'

'Do you ever get used to it?'

'Not really, although I've been told you can create a similar stench by burning human fingernail clippings.' She walked over to one of the stainless steel lockers in the wall. 'Ready?'

I almost wasn't. I almost thought Maurie was right – this was all ridiculous, this was the moment when I should say 'Never mind,' get out, go home and forget about the whole thing. I was cold, I was sweating and I couldn't speak. But I nodded.

She opened the locker, pulled out a sort of body drawer, and I found myself looking at the mortal remains of my imaginary grandchild.

Laid out anatomically, the bones filled only half of the metal slab. The child's proportionately larger skull made the skeleton of the body look stunted, starved, pitiful, and . . .

And subtly wrong.

'That's not my skeleton!' I blurted. 'That's a boy!' I glared at Dr Wengleman, thinking she had tried to pull a fast one on me, but the horrified look on her face made me think again. This skeleton was that of a boy, but it also had a missing collarbone, and fragments of rotting posy-print fabric were laid out below its twiggy, ecru feet.

Feeling pretty much the way Marcia Wengleman looked, I whispered, 'She was a boy, but they dressed her as a girl. And killed her.'

Marcia rushed toward me to place an imploring hand on my arm. 'Shush. Please hush. Beverly, that's information the police are holding back. How in the world did you know?'

'I'm an artist. I know anatomy. I know female pelvic structure when I see it, and that is not it.' Overdramatically, I pointed.

'I never should have let you in here.' Marcia clutched me with both hands. 'If you blab about this, the shit I'll be in, I might as well go flush myself down the commode.'

'Right off the top of my head, I can't think of any reason I would tell anybody.' Extricating myself from Marcia's grip, I opened my portfolio, pulling out both the portrait and the other thing that was in there: the collarbone. Handing the bone to Marcia, I held the portrait at arm's length, gazing, and from the paper an all-but-living child scowled back at me: a square-jawed, hard-faced boy – every contour of his face boyish; how had I not realized that all along, despite the dress? I felt well acquainted with him, as if I ought to apologize for not knowing his name. 'Sorry,' I murmured, and only then could I turn my head to look at his skull. I went over to stand right beside it, my focus darting back and forth.

Meanwhile, Coroner Wengleman positioned the collarbone where it belonged in the layout of his remains, then looked at what I had in my hands.

She was already upset, and the portrait didn't help her any. 'Oh my God, where did you get that?'

Where, indeed? From a haunt? A stubborn spirit? A vengeful paranormal presence? In no way could I tell the truth, so I answered obliquely, 'I told you, I am an artist.'

'*You* painted *that*?'

I only nodded, intent on comparing the portrait with the skull.

'But . . . but it looks one-to-one. Are you a forensic artist?'

The shape of the eye sockets looked right, and that of the jaw and of the skull itself.

Marcia babbled, 'The print of the dress looks just like hers. His. And the head—'

'How old do you think she – the child – *he* was?' I managed to ask.

'The teeth are the most accurate way to tell, and they put him at right around six years old. It's too bad his teeth are not showing in your picture.'

'He had nothing to smile about.'

'I just meant we could compare . . .' The coroner let the sentence trail away into an awkward silence, then said abruptly, 'We still can.' Not quite steadily, she turned to a file cabinet, removed a couple of folders, took them to a photocopier along the wall and proceeded to use it, but not with paper. On to transparent plastic sheets, she copied several photographs of the skull taken from slightly different angles, then said to me, 'Lay your picture down flat, please.'

I did so, on the bare metal slab extending below the child's skeletal feet. Marcia came, looked, chose among her plastic overlays and placed one on my depiction of the child's face. She adjusted it slightly, stood back to scrutinize and said, 'This cannot possibly be a coincidence.'

I did not speak. I suppose I could not speak. Seeing the transparency atop my painting made me feel as if I were seeing the skull beneath the skin of one of my daughters.

'The orbits align perfectly,' said Marcia in heightened tones of incredulity, 'and the lines of the mandible, and the shape of the nasal aperture, and the malar bones, and the curve of the frontal.' She turned on me. 'How did you do this?'

'I don't know.'

'But you even got the length and color of the hair right! You must know something!'

'Really? The hair hadn't rotted?'

'No, hair resists decomposition, and the dress was still there because synthetics such as rayon—' She cut herself off.

I remembered the new, big-deal fabrics of the fifties. Rayon–cotton blends. Permanent press. Drip-dry.

Marcia Wengleman repeated, 'How did you *do* this?'

'I'm not sure. It wasn't normal.' I managed to shift my focus from the painting to her face, to her eyes suspiciously intent on me. 'But I don't know what happened to her. *Him*,' I corrected myself. 'I don't know his name or who he was.'

'So *how* in God's name—'

I interrupted her. 'I'll make a deal with you.'

Silence; her stare softened to a thoughtful gaze.

'You don't want me to tell anybody about . . . him.' I gestured toward the pathetic remains. 'All right, I promise I will not reveal his secret gender, if you will promise not to tell anyone about this painting.'

She looked down and took the transparency away. We both pondered the portrait for a moment.

'It's extraordinary,' she murmured.

'And inexplicable. So, do we have a deal?' I asked.

'Deal,' she agreed, and we shook hands on it.

Flopped on the bed in Mom's guest room, Cassie barely noticed the painted ceiling; she had grown up with painted ceilings. Mom, being Mom, had always painted them. This one depicted a blue-with-white-clouds sky, leafy branches as seen from below, plus robins and various other songbirds, also as seen from below, perched on the branches or flying overhead. It was a damn good thing Mom's birds couldn't poop, thought Cassie as she phoned Creative Java to stay in touch with the employee – a dependable employee, she hoped – the woman she'd left in charge during her absence.

Plaintively, this person asked when Cassie would be back. Wednesday, as planned, Cassie told her, trying to sound reassuring. Secretly, however, she had her doubts.

To assuage her guilt, after hanging up she did some ordering for the business on her smart phone via the internet. Then she checked her email, browsed Facebook, got bored and put the iPhone away. Sighing, she got up to look out the window at the backyard thriving with bushes, vines and weeds that Mom no doubt cherished as wildflowers. This area was beautiful in a tropical way, but daytimes seemed always too hot to go for a walk. Wondering why she felt bored and restless, Cassie realized she was anxious for her mom to get back from seeing her pet skeleton.

Maurie would have a brain seizure if she heard about that expedition.

Or about the collarbone Mom had been stashing.

Or the way it had somehow ended up in the bathtub.

'If it looks like a duck and quacks like a duck and waddles like a duck, around here it's a platypus,' Cassie muttered. 'And Maurie doesn't like platypi.'

Without conscious decision, Cassie ambled out to the studio and stood looking at certain crude paintings done as a senile sort of trick by Mom, according to Maurie, but according to Mom, by . . . something else.

Cassie considered that she had never actually seen a platypus. Nor had she ever actually seen a ghost. So why believe in platypi if she didn't believe in ghosts?

Still, she felt pretty damn uncomfortable thinking that something spiritous had been at work in Mom's studio. But whoever or whatever had drawn the recent pictures, she felt sure it wasn't her mother. The thing about Mom's artwork, remarkable for a picture book illustrator, is that she never used the aww-poor-wittle-baby tricks. No neotene heads, no oversized eyes. Her people and animals were appealing because of their grit and sturdiness. So was Mom herself. If Mom spontaneously sketched a tree, it would be a gnarly old oak with character. If Maurie sketched a tree – Cassie had never seen her sister draw, but she imagined Maurie would draw very straight, symmetrical, orderly trees. As for herself, she didn't feel like sketching a tree or anything else right now. The pictures she was studying made her feel queasy in her mind.

The stick-figure children had big eyes – *huge* eyes – with detailed eyelashes, the sort of eyes drawn by someone very needy indeed. The child lying on the bed was not sleeping but wide awake, with the same beseeching eyes. And all of the pictures sprawled out of control, the bed disproportionately large, the mother so over-powering that her arms and hands had to be distorted in order to fit on the paper. *Her* eyes were just slashing lines. All of the pictures were done with harsh, angular, brutal lines, not the kind Mom would use at all. The flames leaping out of the white box didn't curl; they looked jagged, like a lot of red-hot daggers . . .

Too hot. Dangerous. Could burn.

Something in Cassie's mind either clicked together or snapped apart, and intuitively she knew.

She knew what the white box was supposed to be.

Her insight terrified her.

But at the same time she wanted to cry.

NINE

Waiting in Atlanta for her connection back to Ithaca, instead of phoning her husband – no problem; he wasn't expecting her for another two days – Maurie phoned her Aunt Gayle, her father's sister. Still shocked and shaken by her curtailed visit with her mother, Maurie needed to talk with someone more sympathetic and, face it, more *female* than a husband. Even more than she needed a ride home to her work-in-progress Victorian house in Ithaca, Maurie needed to vent.

Aunt Gayle was a fashionable woman who occasionally invited Maurie to come on down to New Jersey and join her on a jaunt to Manhattan for lunch at a very nice restaurant and some shopping in the most exclusive stores to purchase (Aunt Gayle) or pretend to contemplate purchasing (Maurie) designer shoes and purses. This was not something Aunt Gayle did with Cassie and had certainly never done with Mom. Maurie had noticed at her father's funeral, not for the first time, that her mother and her aunt, while perfectly civil to each other, weren't exactly a mutual admiration society. In full-on brat mode, eager to tattle on her mother, Maurie knew exactly whom to call.

'Hello?' fluted an exquisitely cultured feminine voice.

'Aunt Gayle, you're not going to believe what she's done now.'

'Maurie, dear! Is this Beverly we're talking about?'

'Of course it's my mother. She found a skeleton.'

'No!' Aunt Gayle sounded scandalized already. Maurie felt sure that if Aunt Gayle ever found a skeleton, human or otherwise, even that of a child, she would quickly and decently cover it up again.

'Oh, yes.' Maurie relished dishing the details, facts first, then the bizarre happenings and suggestions that made her frightened and furious – although she acknowledged the fury, not the fright. 'Have you ever heard anything so ridiculous? She really seems to expect me to believe there's a freaking ghost.'

'Honestly!' Aunt Gayle commiserated awhile longer, then asked,

'And what does her next-door neighbor think? That very religious person you told me about once?'

'Um, Wilma Lou?' Maurie could never help showing off her good memory. 'Wilma Lou Ledbetter?'

'Is that her name?'

'Yes, I believe so. I'm not sure how much she's heard about any of this.'

I drove home from the morgue with my mind churning like a washing machine. A boy. My sweet little girl was an angry boy dressed as a girl, and, being a thoroughgoing feminist, I felt infuriated that a dress should be perceived as a shame, not a compliment. Yet, as a reluctant realist, I knew the child had been cruelly shamed. And this alarmed me, the cruelty, and it made me wonder, with a queasy feeling, how he had died.

I walked into the house to find my daughter Cassie looking all too much the way I felt. Rather than relaxing with a book, she was on her feet studying the prints that covered my front-room walls, kind of a visual history of my career: *The Duck That Ate Dirty Socks*, *Petunia Wanted a Pony*, *Cats of a Clowder* and so on.

I set down my portfolio. 'What's the matter, Cassie?'

'Who says something's the matter? Can't I look at your art?' Cassie gave what seemed like a genuine if ghostly smile. 'You know, Mom, your muscular trees show tremendous emotional vitality.'

'Do I hear graphology speaking?'

'Yes. And there's conscientiousness in your details, showing that you never trivialize anyone, especially not children. Unlike most adults, you are constantly aware that children are people. You have been a lifelong advocate for children.'

'Heavens.' I found myself abruptly sitting down. 'Stop it, Cassie, before you make me cry.' Honestly, she had brought moisture to my eyes. 'Did something happen while I was gone?'

She sighed, sat down on the sofa next to me and said, 'First, tell me about your visit with the coroner.'

'It was about as jolly as you'd expect, given the skeletal nature of our business. Cassie, you're being evasive.' I turned to give her a steady look. 'What's going on?'

With another sigh, she said, 'You know the brown snaky thing the big woman is holding in the child's . . . the picture, the one on the easel?'

'Yes?'

'I think it's a belt. And there's more.' She looked at me, and I had never seen her eyes so bleak.

I felt my mouth grow dry. 'What?'

Instead of answering at first, she stood up, took me by the hand as if she were the mother and I were the child, and gently tugged. She led me into the studio, to the big picture on the easel. I felt my heart squeeze; yes, the brown thing in the angry woman's hand was definitely a belt.

Cassie crouched and collected in her hands the many X-ed-out pictures of a child sleeping under a cloud dripping rain. Very quietly, she said, 'I think these mean she wet the bed.' She stood up, clutching the papers in unhappy hands. 'And I think she was punished. You know that expression people use for being in trouble – "I'm in hot water." Wasn't that once literally a way some abusive people disciplined their children?'

Both of us focused on the picture of a white box shooting jagged orange flames. 'Oh, my gosh,' I murmured, for the first time seeing the white box as the bathtub, but I didn't need to say it; we both knew.

'That's why she put the collarbone there,' Cassie said.

I felt a strange, transforming anger take a smoldering hold on me. They had mistreated him. Beaten him. Abused him so badly he had died. My spirit grandson.

Cassie must have seen something in my face. 'Mom?'

'I think my tree of tremendous emotional vitality has just turned to charcoal and stoked a furnace.' I stood up and got moving, smoking hot with wrath and intent on action. Never before in my life had I felt such a vigilante anger. I slammed all over my house searching alien, masculine utility crannies – in the bathroom, the laundry room, the garage.

'Mom,' Cassie asked with caution after a while, 'what are you looking for?'

'The goddamn water heater! Why the hell hasn't it been turned down before now?'

Because nobody could find it; that was why. Cassie started hunting along with me. 'Basement?'

'There is no basement.'

'Attic?'

'Who ever heard of putting a water heater in the attic?'

'We've looked everywhere else.'

So we started to look for a way to get to the attic, and eventually found a trap door in the top of the tool closet. Then we had to pull out dusty boxes and a huge old vacuum cleaner I never used. Grumbling about how people ought to have stepstools, Cassie climbed on to a chair and hoisted herself into the attic. I handed her a flashlight.

'Ductwork, wiring, insulation,' she reported in an echoing voice from overhead. 'Nameless detritus. Nothing that even remotely resembles a water heater.' She climbed back down and dusted herself off, sneezing. I shoved all the junk back in and closed the door on it. Then my daughter and I stood staring at each other.

'A phantom *water heater* now?' complained Cassie, as round-eyed as I'd ever seen her.

Through clenched teeth, I said, 'Certainly not. It must be somewhere.'

'Turn on the hot water.'

'Huh?'

'The hot water in the bathtub, Mom. Turn it on and let it run.'

Aha. I always knew my daughters were smart. With the hot water flowing, we tiptoed from room to room listening for the sound of borborygmus somewhere within the bowels of my house. In the kitchen, Cassie alerted like a bird dog. Then I heard it too: a murmur so muted that I wouldn't have noticed it if I had been, say, washing dishes a few feet away. It was a kind of purring sound, like a big cat hiding somewhere. But I still couldn't tell where the damn frustrating thing was. I confess that, expressing this to my daughter, I used several naughty words.

'Chill, Mom.' Cassie put her palms flat on a countertop.

'Laying on of hands? We'll be dowsing for it next.'

'Not a bad idea. Bring a wire coat-hanger.' But as she spoke, she moved along the kitchen counter, and just about the time I realized she was feeling for warmth and/or vibrations, she yelled, 'Score!' She punched the air. 'Here it is.'

The confounded thing was tucked into the corner of the kitchen underneath the countertop. And completely concealed, as I discovered after I snatched the flashlight off the top of the refrigerator, then peered into the kitchen cupboards on each side of it.

'No expletive entry panel,' I reported to Cassie as she came back from shutting off the scalding water in the bathtub.

'No wonder it's still so damn hot. It's impregnable.'

'Bring me a hammer, would you, sweetie?'

'You've got to be kidding.'

'I am over-my-dead-body serious.' I started yanking pots and pans out of the way.

Cassie somehow found two hammers, dear daughter that she was, and down on our hands and knees, our butt ends pressed together at a right angle competing for space, we battered and clawed at the wooden partitions. They came down eventually, but behind them we found insulation.

'Wait,' Cassie said, 'don't just yank it all out,' and she palpated the fluff on her side as if searching a breast for a tumor. Once I got the idea, I did the same on my side, and felt something like a steel nipple.

'Got it,' I said. She sat back on her heels as I bared the water heater control, studied it with flashlight in hand, then adjusted it down from 145 degrees to 120.

Standing, I felt shaky with relief, which was nonsensical; I had not saved anyone's life. It was way too late for that. But I hoped that somewhere close at hand, somehow, the spirit of a little boy was at least slightly comforted.

After lunch, I marched into the front room and started to take down off the back wall all the artwork I had taped up there.

'I'm not even going to ask,' said Cassie, watching.

This required no answer. I removed *The Duck That Ate Dirty Socks*, *Frog Eyes Dog Eyes*, *A Cow Named Checkerboard* (Holstein with square spots) and more – the entire visual history of my life's work. When I had cleared the beige wall – such a boring color, the reason I had covered it with illos from my picture books in the first place – I took my portfolio and carefully removed the child's portrait. Taping just the very edges, I positioned and flattened it on the center of the wall.

Cassie broke the silence. 'You should mat it and frame it, Mom. Or I could have it done, for the cafe.'

I smiled my thanks at her, not yet ready to say how much I had taken her offer to heart. Hope of a fresh new success in the art world glistened like a dewy imago deep in the chrysalis of my mind, yet to take wing. First things first. Caring for the nameless child in the portrait took top priority.

'Right now I just need to duplicate it.' I went for the camera; some of us still use cameras instead of mutated cell phones or tablets, although I will admit I had succumbed to digital photography.

Cassie asked, 'Duplicate it why?'

'You'll see.' I took half-a-dozen photos of the portrait in hopes of getting one that was nicely in focus, confound my shaky old hands, and then I took the memory chip from the camera and headed for my craft storage-cum-office space, where I booted up the computer. After selecting the likeliest photo of the portrait, I fiddled with it and ran a few copies on the printer before I got what I wanted: the child's face sized for typewriter paper, in black and white rather than in color. I studied it and became satisfied; the tonalities contrasted enough so that it 'read' well. I carried it out to the kitchen, where I found Cassie snacking on Fritos. 'Hey, kiddo, do you want to come to the newspaper office with me?'

I loved her quizzical smile, and her drawl as she said, 'Hey, Mommo, what the heck else would I want to do?' Only after we were in the car and headed down the road past cotton fields and trailer parks did she ask, 'Newspaper office?'

'I hope I'm in time to get this into the Wednesday edition.'

'Wednesday?'

'The local rag only comes out once a week.'

'Oh.' She nodded wisely, as if all was now clear to her, which I knew darn well it was not. But I didn't explain; I was too busy composing my ad in my mind.

The *Skink County Observer*'s office was jammed into one of Cooter Spring's rickety little plank houses, this one even more brightly painted than most: apricot with banana yellow trim. Under the shade of huge live oak trees with branches furred green by vines, we walked up the front porch and inside to find two desks, both unoccupied. This was not unusual for Cooter Spring. There were a few mismatched chairs facing the desks. Cassie and I each sat in one.

About five minutes later, a young woman wearing a tank top, shorts and flip-flops walked in and said, 'Hey, how y'all doing?'

'Fine, thank you,' I said. 'Do you work here?'

She sat behind a desk by way of answer. 'I was on my break.'

'Can I still get an ad in this week's paper?'

'Sure.'

'I want a quarter page.' I handed her the photocopy.

Her eyebrows, which seemed kind of stenciled on to her face, hovered like dragonfly wings. 'Just this?'

I tried not to let my face show how stupid she sounded. 'No, of course I need to write something to go with it. Do you have a form?'

She did – one of those printed sheets divided into spaces to force people to print in neat letters easily counted. I filled it out simply: *If you recognize this child from the 1950s, please call—*

Watching over my shoulder as I filled in my phone number, Cassie whispered, 'Mom, are you sure this is a good idea?'

'No, but I'm doing it anyway.'

'Who is she?' asked the airhead who worked for the newspaper, staring at the photocopied face.

'If we knew,' said Cassie in a far more reasonable tone than I could have managed, 'we wouldn't be placing the ad.'

'But is this an old photograph or what?'

'Or what.' I handed her the completed advertisement. 'How much do I owe you?'

It was not inexpensive; I hadn't expected a quarter page to be cheap. But I was able to pay in cash.

'Hey,' called the space cadet as Cassie and I were on our way to the door, 'I need your name and phone number.'

I paused to look over my shoulder. 'Why?'

'So I can call and ask if you want to renew the ad.'

'I'll call you.' I didn't point out that she already had my phone number.

'Oh.' She looked blank. 'OK, I guess.'

Waving dismissively, I walked out with Cassie right beside me. My daughter waited to speak until we were in the car and had the engine running and the air conditioning blowing at gale force. Then she put a hand out to stop me before I drove away, and she looked at me with frank concern. 'Mom, what's the big idea?'

'There's no statute of limitations on murder. That child deserves justice. I think' – I nearly used the wrong pronoun, but caught myself – 'I think she may *need* justice, and that's why she's so pissed off.'

There were a few moments of silence before Cassie asked cautiously, 'I don't suppose we could leave that up to the police?'

'Can you imagine trying to explain that picture to the police?'

'Right. So what do you think will happen after the newspaper comes out on Wednesday?'

'I have no clue,' I answered honestly enough. 'Probably nothing.'

'I hope. You know I have a plane to catch Wednesday morning. Do you think we could possibly spend tomorrow doing something normal?'

'I'm sure we can.'

But I was wrong.

TEN

Tuesday morning, I let Cassie get up first and go check the studio for spiritous incursions. She came back and reported through the bathroom door to me, 'Handprints. Bony little handprints in paint.'

'On paper or on the walls?'

'The walls and a few on the ceiling.'

To me this sounded more cute than angry, but I asked anyway. 'Did he' – faking a cough, I caught myself – 'did she ruin anything?'

'No, she didn't even make a mess. Are you looking for an excuse to cancel our plans?'

'No, no, not at all!' Cassie and I were going to the beach, the white sands of the Emerald Coast. We had packed beach chairs, beach umbrellas and beach towels, and a kite and tote bags full of sunscreen, sunglasses, sun visors, sun this and sun that in my car the night before. All we had to do was eat breakfast and go.

It took me only my usual commando few minutes to get my khaki cargo shorts on and load their pockets. Then I went to have a quick look at the handprints brightening the studio's boring beige walls. Smiling at their defiant colors forming rainbows and sunbursts up to and including the ceiling, I told Cassie, 'Our little friend had fun.'

'Ya think so?'

'Sarcasm, sarcasm.'

'How did she get up by the ceiling?'

'Think about it.'

'Well, how did she manage it without leaving drips and drops of paint everywhere?'

'Ah,' I said. 'There's the rub. There are more things in heaven and earth, Horatio—'

'Oh, stop.'

I stopped, and I actually cooked us bacon and eggs and raisin bread toast for breakfast, and if we'd just had cereal as usual, we would probably have been out of there before officialdom had time to ruin our day. But as it was, we were not yet finished eating when we heard someone knocking at the front door. Cassie got up to look out the front window. 'It's a cop.'

It was, indeed, a cop I knew: Deputy Nick Crickens, as I discovered when I opened the front door. I beamed at him. 'Why, hello! What can I do for you?'

He didn't smile back at me, and I noticed he had trouble facing me eye to eye. 'I, um, Mrs Vernon, ma'am, actually I'm here as provided by the authority of the Baker Act to serve a seventy-two-hour notice of protective custody on you.'

My life had been spent far from the world of officialdom; I simply didn't understand at first. 'What?' The nice young man's words seemed to float in the air like a big, bright orange Gulf fritillary that sailed by at that moment, and the butterfly seemed more important than what this doofus in uniform was saying.

Cassie, who stood beside me, asked stridently, 'Who is she supposed to be protected from?'

'Um, herself, miss.' Deputy Crickens held out a document that looked like one of those summonses you see on TV. Because my reactions had hit a speed bump, Cassie grabbed it and opened it.

'You need to come with me, Mrs Vernon,' said Deputy Crickens.

'Come where?' I asked reasonably enough.

'The hospital, ma'am.'

'What for?'

'Please stop stalling, Mrs Vernon.'

'I'm not. I just—' I was having a delayed reaction, and I was going to explain that I just wanted to know what was going on when Cassie enlightened me.

Actually, she yelped. 'Mom, Wilma Lou next door got some sort of order saying you're a danger to yourself and others, and they're going to put you under psychiatric evaluation!'

Realization, fear and adrenaline kicked in. My heart started to pound.

Deputy Crickens said, 'Mrs Vernon, come along now, and don't make me handcuff you.' He reached out to take me by the arm.

I started to pull away, but Cassie ordered me in heightened tones, 'Don't resist!'

I managed just enough self-control to obey her, and just enough sensible thought to yell at her, 'Call Doctor Roach!'

'Don't you want a lawyer?'

'Call Doctor Roach first!' I hollered back over my shoulder as Nick Crickens towed me by the elbow toward his cruiser. I had seen the doctor almost weekly during the previous flu/bronchitis/viral pneumonia season and, while I considered him kind of a prick, I still hoped he might verify that I was as sane as the average patient.

Cassie called Dr Roach first, and after shouting between her teeth at receptionist and nurse she got through to him, only to have him shout similarly at her. 'Roach here! *What* is the matter?'

To her astounded dismay, Cassie found herself sounding like a teenager. 'Um, this is Cassie Vernon, and they just took my mother, Beverly Vernon, in for a seventy-two-hour hold—'

'Chronic undifferentiated assholery!' he barked, hanging up on her, leaving her unsure of whom he was speaking and lacking any sense of reassurance. Next, she searched her mother's desk until she found the business card of a law firm in Cooter Spring, and she called them. A secretary picked up; no lawyers were available to consult at the moment, but the secretary herself was alarmingly knowledgeable, explaining to Cassie with relish that yes, anyone

– family member, friend, neighbor, *anyone* – could go to the courthouse and fill out a form to Baker Act someone – she used it as a verb – or heck, the form could even be downloaded from the internet. Anyway, most times the judge would sign an *ex parte* order as a matter of routine, and then the person being Baker Act-ed could be involuntarily hospitalized.

'But only for seventy-two hours,' said Cassie, trying hard to find a bright side.

'Actually, no.' The secretary's zest for misfortune audibly increased. 'If the doctors decide the person needs IIP, then they have five days to come up with a treatment plan.'

'Five days *after* the first three days?'

'That's right. In fact, if they want to, they can hold people indefinitely. That's what IIP means: Involuntary Inpatient Placement. Civil commitment.'

Having rendered Cassie temporarily speechless, the secretary then told her to have a nice day and disconnected.

Have a nice day? Cassie considered, with a momentary sense of irony, that she had come here specifically because she feared that Mom might need mental health care, but so what? And some strange things had happened, but screw that! Wilma Lou had no damn business, and Maurie had bailed, meaning she had even less. What the—

Suppressing the F-word, feeling incandescently pissed, Cassie phoned Maurie, who was sure to be busy tutoring or mentoring or something, and left a white-hot message for her. Finally, her mind sizzling with adrenaline and her muscles likewise, Cassie slammed out of her mother's house and headed across the yard toward the stodgy brick place next door.

She knocked on Wilma Lou's front door so hard she rattled its cross-shaped fake-flower wreath, and she rang the doorbell, and kept on knocking and ringing until the door was opened by a woman very nearly as skinny and bent as a fishhook.

'Why did you do that to my mother?' demanded Cassie with volume she usually reserved for deaf people.

Perhaps Wilma Lou *was* deaf. She peered back without replying and, Cassie realized, very likely without comprehension. Wilma Lou could have no idea who she was, as the two of them had never met before. Duh.

'I'm Beverly Vernon's daughter,' explained Cassie only slightly less loudly, pointing in the direction of Mom's house. 'And you *are* Wilma Lou Ledbetter, right? *Why* did you send the sheriff to take my mom away?'

The old woman's face shirred into an expression of righteous defense and she spoke up with twanging vigor, like a bluegrass band. 'What I hear, she's got bees in her bonnet and funny business in her brownies, what with her make-believe ghost and all, and worshiping animals and sleeping with the Devil.'

Luckily, Cassie's business experience, somewhat equivalent to survival training, had taught her mind to sort through a bombardment of data and seize upon the one thing that had to be taken care of first. 'You *heard*?' Cassie remembered quite clearly Mom saying Wilma Lou knew nothing about 'any of this,' meaning things that painted pictures in the night or went bump, whatever. Cassie stepped toward the rickety old woman, not exactly threatening but definitely pressing. 'You heard? How?'

'That poor heathen woman needs help, what I heard.' Just because Wilma Lou stepped back didn't mean she was retreating. She stood arms akimbo, sharp elbows deployed, chin up and trembling with indignation. 'I ain't done nothing but my Christian duty, and the lady on the telephone agreed with me.'

'*What* lady?' Oh, God, Cassie thought, please let it not be Maurie – but who else could it have been?

'Beverly's sister, she said she was.'

That made no sense. Mom had no sisters. Try again. 'Somebody phoned you?' Cassie asked a little more quietly, stepping into Wilma Lou's house, which was dark, heavily blessed with prayerful cross-stitch in picture frames, crowded with Victorian furnishings and smelled like Pine-Sol.

'The lady phoned me special because she don't live around here, see, so I had to do it, get Beverly committed because she has clearly lost her mind or else got herself Satan-possessed, what with messing up her own house and saying a ghost did it and making nasty pictures and saying a ghost did that too, and all sorts of sinful lies ever since she found that skeleton in her backyard, which might have been some sort of trick too.'

Cassie had several thoughts seemingly all at the same time.

Wilma Lou hadn't seen the messed-up house or the pictures; 'the lady' had told her. 'The lady' was the cause of Mom's being driven away by a skinny, carbuncular parody of a deputy sheriff. How much had Wilma Lou done to make it happen? Was it just a matter of filling out a form, or did she have to know somebody? No problem if so; Wilma Lou knew or was related to nearly everybody in Skink County. Trying to connect the dotty people involved was no use in getting to the source.

'What's this lady's name?' Cassie demanded.

'Well, you ought to know what her name is – she's your mother's sister!'

'My mother doesn't have a sister. What did she tell you her name was?'

Wilma Lou's scrawny hands flew to cover her mouth. Her old eyes, sunken in their orbits, tried to widen. She shuffled backward a couple of steps, bumping into a whatnot on top of which large porcelain figurines of Pinkie and the Blue Boy flanked her, standing blind guard.

'Her *name*,' Cassie insisted.

'She – your mother – really don't have no sister?'

'I just said so, didn't I?' Hearing her own tone, Cassie warned herself to cool it before Wilma Lou called the cops on *her*.

'She *lied*? The lady on the phone, she lied to me?'

The frail old woman seemed so rattled that Cassie calmed down. 'It looks that way. Do you remember what she said her name was?'

'Um, no, not rightly. Maybe it was *your* sister she said she was.'

'Maurie?'

'Um, I don't rightly recall.'

'Berthe? Berthe Morisot? Maurie Vernon Madison?' The old woman looked increasingly more blank as Cassie ran out of patience to wait for answers. Seemingly on their own, her fists clenched. Cassie felt a strong urge to hit something, break something, conk Wilma Lou's wobbly head with Pinkie or Blue Boy or both. So she turned to get herself out of Wilma Lou's claustrophobic house before she made things worse than they already were.

Just before Cassie slammed the front door behind her, she heard Wilma Lou quaver, 'No hard feelings.'

No hard feelings? No problem, thought Cassie. She was reserving her hard feelings for Maurie, who damn well better return her phone call.

ELEVEN

I sat in the back of the cruiser trying hard not to act like a crazy person, allowing myself no hysteria, thank you very much. To distract myself from my frantic anxiety, I deployed my regrettable sense of humor, thinking, *They're coming to take me away, haha, hehe, hoho, to the funny farm* . . . Separated from Deputy Crickens in the driver's seat by a mesh barrier, I nevertheless could talk to him, desperately trying to joke. 'How come they sent you instead of the little men in white coats?'

As I might have expected, he took me seriously. 'When we get one of these psych holds, I'm supposed to check it out, and if I need backup, I call for it.'

I persisted. 'And then they bring the wacky ward wagon with the straitjackets?'

'I wouldn't know, ma'am. To tell the truth, this here is the first psych hold I ever been sent on.' He sounded boneheadedly dutiful about it.

Giving up on him, I turned to another of my distraction strategies for scary times, watching through the car's window for another butterfly, or a showy clump of mushrooms, or a mockingbird on the wing, anything bright and beautiful. There was always something, no matter how bad things got. There: we drove into town, and there were the cypress trees of Cooter Spring, standing up to their knobby knees in sleek water, and cooters (or perhaps sliders) sunning on logs, smaller turtles stacked on top of larger ones to resemble squat pagodas.

Half in challenge and half in appeal, I asked Deputy Crickens, 'Do you seriously think I am *non compos mentis*?'

He didn't answer. He probably didn't understand the Latin phrase, right? Or so I reassured myself until he pulled up at the hospital door marked *Emergency*. A number of people in scrubs and, yes, white coats came hustling out to surround the cruiser or, more accurately, me. For a moment, my panic took over and turned me stupid, urging me to fight and break free and flee. Only Cassie's remembered voice, *'Don't resist,'* kept me from making a mental patient of myself.

They 'helped' me out of the cruiser, two of them flanking me to take firm hold of my arms, and escorted me inside, past all the people in the waiting room, toward the curtained cubicles in the back. Aaak. I looked mostly at the floor—

'Ex*cuse* me,' said a strident voice that in no way expected to be excused. Jerking my head up, I nearly choked on my own gulp of relief; Cassie had gotten through to Dr Roach, evidently, because here he came, all five foot nothing of him, striding toward us. Seeing him always reminded me of an inverted exclamation point because of his emphatic personality, plus his perfectly erect posture right up to and including his amazingly spherical bald head. Factor in his Napoleon complex sticking out all over him, and he took up so much space that his one-person presence in the corridor halted the little posse that surrounded me. I had often wondered whether Dr Roach abused energy drinks. Like a wasp, he packed dynamo clout into his comparatively small self.

'*I* am this patient's personal physician,' he decreed with barely a glance in my direction, 'and whoever initiated this farce might have had the courtesy to consult me.' He directed his pit-bull glare up at a white-coated man who emerged from a nearby examination room.

'Just let me get her examined and settled in a room, Doctor Roach,' said this individual, a tall yet droopy medico, with admirable restraint.

'*No*, she is *not* to be admitted. I am telling you as her primary care provider, she does not require treatment.'

'That will be my call. I am the supervising—'

'I don't care if you're the head bedpan! I am a *founder* of this hospital.'

The doctors glared at each other, and the surrounding hospital personnel shuffled their feet, then disbanded, although I could barely hear their retreating footsteps because my heart thudded so loud. I very much appreciated how greatly Dr Roach was indeed a prick, as I had thought, and how lucky I was that his prickitude was directed at his colleague on my behalf, as I had hoped it might be.

The supervising whatever-he-was, with his stooped shoulders, pendulous face and basset-hound eyes, was no match for Dr Roach in the face-off. He turned away first. 'Let me call one of my colleagues, and—'

'No, I'll let you call the *judge* and arrange a hearing.' For the first time focusing on me, Dr Roach said, 'Mrs Vernon, I don't suppose anyone bothered to inform you that you are entitled to challenge their jackass-wipe piece of toilet paper?' He swung back to the other doctor. 'I have not yet seen the so-called court order. Where is it?'

The unfortunate man handed Dr Roach a folder from which he extracted the legal document, opening it to scan it.

I remarked, 'I haven't really seen it either.'

My hint went unacknowledged.

'The original intention of the Baker Act,' lectured Dr Roach to the hallway at large, 'was to *prevent* the egregious imprisonment of unfortunate individuals in the name of mental health provision.'

I squeaked, 'Imprisonment?' I heard a gurney rattle down a nearby corridor like something out of a Victorian novel, stealthy footsteps behind me and, not far away, someone gave an anguished scream. I hoped it was not a mental patient. The footsteps I disregarded; if there was someone standing behind me, it was probably just a returning member of the white-coat posse.

'No, no, we don't *imprison* patients here, not at all.' With an eloquent sigh through his large nose, the doctor I knew as Head Bedpan turned to me. 'Mrs, um, Vermin—'

'Vernon.'

'Mrs Vernon, do you wish to contest?'

'Yes!'

'Good,' growled Dr Roach, still giving off the impression of being fireworks about to explode. 'I have work to do. Get yourself a lawyer,' he instructed me, handing me the paperwork. Then he strutted away, leaving me on my own.

'Am I free to go?' I asked Head Bedpan.

'Not until the judge—'

'I'll take care of that, ma'am!' piped a voice behind me. 'I'm an attorney.'

I swung around to see an eager lad in a suit, hair freshly cut and slicked, who looked all of sixteen years old.

'Ambulance chaser,' muttered Dr Bedpan as he strode away.

'Scott Clayton,' the youngster introduced himself, offering me his hand, which I accepted and shook with warmth and without hesitation. I had no doubt he was just out of law school, had heard about me on the police scanner and had come to my rescue more for a fee than for the sake of mercy. But I didn't care if he was a toddler in diapers as long as he got me out of there.

'Could I see the paperwork?'

Of course he could. I handed it over.

He took one look, handed it back and deployed his cell phone and his thumbs, texting. 'Less intrusive, easier on everybody,' he explained to me. 'Now we just wait to hear back . . . boom.' He pulled an InkJoy pen and a card from his shirt pocket, wrote on the latter and handed it to me. 'See you there!' He hustled away. I wondered where he was going in such a hurry, then realized: he'd heard the siren call of, well, sirens outside the ER.

I looked at the card. It was Attorney Scott Clayton's business card, with a phone number but no address. On its back were noted the date and time, the next week, of my hearing.

Finding it hard to comprehend anything that was happening, I must have stood there like a pillar of salt in the middle of the hospital hallway, and why salt, let alone a pillar, of all things? But finally my mental ducks began to arrange themselves, thus: it did not appear that Deputy Crickens was going to drive me back to my home, nor was Dr Roach or Dr Bedpan or my so-called lawyer or anyone else. I needed a ride. I needed to phone Cassie.

I found an orderly and asked to use a phone. He looked at me as if this request alone were proof of mental incompetence, then passed me off to a nurse, after which I was volleyed from nursing station to nursing station to front desk to administration. There was a pay phone in the lobby, but it was out of order – why were they always and forever out of order when needed? And no, I was not allowed to use the one sitting right there on the secretary's desk. Shuffled hither and yon like a refugee, finally I realized I was asking the wrong people, so I approached a humble, scruffy man in work clothes who was mopping a floor, his olive-drab sleeves rolled up. He said, 'A'course, ma'am,' and handed me a cell phone he carried clipped to his belt.

First I called myself, at home, hoping Cassie would pick up. A moment later, it occurred to me that, duh, I should have used her cell phone number, but by then it didn't matter because I was talking with her.

'Mom!' She sounded vastly relieved to hear my voice.

'How are you, sweetie?'

'Mom, if we were standing on the deck of the sinking *Titanic*, you would be asking me how I was. I'm worrying about you, that's how I am! What's going *on*?'

'Nothing. The redoubtable Roach rescued me, at least for the time being. All I need right now is for you to come pick me up.'

'All right! Where are the keys to the Vo?'

'They're . . .' I groped myself. 'Oh, shit. They're in my pants pocket.'

I suppose the expletive clarified that they were in the pants I had on. Cassie asked, 'Spare keys?'

'Of course I have some, but I'm not sure where . . . try under the bananas.'

Rather blankly for such an intelligent person, my daughter echoed, 'Under the bananas?'

'You know, in the basket on the kitchen table.' Which was not actually located in the kitchen, as the kitchen was too small, but between the kitchen and the studio, in what was rather grandiloquently known as the Florida room. Bananas resided in one of the baskets on that table, but other objects tended to collect around and beneath them, as if they were yellow dragons lying in a nest of treasures. 'Try the everything drawer in the kitchen, too. And the everything basket on the coffee table in the front room. And the everything box on top of my dresser.'

'Hold the phone, Mom.'

I did so, following its owner down a corridor. His life seemed to consist of slop, wring, mop, trundle the wringer forward on its tiny wheels, repeat. Brown, grizzled, bent, his arm muscles like thick ropes under his brown skin, he took time to smile at me, and I asked him, 'Have you worked here long?'

'Close to forty years.'

'That's a long time. Do you live close by?'

'Not too far. Up Esto way.'

'Esto!' As usual, I remembered something but didn't know what. 'Somebody was telling me not long ago . . .'

The friendly custodian knew a senior moment when he saw one happening. 'Two-Toed Tom Festival's coming up soon,' he diagnosed.

'That's it! Esto's the place with the giant alligator.' Gesticulating, I pointed his own cell phone at him. 'Have you ever seen it?'

'*Seed* it? Heck, no, ma'am.' Growing animated, he took a break from his work and stood up to talk with me, leaning on his mop. 'Ol' Tom don't let nobody see him, not in my lifetime. What a person gets to see is the carcass laying dead an' all ripped up, the cow or the colt or whatever it was, and the big ol' drag marks where that gator done come and went, and the tracks of that foot ain't got but only two toes on it. Years go by. Just when you think he gone it happen again. How he live so long nobody know. Maybe he a ghost now. He don't stay in no swamp like a regular gator. He—'

'Mom?' spoke a voice from the phone in my hand.

I gave a startled jump before I put the phone to my ear. 'Cassie! I forgot about you.'

She laughed, sounding both frustrated and relieved. 'Nice to know you're functioning like your normal self.'

'Did you find the car keys?'

'Yes, finally, in your craft room in a basket full of stickers. So where exactly in Cooter Spring is the hospital?'

I gave her directions, clicked off and handed the phone back to the janitor. 'Thank you so much.'

He nodded, smiled and lifted his mop, ready to get on with his work.

'Do you believe in ghosts?' I asked him. 'Alligator or otherwise?'

He paused to think, eyes wide; the whites showed, making his eyes look like hollow moons in a dark, dusky sky. 'Now you ask, ma'am, I don't rightly know. I always figured them was just stories.'

I smiled, nodded, walked away and sighed.

TWELVE

Fifteen very long minutes later, Cassie pulled up in front of the hospital, where I was waiting, sweating in the sun, but, damn, I was not going back inside that place, air conditioning notwithstanding. As I got into the Vo, which remained loaded with towels, chairs, rainbow kite and so on, I said, 'We still have time to go to the beach for a couple of hours.'

'Are you crazy, Mom? No, forget I said that; just tell me how you engineered your great escape.'

'We can talk while I drive. Move, please.'

'Sheesh!' But, relinquishing the driver's seat, Cassie looked relieved that I was acting so normally annoying. Truth was, I needed the feeling of taking charge and being in control, although I found myself being especially careful to drive sanely.

'Doctor Roach engineered my great escape,' I told Cassie, keeping my tone very matter-of-fact as I described the clash of the Great Ones in White Coats and explained how it had been resolved: I was to show up at a court hearing the following Monday.

'So you're not out of the woods yet.' She did not sound matter-of-fact at all; her voice rose with each word. 'I can't believe Maurie is doing this to you.'

'Maurie?' I screeched, as did the brakes; I slammed them on. We were passing through a small town with no traffic lights, one grocery, no houses larger than a shack and not a soul on the sun-baked sidewalks, but I reacted as if a child had darted in front of me. 'It couldn't have been Maurie!'

'It has to be Maurie.' Cassie sounded almost as upset as I now felt. 'Wilma Lou didn't know all that stuff about you. She says some woman phoned and told her.'

This shook me more than being taken away in a police car, the fact of the psych hold and the confrontation with Dr Bedpan combined. I swerved to the curb, stopped the car, put it in park and turned up the air conditioning because, for some reason, I felt hot. 'It could *not* have been Maurie,' I repeated, as if saying it louder would help.

Cassie spoke softly, sensibly. 'I don't like it either, Mom, but try to calm down and think—'

I hated being reasoned with, and I interrupted most rudely. 'Call Maurie,' I ordered Cassie.

'I already did and left a message. She hasn't returned—'

'Call her again.'

Rolling her eyes only slightly, Cassie pulled out a high-tech (to me, anyway) phone, hit a preset button, then speaker. I could hear for myself that the phone rang and rang and no voicemail picked up.

Cassie poked, swiped and started to put the phone away.

'Call Rob,' I ordered.

'This time of day he'd be at work, Mom.'

'Then call him at work.' Even to myself I sounded a bit shrill, so I took a deep breath, made my voice calm and explained, 'I want to get this thing settled.'

'You're pissed off, you mean.'

'No, I'm not.' I truly wasn't, not after the first shock. Already I had made up my mind. 'Maurie might be rigid, sweetie, but no way does she want to get me committed. Have some faith in your sister. Maybe Rob knows what's going on.'

'I don't have his work number.'

'Then call information! Loomis, Badcock and Madison, Attorneys at Law, Syracuse, New York.'

Sighing, Cassie humored me, leaving her phone on speaker so I would suffer martyrdom with her as she was passed from operator to New York operator to office receptionist to aide to secretary to executive secretary to paralegal assistant before Rob finally picked up. 'Madison.'

But speaking with Cassie, it only took him a moment to transform himself from lawyer to brother-in-law. 'I only saw her for ten minutes, Cass. She stopped by the office to tell me she was on her way to the cabin to do some primal screaming.'

Good for Maurie. I loved the isolated cabin in the Adirondacks, which had been in my husband's family for generations without much change. Not only was it safe from any cell phone reception, but there was no electricity, only a wood stove, and bathing meant

skinny-dipping in a frigid, glacial lake. To me, Maurie's going to
the cabin showed that she knew exactly how to deal with the slings
and arrows of outrageous relativity.

'She said your mother hadn't completely lost her marbles,
but there was definitely a hole in the bag,' Rob added. 'What's
going on?'

'I am an old bag with only the usual orifices,' I hollered into
the phone.

'Oh my God, Beverly, I didn't know you were there! I'm
sorry! I—'

'It's OK, Rob! I'm just joking around. What's happening is I
got pulled in this morning on a psych hold.'

'*What?*'

'A Baker Act,' I clarified, as Rob was a lawyer and maybe
would know what that was.

But he didn't. 'Pulled in? What are you talking about?'

I tried to explain but Cassie took over, concluding, 'So they let
Mom go, but she has a court hearing next week. Mom's OK for
the time being, but I am seriously pissed at Maurie if she had
anything to do with this.' With her tone getting edgier by the
moment, Cassie ended the call hastily. 'So we need to talk with
her, that's all, Rob. When she gets back, could you tell her to call?
Gotta go. Thanks.'

Snuffing the phone, Cassie told me, 'Your sense of humor sucks,
Mom.'

'Always has,' I acknowledged. 'What the heck is that thing
we're parked in front of?' I'd been eyeing it and trying to figure
it out for the past several minutes.

Rolling her eyes, Cassie sat back, looked out her side window,
and stiffened. 'No way! Has that been there all the time?'

'Presumably. It's a solid stone statue. They don't move around
much.'

'Of a *possum*?'

My view cleared since her head was no longer in my way, I
was able to say, 'Several possums, actually.' The monument, at
least six feet tall, enclosed by iron railings, stars and stripes waving
overhead, featured a bas-relief sculpture of daddy possum climbing
a tree trunk to mommy possum, identified as such by baby possums
riding on her back.

'But – but *why*?' Cassie bleated.

Trying to find an answer for her, I scanned the text carved into the stone below the bas-relief:

> Erected in grateful recognition of the role the North American possum, a magnificent survivor of the marsupial family pre-dating the ages of the mastodon and the dinosaur, has played in furnishing both food and fur for the early settlers and their successors. Their presence here has provided a source of nutri-tious and flavorful food in normal times and has been an impor-tant aid to human survival in times of distress and critical need. The 1982 Session of the Florida Legislature further recog-nized the possum by passing a Joint Resolution proclaiming the First Saturday in August as Possum Day in the Great State of Florida.

'Cassie,' I said, 'do me a favor and take a picture with that magic phone of yours?'

'What for?'

'So I can show it to the judge next week, as proof that other people, including the Florida Legislature, are crazier than I am.'

She stared, then cracked up laughing. I tried not to smile, not to show how glad I was to help her laugh.

When we got to Panama City Beach, we first checked what was waving atop the flagpoles all up and down the coast, and we sighed with relief: yellow flags, meaning only slight surf hazard, not red for dangerous rip tides or purple for jellyfish, sharks, Nile croco-diles or whatever. Yellow meant mellow. Thus reassured, we found an outdoors-in-back table at one of the little seafood shacks that squeezed between all the towering hotels and condos. Given those obstacles, sitting on an open-air plank deck to eat was our only immediate way to access a view of the ocean.

OK, technically it was not the ocean but only the Gulf of Mexico, with waves no surfer coveted, but with beach sand as white as powdered cane sugar and turquoise water shading to a vast bottle-green horizon. We sat on cast-iron chairs, the briny breeze messing with our hair, the seagulls swooping and keening, and neither of us minded how slow the service was. I know this because Cassie looked as entranced as I felt, both of us watching waves dancing their free-form minuet, an old man with a metal detector snailing along the shore, a parasailer billowing by in the sky. And I knew it because she ordered beer to go with her catch-of-the-day platter.

By the time we had finished our lunch, fetched our gear from the car, claimed a spot on the beach (it wasn't terribly crowded) and changed clothes in a grungy public locker room, I felt so in the moment that I had nearly forgotten about psych holds, Dr Bedpan, my instant lawyer and all the weirdness of the morning. I put sunscreen on Cassie's back, and she did the same for me, deploring my swimsuit. 'Mom, how many years have you been wearing that old thing?'

'Who's counting?' The one-piece old thing had a ruffled skirt that started just below the bust to conceal my potbelly, not to speak of everything else that needed to be hidden. I headed for the door. 'Last one in the water is an old thing!'

I did not actually intend to race, but the sand was so burning hot that it forced me into a jog, and I waded into the surf not much behind Cassie.

'Do the sting ray shuffle!' I hollered at her.

Bounding ahead, she paid no attention. I stood in a foamy wash of water up to my knees, then my ankles, then my knees again, and watched Cassie give the waves a frontal assault, then expertly dive beneath the curl of a big one. Well, no reason she shouldn't. The flags were yellow, which was almost as good as green, Cassie was a strong swimmer, and her bikini, while quite attractive, was substantial enough not to fall off her.

Smiling, listening to the siren song of the surf, I waded in a little deeper . . .

Sploosh, and a rude, crude, saltwatery assault knocked me head over teakettle, as my mother used to say, although I never knew exactly what 'teakettle' signified. Nor, with my head submerged and water invading my nose, did I care. I tried to stand up, but the water seemed to grab me by the ankles and tug me deeper. *Sploosh* again, inverted again, first sand in my face and then water and then sand once more; I felt myself being tumbled like washing in the dryer. I no longer knew which way was up, but I knew that sometime when I wasn't watching I had become too much of a wobbly old woman to stand up to waves, and realized with dreadful clarity that I was about to drown in ridiculously shallow water. My lungs screamed. I needed to breathe or die.

I dug my toes into the sand, then my fingers, and on hands and knees I crawled uphill – only by the slope of the sand could I tell which direction to aim myself. The water whammed me first one way and then the other, swooshing the sand out of my clutch; I dug in deeper and kept on keeping on. Even when the saltwater finally swirled away from my head and allowed me a gasp of air, I knew better than to try standing up. Submerged again as the next wave came in, I held on, then crawled some more. Inch by inch, between waves, gradually I emerged, like some sort of primeval life form, from the briny deep. I crawled until I reached dry sand, where I thought I could stand up. Ha! I wobbled halfway to my feet but found myself sitting right down again, facing my enemies, the waves. Shaking, coughing and gasping, I looked over both shoulders. Nobody on the beach seemed to have noticed me at all. Nor had Cassie, who was swimming about twenty feet out from shore, bobbing in the waves and grinning like a kid.

I sat on my big butt (aka teakettle?) in the sand, blew salty residue from my nose, caught my breath, stopped shaking and decided there was no need to tell Cassie what had just happened, because what was the point? I had found a skeleton in my backyard, a dead person was visiting my house, a shadow of doubt had been cast upon my mental stability and I couldn't seem to keep my balance in the water either? Nearly drowning was just another reminder of transience and mortality. It was just another tap on the shoulder.

How many times in my life had something like this happened? More than I would have realized, now that I thought about it. A drunk driver nearly ramming my car head on, a fall that would have split my skull if it weren't for a scrunchy, a gunman in a convenience store, a lightning strike, the Vo sliding nearly over a cliff on a snowy road . . . I had always felt safe and secure to the point of being boring, yet the way life was, hadn't I always been living with a ghost?

That evening Cassie somehow (I don't understand these things) sent her photos of the possum monument from her cell phone to my laptop computer, then showed me how to access them. Not trusting myself to remember all this technology until the next week, I printed them out, just in case I really did want to show them to the judge.

Emerging from my office/junk cave, I found Cassie in the guest bedroom with her luggage lying open on the bed; apparently, she was trying to get packed for her flight. I say 'apparently' because all I actually saw her doing was pacing and looking grim. I knew she was worried about the court hearing; I was tired of reassuring her about it while concealing the fact that I was worried myself, and I hoped she was not trying to decide to stay with me longer. I loved her dearly and enjoyed her company, but, apologies to Einstein, there can be such a thing as too much relativity, even in difficult times. Perhaps especially in difficult times.

Bracing myself for more advice about getting a good lawyer, I asked, 'Sweetie, what's the matter?'

To my surprise, she answered. 'Maurie!' Fists clenched, she glowered, although not at me. 'I'd like to hang her by her lovely superior ears!'

Was that all? I smiled, almost laughed, which I suppose would have been dreadfully inappropriate. Teasing, I said, 'And here I thought it was all about me, me, me and my questionable brain-power and my dubious paranormal visitor and my psychological balance being under investigation. But it's just sibling rivalry?'

By now Cassie had transferred her glower to me. 'Mom, it *is* about you! What's going to happen to you because Maurie—'

'Honey,' I interrupted, 'you're forgetting your name is not Cassandra.' She still hated the occasional times people had mistakenly made that guess at her full name, and hearing it coming from me, she looked angry and hurt, but I was trying to tell her something. 'You are not a seeress or a prophet of doom. You cannot predict what is going to happen. Right now you think Maurie did something, but in fact you don't actually know. Remember the magnificent survivor of the marsupial family?'

Even when Cassie had been a baby, the best way to calm her down had been to change stimuli. Necessarily, she stopped clenching her jaw, because it dropped. 'What are you talking about? That wacko monument we saw today?'

'Yes, that wacko monument. It failed to list all the virtues of the splendid opossum. Or spell out its correct name.'

'Mother, sometimes I think you *are* crazy.'

'It helps,' I acknowledged. 'Honey, a person can be clueless and a mastodon, yet still have some faith that life will go on. Don't jump to confusions about your sister, please?'

I spoke to her with my eyes while talking, and her eyes answered; I saw beginning in them a glimmer of a smile.

I said, 'Another virtue of the splendid opossum is knowing when to just play possum.'

Cassie rolled her eyes hugely, turned her back on me to resume her packing and firmly changed the subject. 'Mom, do you want to package that portrait for me to take with me? I could have it archivally matted and framed and on display within a week.'

'Good idea,' I said slowly. It would be a heck of a lot easier, and safer, to sandwich the portrait in tissue paper between two cardboards and send it with Cassie, than it would be to mail it. And much more quickly than I had thought, I could have a career again.

In the eyes of the people who counted – the critics and connoisseurs and doyens in the Big Apple – I could be an artist again.

So what was slowing me down, not just my speech but my entire inert body?

'Right,' I muttered, and once I got myself moving, I strode more than soodled into the front room where the child's portrait remained lightly taped to the wall. As this was not good for it, I took it down and removed the tape with extra care before I took it into the studio and placed it on the easel. I needed to sign it. With a tiny brush, somewhere inconspicuous, at the bottom. In indigo?

I stood there.

I needed to choose the brush and the paint.

But I stood there staring at the child, who glared back at me, and in his glare I felt the force of my responsibility for his flimsy existence. *I know it's not about me*, I had told him. I had thought of myself as his grandmother and his rescuer. If I now chose to sign off on him and sent him away, then what was I? Compared to, say, Judas?

'An artist,' I muttered, defiant.

Still, I didn't touch the brushes or the paint. But I wanted to. I did. I so terribly wanted to be a capital-A Artist again.

'Dammit,' I said, turning away from the child so he wouldn't think I meant him. 'Damn everything,' I said, huffing, but then I sighed and slogged back to Cassie's room. 'The kid's not finished with me,' I told her.

'Huh?' Suddenly upright, she spun to look at me.

'What I mean is I might need the portrait in case anybody answers my ad. Or in case I want to show it to the judge. I'll send it to you later, honey.'

She did not actually roll her eyes, but she might as well have. '*What*-ever,' she said, turning back to her suitcase.

THIRTEEN

The next morning, Wednesday, I needed to get Cassie to the airport. I drove the old Volvo, and we set out early, both of us still sleepy and sipping on second cups of coffee. Once south of Cooter Spring, we drove past nothing much except pine forest and cypress swamp and shallow pools quilted with water lilies. Human interruptions were sparse: occasional houses, one with a fire tower in the front yard; a rustic bait shop/raw oyster bar; a welder's shop displaying tacky lawn ornaments; a completely isolated dog racing track. The Vo was just about the only car on the road. After the first half hour, I had processed things enough and felt sufficiently awake to remark, 'Wednesday. It's been exactly a week since I found the skeleton.'

Cassie bolted upright in the passenger seat. 'Oh my God, Mom, I forgot about the newspaper coming out today, with your ad in it!'

'Right. Note to self: pick up a copy on my way home.'

'But what's going to happen now? I mean, are you going to be *OK*?'

I gave her the best amused glance I could while keeping my attention on the road. 'OK compared with what?'

Silence. Without looking, I could tell I had embarrassed her, and I hated my smart mouth. As gently as possible, I said, 'I know when you and Maurie came down, you were worried about my marbles, and the reason I knew was because I was getting worried myself whether I had one oar out of the water, cheese sliding off my cracker, wheel still going but the hamster dead, a couple fries short of a Happy Meal—'

Cassie protested like a teenager. '*Mom*, stop.'

'Porch light on but nobody home,' I concluded. 'And what's happened since hasn't exactly been reassuring, has it?'

'Understatement of the century.'

'Yet I don't worry about bats in my belfry anymore. Some might say I'm too far gone. What's been happening frightened me at first, but now it—'

I stopped to edit myself. No way would I ever tell either of my daughters that I had longed for grandchildren and that this was my reason for starting to paint the portrait. The truth was I felt as if I actually had a grandchild now, one who needed my care, and if that made me crazy, so be it.

'But now . . .' Cassie prompted.

'Now, legal papers and shrinks and judges be damned, the question of my marbles is moot. Things are not all about *me* anymore. Since the child came, he – I mean she – just totally overrides worrying about myself. I feel as if I've become part of something way bigger than I am.'

Silence. I got the feeling Cassie was mulling this over.

Then she blindsided me. 'Did you check your studio this morning?'

I gasped. 'Summonabinch, no, I didn't! We were in such a hurry . . . Did you look?'

Instead of answering, Cassie teased, 'So this kid that goes bump in the night is your new reality, isn't she? Practically routine.'

'Almost but not quite. Did. You. Look?'

'I took a quick peek. She sorted your paints by color and put them in kind of a wheel, a circle, on the floor. Unless you did that.'

'Sure, I do that all the time.' Meaning no, not likely.

We turned on to the airport road, driving between acres of slash pines interrupted by swamps and ponds, much as before. This part of Florida was very much of a muchness. Beautiful and lonely. I loved it.

Cassie said, 'Mom, what if they really do put you away?'

'They won't. And even if they did, that wouldn't be the main problem.'

'Mom—'

'And I'm sure I could appeal.' I stopped the car in one of many available parking spaces. This was not the world's busiest airport.

'Mother.'

Cassie's tone demanded me to face her. I did so.

Very seriously, she said, 'I want you to call me every day.'

I smiled. I wouldn't mind that at all. 'OK.'

In the Skink County Sheriff's Department's small building, the new issue of the *Observer* lay open on the break-room table, competing with Styrofoam cups and coffee spills for space. Usually, somebody would have been reading some news or sports article, but not this time.

Standing over it as he stirred creamer and sugar into his coffee, Nick Crickens eyeballed a sizeable picture on the advertising page. Seemed to be a photo of a painting of a child, and not a very attractive child, either. Kind of scruffy and sour-looking. The whole quarter-page ad consisted of the kid's unsmiling face plus a caption: *If you recognize this child from the 1950s, please call* and then a phone number.

He was not the only one staring. Looking over his shoulder, his boss, Chief Pudknucker, growled, 'I'd love to know what the hell that's all about.'

Nick felt an uncomfortable inkling that he should have a clue.

'Probably just somebody doing whatchamacallit, genealogy,' said another deputy.

'Pay for an ad like that just to fill in a blank on their family tree? I don't think so. I feel like calling that there number just to find out who it belongs to.'

Nick said, 'Nut case is going to get a lot of crank calls,' but only with the part of his brain that moved his mouth. Other parts of the rumpled lump of gray fat in his head were busy making connections. Nut case: 10-96. He had recently answered one of those – old lady who did painting and drawing, had goofy pictures taped all over her walls. Folded paper stuff hanging from the ceiling. Talkative. Which call . . .

Right. The 10-54 with a difference. Skeleton in the backyard.

A cold, cold case of probable homicide, on which the State Police detectives had made no progress at all, Nick had heard. They had counted on records of who had first built and owned the property, but those hadn't helped, because those people had leased the house to one renter after another before they sold it. And nobody had kept track of the renters. Why should they?

So that blew the only lead.

Unless this picture in the paper was somehow another lead.

Just before the chief told everybody to get back to work, Nick did. At his desk, he flipped open his notebook and found the right page, then looked at a name, Beverly Vernon, and the phone number he had recorded next to it. Then headed back to the break room and had another look at the phone number appended to the newspaper advertisement.

'Bingo!'

'What?' growled the chief, who had sat down at the table to suck on his coffee.

Deputy Crickens showed him. On Pudknucker's face the frown lines deepened as he compared the two phone numbers. 'Are you saying this picture got something to do with that skeleton?'

'I'm just saying "Bingo."'

'Well, bingo on out to your patrol car and get rolling.'

'Yes, sir.'

But on his way out of the room, he heard his boss mutter, 'Tadlock is going to *love* this.'

When I got back from the airport, my house seemed terribly empty, as it always did when my daughters left. Even when Jim was still alive, I'd felt the empty-nest blues whenever Maurie and Cassie had gone away after a visit. And living in such an isolated house now didn't make it any easier. As always, I drifted from room to room, feeling like a mama cat searching for kittens that had grown up long ago.

I happened into the studio, saw most of my paints set out on the floor in a big, elaborate array, and felt a smile start in my heart and bubble up to ease my face. The house was not empty after all. There was a child in it.

A child who had at first been angry but now made handprints on the ceiling and played with my paints.

Suddenly more contented, I sat in my Joseph chair and leaned back to study what the child had done with my paints. From Cassie's description, or perhaps from memories of my own childhood play, I had expected a lovely rainbow color circle blending the primaries, secondaries and tertiaries, hues and tones and . . . bullshit. This was not an art class or the creation of a little girl who loved beauty; I was seeing my studio as transformed by a combative little *boy* at play. He had marched my paints into rank and file, reds in one regiment, blues in another, yellows and greens divided into squadrons and platoons or what the hell do I know, with all of the bright colors facing off against an army of gray, brown and black. Every can or tube or jar of paint I owned was on the floor, but the white, off-whites and other soft hues were thrust aside, sprawling.

'Somebody doesn't like pink,' I murmured, still smiling like a proud grandma. The dress I had painted him in was lavender – bad enough from his point of view – but the dress some horrible person had buried him in might have once been pink. At the thought, my smile faded like the posy-print fabric, now bleak.

I muttered to myself, '*Why* did they make him wear a dress?'

The phone rang. Being an old phone, it jangled rather than warbled. Reflexively, my response to that sound being thoroughly conditioned since childhood, I hustled to get it, grabbing a pen and notepaper. Only as I picked up did I notice that my answering machine was flashing like a danger signal.

'Hello?'

Someone audibly gasped, almost choking.

'Hello?' I repeated with some concern.

I heard rapid, ragged breathing, and then someone – maybe a woman, maybe a child – whispered, 'Sorry,' and click, the line went dead.

'Hello? Hello?' I insisted, irrationally coaxing the silence before I hung up. The aborted phone call gave me the same odd feeling as tiny handprints on my studio wall. I had to pull myself together before I listened to the messages on my answering machine.

Man's voice: 'I'm just curious, where'd you get that picture? It looks kind of like one of my cousins, maybe.'

Woman's voice, querulous: 'That there picture, is that supposed to be a boy or a girl?'

Woman, plastic professional voice: 'Are you having difficulty locating a family member or loved one? Let me offer my confidential psychic services . . .'

I skipped the rest of that one. Then the next two calls were moments of silence after which someone, apparently hesitant, hung up.

The next call advertised the services of a genealogical researcher. The one after that recommended prayer and invited me to a tent revival. Then a stern female voice informed me, 'I taught school here for sixty years and I never seen no such youngster.'

Very helpful. By then I had started doodling a border of flowers on the notepaper, and I barely blinked when a man's recorded voice asked me with gratuitous profanity who the bleep I thought I was and what the bleep I thought I was doing. Humming to myself as I often do when in abeyance, I found myself drawing children romping among the flowers – happy, androgynous children in T-shirts and shorts.

I listened to another message that was not a message. Someone hesitated, then hung up.

I realized I was humming 'Sounds of Silence' by Simon and Garfunkel.

End of messages.

After a lunch of sorts – potato chips dipped in applesauce – I sighed deeply, rolled my eyes and made myself go look for the ambulance chaser's card. Fortunately, I found it still in a pocket of the shorts I had worn the day before. Scott Clayton, Attorney. On the reverse side, I found a date and time, which I wrote on my calendar with a sense of disbelief: the next Monday I needed to convince a judge I was sane, and how was I supposed to do that? Already the whole psych hold episode seemed like a bad dream, but I could not afford to be an ostrich about it. I marched myself over to the phone and dialed my so-called lawyer.

Instead of saying hello, he said, 'Scott Clayton, Attorney.'

'This is Beverly Vernon.'

'Who?'

'Psych hold.'

'Oh! Yes.'

'You never did tell me what your fee is.'

'You sound quite sane to me, Mrs Vernon,' he said coyly, and
the conversation went downhill from there. He wanted to meet. I
wanted to know how much that would cost. He stressed the need
for us to 'put our heads together,' telling me all the important
things he needed to do to ensure a happy outcome for me. Taking
notes, I asked again how much his doing all of those important
things would cost. He hedged. I insisted. He divulged. I fired him,
partly because I couldn't afford him but mostly because I didn't
like him.

I then phoned Marcia Wengleman. A woman of wisdom and
foresight, she had given me her private cell phone number, which
I took the liberty of using. She greeted me eagerly. 'I saw the
newspaper. You aced it, Beverly! You didn't let the cat out of
the bag at all; you covered our mutual ass beautifully.'

'Whoa, Marcia! Can anyone overhear us? I mean, is it OK for
me to talk about stuff?'

She chuckled. 'The minute I saw your name on the phone, I
retreated to a very private bathroom. Any responses to your ad?'

'Not any live ones, not yet. Marcia, I called to ask you about
something different. Can you recommend a good lawyer who won't
bankrupt me?'

'Lawyer?' Her tone switched instantly from chipper to concerned.
'For what?'

'For a court appearance.'

'*What?* Beverly, what's going on?'

I told her.

'Great galloping cooters,' she said, clearly stunned, 'I can't
believe it.'

'Why not? Given a skeleton in my backyard and so on, what's
a little ol' psych hold?'

'It's nice you can keep a sense of perspective, Beverly.'

She paused, and I kept my mouth shut, because I seemed to
hear her thinking, although I suppose really all I heard was the
ghosts that always seem to gibber within telephone lines.

'Beverly,' she said finally, 'I've been thinking of all the lawyers
I know, and, frankly, they're all more or less assholes, at least in
this area, and – do you think I'm crazy, or might you be better
off without one?'

'Nobody thinks *you're* crazy.'

'Right. Dumb choice of words. Listen, Beverly, what we're talking about is not a trial, full of legalese; it's an informal court hearing. But a lawyer would get between you and the judge, trying to portray you as a stereotypical little old lady, just a bit scatty and a Sunday School teacher. What if you just talk with the judge yourself?'

I said, 'Hoo boy.'

'Within reason,' Marcia said. 'Practicing a certain degree of diplomacy. You can pull it off. Can't you?'

'Let me think about it.'

Actually, I tried not to think about it for the rest of the day. This approach to problems, artistic or otherwise, had worked well for me in the past.

For purposes of thinking about something else, I went back to the junk-cum-craft room and started looking through a big cardboard carton of pictures I had bought at yard sales and thrift shops. More accurately, I should say I had bought good wooden frames fitted with glass; the pictures themselves I would discard, often with a shudder.

I pulled out several frames that were the right size, laid them on the floor and looked at them, feeling very choosy, even more so than usual, for the child. I wanted to frame his portrait. Temporarily, I told myself and/or the child. Just to safeguard it until I was ready to send it to Cassie.

I personally tend toward ornate, Victorian-style frames, but eventually I chose a plain, sturdy, burl oak frame I thought the boy might like. Not bothering to put the others away, I took it out to the table in the Florida room and got to work. After ripping off the backing and pulling out the old brads, I got rid of a fairly hideous still life (sunflowers drooping over the bulbous fruit of the eggplant) and settled down with a soft cloth and some Murphy's Oil Soap to clean the frame's fine wood.

At random intervals the phone rang, and of course I answered it each time, hoping for some helpful response to my advertisement.

I got responses, all right, but not helpful. Sheriff Pudknucker: 'Mrs Vernon, you got something you need to tell me?' Wilma Lou: 'I seed you're home and I seed your phone number on that heathenish pitcher in the paper and I don't know but maybe you should be put away like your family said.' Anonymous female: 'What for relation is that child to you-all?' Anonymous male: 'How come you looking for this here kid? You offering some kind of reward?'

After I had shined up the frame to my satisfaction, I took the glass to the kitchen sink and cleaned it with dish soap and running water, dried it with a clean dishtowel, then kept at it until there was not a speck or a fleck of dust or lint on it anywhere. The main reason I did my framing in the daytime was so I could see for sure that the glass was crystal clean.

The phone rang again. I was becoming reluctant to answer it, but I picked up anyway, then smiled; it was Cassie. 'Hi, Mom, my plane just set down, so I'm fine and how are you?'

'Coping.'

'With what?'

'Crank phone calls.'

'Oh. Because of your ad?'

'Yup.'

'Bummer.'

I thoroughly agreed. Then she had to go; her flight was disembarking or debouching or whatever it is planes do. Back at the studio table, I rigged spacers around the edges of the glass so the painting would not touch it. Very lightly I taped the edge of the portrait to the top of the backing. Then I began putting my frame job together, super careful not to let any dirt into it – difficult in my less-than-pristine home. But I managed. I was even able to find my brad pusher, and some brads, and eyelets and new wire. Triumphantly, around supper time, I held the child's portrait up to see how it would look in the middle of the space I had cleared on the front-room wall.

The phone rang. Carrying the picture with me, I answered. 'Hello?'

Silence, except for a faint sort of whimper that sounded quite involuntary. At once I knew which caller it was. Gently, trying to sound like the nicest of all possible old ladies, I begged, 'Please, talk to me. I don't bite.'

But I heard only another muted sound – a gasp or choke or a throttled sob – before the line went dead.

*   *   *

Getting the child's picture up on my front-room wall was not simple – one of the drawbacks of living in a house made of concrete. But eventually I found the electric drill and the masonry bit and the concrete screws, then managed to position the damage correctly on the first try, and hung the portrait that evening. Afterward I sat looking at it, feeling replete and needy at the same time. Such masterful art, worthy to be displayed in some Manhattan gallery. But such a messed-up 'pretend' grandchild I'd gotten myself. OK, I'd always believed in a spirit of goodness, and sometimes I had even believed in the soul, and maybe I was all wrong about an afterlife or even about resurrection, but I felt sure to my core my grandghost needed help. Having to be a ghost wasn't right.

FOURTEEN

Mauric felt better driving home after two nights and one full day of healing seclusion in a place almost completely silent except for a heron's crake, a kingfisher's ratchety call and the occasional slap of a beaver tail. Sunup to sundown she had spent either swimming in the lake or paddling it in the kayak, chilly evenings reading by firelight, and now, enjoying the drive along secondary roads meandering through the upstate mountains, Maurie had time for unhurried mental rehearsal of re-entry. First, she had to return the rental car. Rob would pick her up, and she hoped they could eat out, catch up, reconnect before she actually got home, unpacked and tackled tomorrow's schedule. And before she dealt with messages. There were sure to be scads of phone messages. And even if Cassie hadn't called her, she had to call Cassie, to clear the air. And Mom, for the same reason. Meanwhile, she had plugged her iPhone into the car battery to charge. She noticed when, halfway home, it started murmuring like a contented baby waking up. Lying there on the passenger seat, it tempted her, but she knew better than to text and drive.

The phone chimed Chopin. All of Maurie's ringtones were classical music, but Chopin was reserved for her husband. Her eyebrows shot up. Rob hardly ever called during work hours. Because the road was challenging, hairpinning down rocky terrain, Maurie did not pick up, but as soon as she found a place to pull over – a runaway truck ramp – she called him back.

'What's wrong?' she demanded.

'Greetings and salutations to you also,' he said, sounding a bit punchy. 'Global warming is wrong, terrorism is wrong, North Korea's having nuclear weapons—'

'Get over yourself, Rob! You wouldn't have called unless something was upgescrod.' This was 'German' for screwed-up.

'How well you know me,' he said, sounding whimsical, not sarcastic. 'You're not driving, are you?'

'I pulled over. What's the problem? Is it about Mom?'

'Yes and no. Somebody tried to have your mother committed to a mental facility, and Cassie thinks it was you.'

Gobsmacked, almost speechless, Maurie barely managed to squeak, '*What?*'

'You need to straighten things out with your sister.'

'Cassie, Schmassie. Is Mom OK?'

'She sounds only slightly inconvenienced by the prospect of a court hearing next week. Listen, hon, I gotta betake my ass unto a meeting. Drive safely, OK?'

Maurie assured him that she would do so and that she loved him, but once Rob clicked off, Maurie did not move to get her car back on the road. Instead, she watched unidentifiable flits of motion in the trees – birds, squirrels, leaves in a mountain breeze? Her nights at the cabin, isolated from traffic noise, TV or light pollution, had been a poetry of primal darkness punctuated by the mystery calls of unidentifiable presences – foxes, frogs, insects, owls or why not ghosts? She could somewhat better understand now why some people might believe in ghosts.

No. No, she hadn't just thought such a thing. It was insane.

The runaway truck ramp felt like all too fittingly ironic a place for her life to be parked right now. She wondered how her mother was doing, really and truly, whether she was delusional, whether it mattered if Mom was happy. After a moment, she listened to the voicemail message from her sister. Outside of her air-conditioned rental car, the weather was sizzling hot, but Cassie's message was even more so – scalding, scorching, blistering. The accusation implicit in Cassie's account of events and tone of voice impacted Maurie physically, making her gut knot and her butt tighten as if stung by a paddle. She dismissed her reaction as childish, like her urge to text back, *I didn't do it!* Of more concern were the questions raised: was Mother in genuine danger of being labeled, packaged and shelved as insane? Would she, Maurie, have to go rescue her? Was Cassie in the air right now as planned, en route to Newark Airport, or was Mom's situation actually dire enough to keep Cassie in Florida?

Either way, Maurie decided, she had to get home, back to her own turf, settled in with her back up against the wall of her own tastefully decorated living room, before returning Cassie's call.

Sighing, double-checking for traffic both over her shoulder and in the rear-view mirror, Maurie eased back on to the road, driving safely.

Around suppertime, I heard somebody drive into my yard.

I put the microwave dinner I had just chosen back into the freezer, then hurried to look out the front-room window, where I saw, bumbling like a hamster over my uneven yard, an old car partly held together by duct tape – a practice not uncommon in Skink County. What color car? So faded by the Florida sun, I couldn't say. The front bumper seemed to be sagging at one end, probably clinging to coat-hanger wire.

In other words, a pretty much representative sort of car for this area. In no way did I scorn it, because I foresaw that, after a few more years on social security, unable to make any art sales, I myself would probably be driving a car like that.

The junker stopped in front of my house, but nobody got out, not for a couple of minutes. Because of the way the light hit the windshield, I couldn't see who was in there, and I started to wonder what was going on. But finally somebody opened the driver's side door.

And as she faltered to her feet, I could see her.

A woman not much younger than I was, but a lot skinnier – not the stylish kind of skinny but the eroded-by-life kind – in T-shirt and shorts and flip-flops that showed some wear. No glints of polish on her nails, and nobody had ever taken much care of her rough feet or her dry hair frizzing out all around her plain, scared face.

Scared. Hesitating halfway between her car and my front door on my so-called lawn of wiregrass and pine bark.

It was so ridiculous for her to be afraid of me that I stopped wondering who she was or what she wanted; I just hurried to open the front door. 'Hello,' I called, friendly as a beagle.

She stared at me, apparently unable to speak but trying to smile. I felt a slight inward slosh as something about her bony, kind of square face gave me an inkling of déjà vu.

My interest heightened so that I positively radiated warmth and welcome as I asked, 'What can I do for you?'

The weathered-looking woman managed to speak, her voice barely more than a whisper. 'Um, hi, I'm Bonnie Jo . . .'

She stopped there, apparently running out of traction.

'I'm Beverly.'

She nodded, still wordless.

And I knew. Even though knowing seemed an audacious leap in defiance of logic, I just knew, but I tried to keep my voice soft and supremely non-threatening. 'Are you the one who's been trying to phone me?'

Her clay-brown eyes widened, but I swear she looked relieved. 'Yes.'

'Well, I'm so glad to meet you!' With acute effort, I remembered her name. 'Bonnie Jo.' I'm very bad at remembering the names of people I just met. Making welcoming gestures, arms lifting almost as if to hug her, I beckoned her to enter my house.

'The picture,' she said, her voice so low I could hear her only because she took a few steps toward me, 'the picture in the newspaper kind of looks like . . .'

Silence, and she stopped where she stood. She seemed to have run into an invisible wall. 'Come on in,' I urged.

She did. She walked forward but then paused on the doorsill, eye to eye with me and close enough to touch. 'I'm not sure, but it might be my brother.' Her hands flew to hide her mouth; she acted like a child who has just blabbed. 'I mean, my sister.'

Oh. Oh my God in whom I did not believe, she knew the secret. Feeling my heart beat fast, trying to hide my excitement, I guided her inside, babbling, 'Well, I wish I could tell you my house wasn't always this messy, but the truth is, it's usually worse.' I led her into the front room. 'Here he is. I mean, she.'

It's amazing how much more vital a portrait is than a print or a black-and-white photo, let alone a copy in a newspaper. From his place on the wall, the phantom child seemed to watch us walk in. I felt the impact of his scowling gaze.

I think Bonnie Jo felt it too. She stopped short when she saw him, her knobby hands still hovering near her mouth but not hushing her; a mewling sound escaped, then took shape in words. 'LeeVon,' she whimpered. 'LeeVon!' she cried aloud.

In the portrait's eyes, tears formed and overflowed, slipping down his paper cheeks to become watercolor, part of the painting.

Bonnie Jo screamed, her arms flying up as if to fend off a blow, and she fled the house so impetuously that she tripped and nearly fell but darted away anyhow, her flip-flops slapping like an angry mother as she ran.

Being pretty damn poleaxed myself, I couldn't stop gawking at LeeVon, at his tears drying on his stark, still face, until it was too late to stop Bonnie Jo. But her coughing old car backfired when she started it, and that jolted me out of my trance. I recovered just enough presence of mind to grab my camera and, through the picture window, take a few hasty photos as she slewed over sand and pine straw to the road, then sped away.

Once Maurie got home, once she had checked the mail, kissed her husband and debriefed him, prepared a healthy supper (breast of chicken in tomato and basil sauce, brown rice, asparagus) and eaten it with him, once she felt settled in and the sun had gone down, Maurie felt ready to call her sister – but she reached for her iPhone just a minute too late. It tootled Vivaldi, musical code for family. The caller ID made her cringe.

I am the clear-headed, logical one, she reminded herself, putting the phone to her ear. 'Sis. Hi. I just got home a few hours ago. How about you? Are you home, or—'

'Berthe, cut the bullshit. Of course I'm home.'

'Your message had nothing "of course" about it.'

'Do you blame me for being upset?'

'Unclench your teeth, sis. I plead not guilty. How could you think—'

'Well, the way you stormed out of there—'

'I didn't storm. I fled, I ran, I retreated in disorder. I admit, Mom's most recent weirdness totally unwomanned me. But that doesn't mean I would—'

'Well, then, who did?' Cassie sounded as if her bite was tightening by the moment. 'Somebody had to tell Wilma Lou those things! Berthe, it had to be you.'

Maurie wanted to tell her to go get screwed. Instead, she took a deep breath, then spoke as if addressing freshman orientation. 'Cassie, be reasonable. If you can believe Mom even halfway, why can't you believe me? As if I spend hours on the phone every day with Mom's neighbor? I didn't call her. I've never called her. I didn't tell Wilma Lou anything.'

'Well, then, who did?'

'I don't know.'

There was a long pause, and then Cassie started talking again in a different, calmer tone. 'OK, Berthe, I hear you. So who *have* you been talking to?'

'Nobody!'

'Come on, Berthe, get back in touch with your inner bitch. You were upset when you left, which makes it almost a sure bet that you spilled your guts to somebody. Who was it?'

Maurie opened her mouth but didn't speak. Mom and Monday morning seemed so far gone. But . . .

'Berthe?'

'I'm thinking.'

'And?'

'You're right. I remember now. I called Aunt Gayle.'

FIFTEEN

I forgot to eat any supper after Bonnie Jo bolted, which goes to show how preoccupied I was. More than preoccupied. Stunned. Dumbfounded. Unable to do anything except sit in the front room staring at the portrait – LeeVon. LeeVon had a name. LeeVon had cried watercolor tears. They were still there. I gazed at him in a trance of sheer wonder. The telephone rang repeatedly, but I did not get up to answer it. Just more crank calls about the picture in the newspaper, I figured, and anyway, in my humbled yet exalted state of mind, I barely heard the phone. I sat there in a sort of spiritual pregnancy, my heart swelling, yearning, tender.

The child.

LeeVon.

How had a portrait become so much more than just a portrait?

The whole thing felt like a dream.

And then it was. Exhausted by my own turmoil, I fell asleep on the sofa in the front room. Sometime much later I woke up, turned off the lights and went to bed.

The moment I awoke the next morning, I hustled out of bed and went to see what LeeVon had done during the night. When I found the paints arranged on the studio floor just the same as before, not moved at all, I felt disappointed. But then I stepped into the front room. Stopped. Stared. Felt a toasty warm smile dawning on my face, and said to myself, 'O frabjous day.'

The child had been busy with crayons on the beige plaster of the front-room wall. There, in the brightest colors wax could convey, he had created so many things: airplanes, yellow dogs, firecrackers popping, pickup trucks, wedges of watermelon, speedboats, tree frogs, gum balls, ice-cream cones, tractors and more, and some objects I couldn't identify, but all scribbled with such fervor, layer upon layer, that they shone.

And, all together, they formed a big oval glory around the portrait of – of himself.

Thursday morning, Maurie cancelled everything on her schedule because she was unprepared and needed to get in touch with her mother before she could focus on anything else. And she felt increasingly anxious, because she had tried to phone her mother several times the previous evening and Mom had not picked up. Frustrated, she had texted her sister, *Phoned Mom ten times no answer.* Cassie had replied, *Me too maybe she went to bed already it is central time there*, and Maurie had vented to Rob, denouncing time zones and her mother's biorhythms. She had managed to sleep some, but the fact that she was dipping into a treasured package of Ghirardelli Squares for breakfast bespoke her state of mind as she tried, once again, to contact her mother. That, and the fact that she had seated herself on the pink-cushioned ledge of her favorite bay window – a turret window, in fact – looking out over Lake Cayuga.

Mom picked up. 'Hello?' Of course she didn't know who it was; she had no caller ID on that troglodytic phone of hers.

'Mom!' Relief, frustration. 'I've been trying and trying to—'

'Maurie! How are you, sweetie?'

She sounded just the same as ever. Unbelieving, Maurie asked, 'Are you *OK*?'

'Of course. Maurie, I repeat: how are *you*? I take it Cassie told you about the psych hold?'

'Yes, and I'm so sorry—'

'Why? I know you weren't the one who put Wilma Lou up to it. I told Cassie it couldn't be you.'

Hearing that, Maurie felt childishly close to tears. She blurted, 'I blabbed to Aunt Gayle.'

'Ah,' said Mom, in her voice the hush of epiphany. 'Aha.'

'Ah, aha, what?'

Mom's tone remained meditative. 'I never said, because I thought I shouldn't interfere if you and your father's sister got along.'

'Never said what?'

'That I consider Gayle a shallow, selfish, materialistic woman.'

Despite her excellent view and her Ghirardelli fix, Maurie began to feel annoyed. 'It was pretty evident at the funeral, if not before, that you and she *didn't* get along. So?'

'So there's a pretty fundamental lack of understanding between us. After your father died and I decided to move to Florida, Gayle wanted me to give her the Montclair house.'

'*What?*' Maurie yelped, thankful she was already sitting down. '*Give* it to her? Seriously, without her paying for it?'

'Seriously, yes.'

Often, when dealing with her mother, Maurie felt a humiliating sense that her PhD was a useless piece of paper. This was one of those times. 'But that makes no sense,' she bleated.

'Actually,' Mom elaborated, 'she didn't ask me to give it to her as such; she wanted me to give it *back*.'

'Back?'

'Give it back – those were her words. Because she, like your father, grew up in that house, she seems to think it rightfully belongs to her. As she told me repeatedly and at length less than a week after the funeral. She came clopping in when I was trying to pack a few boxes. Silly me, I thought she was dropping by to commiserate.' As Mom spoke, Maurie imagined: Gayle, always in high heels with her hair in a vivid red wedge. Mom, sluggish from grief, trying to function; Mom had been an old woman when she lost Dad, much more so than she was now. Gayle reacting to her brother's death by wanting his house.

Repeatedly and at length? 'But that's irrational!' Maurie protested. 'Grandpa left it to Dad, and you married Dad, so now it's yours, isn't it?'

'Since I hold the deed to the property, yes, exactly. Gayle is arguably more out of touch with reality than I am.'

That jolted Maurie, hearing her mother describe herself as out of touch with reality. Miserably unable to disagree, she sat with her mouth open but silent. It didn't matter; her mother kept right on going.

'Your aunt is used to getting whatever she wants.' True, Gayle had scads of money, reaping the alimony of three failed marriages to three CEOs, each one obscenely wealthier than the last. 'She couldn't believe I stood up to her, and, wowsers, did she get bent out of shape.'

'She yelled at you?'

'For two solid hours. She cursed me out, she threw things, and her face got as red as her hair before she stormed out. It makes perfect sense that she would try to get me declared incompetent.'

'She thinks she would get the house that way?'

'Maybe.' Mom's voice conveyed a shrug. 'Or maybe she's just getting even. Either way—'

Feeling no inclination to shrug, Maurie interrupted, 'I would like to hang her by the thumbs.'

'Settle down, sweetie. Don't you have to get to work?'

'I cancelled everything and I'm sitting here eating chocolate. What can I do about Aunt Gayle?'

'Nothing! She's not trainable, and, Maurie, it doesn't matter. It's very good news that you told Aunt Gayle about me. I was going to need to round up character witnesses, but now it sounds like all I have to do is tell the judge I was Baker Act-ed by a person who hasn't seen me in nearly two years, and the whole psych hold thing will disappear.'

In Maurie's world, lawyers were a given, so even though Mom was using the first-person singular, Maurie failed to realize her mother was going to court without a lawyer. Instead, mention of the psych hold made her say, 'Aaak.' Suddenly subdued, uncomfortably reminded of the underlying issue, Maurie ventured to ask, 'Mom, do you still have, um, paranormal phenomena happening in your home on a nightly basis?'

'Yes. But you don't really want to know all the woo-woo details, do you, honey?'

It took Maurie only a moment to admit, 'No, I guess I don't.'

After Maurie and I finished talking, I phoned Cassie just to say her sister and I were OK. In the background, I heard the atonal music of conversation and crockery; obviously, Cassie was at work and Creative Java was slammed. 'I'll let you go,' I chirped, and hung up. Cassie had asked me to call every day, and I had called.

I had not told her a thing about Bonnie Jo's visit or LeeVon in tears. My daughters still did not even know LeeVon was a boy.

Vaguely upset with myself for keeping that secret from my daughters, I went and had breakfast, then a second cup of coffee, and headed into the studio. Figuring the child was done with the cans and tubes of paint on the studio floor, I started picking them up and putting them away, rediscovering a few in the process. After musing over the child's paintings, I hung most of them on the studio walls with Poster Putty. I didn't usually put anything on the intentionally neutral-colored walls of the studio, but for the child I made an exception.

Then, purposeless with no project to paint, I wandered back into the front room, slumped on the front-room sofa facing the image I had created for my grandchild, blew air out between my lips like a tired horse and said to LeeVon, 'Why do I have to be so damn maternal?'

Paper and pigment, he looked back at me from the place of honor he had taken over from my testament to my art career.

Still shaken from yesterday's events, confronted by the tears on his face, I said, 'I wish I could give you a hug.'

I had chickened out when I was talking with my daughters. Not telling them I wanted grandchildren had always seemed noble, but not telling them about LeeVon felt cowardly, and I ached, heart and soul, because I couldn't admit to them how grandmotherly I felt about the dead kid who lived in my house. How had everything become so very much all about LeeVon?

But it was. I felt for that suffering child even more than I did, sometimes, for my own grown children. I terribly wanted to dry his tears. Because I was a mom and therefore a rescuer, nothing mattered more than saving him. I had welcomed him into my life with real sable paintbrushes and wistful dreams; he was my child now, and I had to help him somehow.

But save him from what? Help him how?

Sunshine streamed in the picture window behind me, but through it flew a large raptor of some sort, casting a hawk shadow as it passed.

'LeeVon,' I said, 'is it all right for me to call you LeeVon? I'm scared,' I admitted. 'And clueless. I feel like I'm in a foreign place where I don't know the language or the rules.'

Face it: I was blundering around in the country of the dead, and what did I know?

'I know you're angry,' I whispered. 'I know you're sad. But what can I do about it?'

Even if he hadn't been dead, he was a young child, and to parents and other adults, the thoughts and actions of small children are a mystery. Cognitive aliens, the shrinks called them. Trapped in their own worlds, centers of their own universes, taking credit for everything but also taking blame.

'Well,' I said, 'I guess I can start by telling you it's not your fault. Nothing that happened when you were a child was your fault.'

I listened to the silence following that little speech of mine, silence so vast and hollow I could hear only the faintest echo. Fault . . . fault . . . fault . . .

'It was her fault,' I said. 'The big one with the belt and the boiling water – it was all her fault. And you want somebody to punish her, don't you.' This wasn't even a question. It was the answer.

SIXTEEN

It was also a considerable problem.

It took me hours to figure out how to proceed. For me, the best way to get a handle on things is usually not to think, so I went outside and wandered around my yard, where I knew I would be incapable of paying attention to anything except the way the morning light played on every single leaf, the touch of a moist breeze, the latest mushrooms – resembling crepes this time – and the snail tracks etched on my mailbox, the pastel lichens impasto on the tree trunks, and the celadon green froth of deer moss looking so deceptively delicate but feeling like lava to the touch as I collected some to take inside. And, of course, lizards, songbirds, a moth flattened on my door in a brindle half-circle – I saw that, and admired it, on my way back in.

Feeling much more steady and resolute, I phoned the woman I was coming to depend on as my closest local ally. 'Hi, Marcia, it's Beverly.'

'Beverly! Has something happened?'

'Is the coast clear?'

'Yes, I'm closeted in the john.'

'OK. I had a response to the ad—'

'Wow! Really?'

'Really. A woman named Bonnie Jo. She positively identified the child as her brother LeeVon.'

Silence, except for an audible gulp. Then, rather inanely for such a professional, Marcia said, 'Are you *sure*?'

'Sure she was for real? Yes. She knew where the house was. She knew LeeVon was a boy. She had a very strong reaction when she saw the portrait.'

'She came to your *house*?' Evidently, Marcia was having trouble keeping up.

'Yes, but then she got scared and ran away.' I saw no point in straining Marcia's credulity with details concerning the portrait's tears. 'I'm calling you first, before I call the police, to promise you I will not get you involved.'

'What?' Her voice had gone up an octave. 'Beverly—'

'Marcia, trust me, please. Could you tell me the name of the homicide detective handling the case?'

'Beverly, you've got to be kidding! How are you going to explain the painting?'

'I saw the skull when it was in the ground in my backyard. I saw the dress fabric. I painted a, um, whatchacallit—'

'Forensic facial reconstruction.'

'Right. I didn't really expect any response to the ad. I'm surprised, astounded, dumbfounded that my visitor said it was a boy and I feel the police ought to know she knew.' Pause for breath. 'As a wise person once told me, I can pull it off.'

Marcia did not answer right away, but finally she said, quietly enough, 'I believe you can.'

'Of course I can. I'm a harmless little old lady and if I had any eyelashes left, I would bat them. Which cop should I contact?'

She gave me a name: Tadlock. State Police Detective T.J. Tadlock.

I didn't like to drive after dark anymore, now that I was old enough for my eyes to spaz out when confronted with oncoming headlights. However, for LeeVon's sake, I did it anyway, peering at the shoulder of the road when my eyes wanted to panic, eventually finding my way into a strange parking lot without accident. State Police Detective T.J. Tadlock had asked me to come in to headquarters that evening to talk with her. Yes, *her*. T.J. Tadlock was a woman, as Marcia Wengleman had explained to me. 'Like "padlock," but with a T. T as for tadpole.'

'So like a tadpole plus a padlock.'

'Exactly.'

Marcia went on to opine that, because of qualities innate in T.J. Tadlock's gender, she was less likely than the other detectives to stonewall me.

Wondering whether I dared hope so, I saw the detective through an opening doorway as I stood at the bulletproof-glass window awaiting my turn. Glimpsing the cloistered squad room on the other side of the security-coded buzz-in entry, I picked out the one female among a group of plainclothes cops clustered around the coffee pot. I saw a stocky woman in a blouse, knee-length skirt and sensible one-inch heels. But my artist's eye approved of her in a way that would never occur to most males. Her body was thick but perfectly proportioned, as if classically sculpted in accordance with a Platonic norm. She would never be a fashion model, but at least she could buy clothes off the rack and they would actually fit her.

When she came to escort me in, however, I saw that she would never be a beauty either. Nodding to me and offering her hand, she surveyed me with wary tan eyes minimally enhanced by mascara. Hers was an unfortunate face with a low center of gravity, the features larger and heavier as it progressed downward. A smudge of lipstick attempted to center a mouth that was clownishly wide, especially given her thick neck and hefty body. As bad boys of my generation used to say, she was 'built like a brick shithouse.' Not fat, just solid. Strong. A middle-aged woman, T.J. Tadlock was not pretty, probably never had been pretty, but wore her very pretty blouse-and-crochet-vest outfit with confidence.

From behind her battered metal desk she watched and listened as I launched into my routine much as I had described it to Marcia: I had seen the little girl's dress and skull when I had first uncovered them in my backyard; as a professional artist, I had attempted a facial reconstruction of the victim; I had advertised in the *Skink County Observer*, receiving a response and, very much to my bewilderment, the little girl's sister had identified her as a boy named LeeVon. My witness had then fled; I had snapped some photos of her car, and by enlarging them on my computer I had been able to come up with a license plate number – see?

T.J. stopped me with a gesture as I started to hand her the printouts. 'Let's go back.' Her voice was as husky as her build, but not ungentle. 'Please describe this Bonnie Jo person.'

'About the right age, sixty-ish, and looked like she'd never been to a hairdresser or a dentist. Big hands like a manual worker, no nail polish. Long hair the color of putty with split ends. Her face . . .' I hesitated, then said it. 'The shape of her face reminded me a lot of the child's.'

'Is that why you're so sure she is the victim's sister?'

'Partly that, and partly the simple fact that she showed up at my house. Question: how did she know where I lived? Answer: she had been raised there, at least for a while. A long time ago, she probably saw whatever happened to LeeVon.'

Detective Tadlock neither smiled nor frowned, but her homely face hardened. 'Mrs Vernon, can you understand why I feel skeptical about your story?'

I lied, answering stoutly, 'No.'

'Well, for one thing, having come forward, why did this purported Bonnie Jo then run away?'

I sighed. No way was I going to tell her how LeeVon had wept when his sister called him by name. But I reached down and pulled his portrait out of a large tote bag in which I'd been carrying it in case I needed it. 'This,' I said, propping it up so it faced the detective on her desk.

At first just glancing at it, she then did a genuine double-take and studied it intently. I hoped that maybe in the artificial light, with overhead lamps glaring off the glass, she didn't notice the tears. I certainly did not intend to point them out to her.

'Cripes,' she said, 'you really can paint.'

Call me rude, but I didn't feel like thanking this woman for observing the obvious. I simply nodded agreement as I put the portrait away.

The detective's wide mouth turned out to be flexible, quirking into a quizzical smile. 'Mrs Vernon, didn't you get pulled in on a psych hold a couple of days ago?'

I should not have been surprised, of course; Cooter Spring is a small town. But I *was* so surprised that I laughed, joyfully amused; life has that effect on me sometimes. 'How in the world did you hear that?'

'Never mind. You have psychological problems?'

'No more than most people. Do I seem like a psych case to you?'

'Not at all. That's what bothers me.' Detective Tadlock leaned forward to give me a penetrating stare from her close-set eyes. 'Something doesn't feel right. Why haven't you asked me whether the victim was really a boy? And why did you make the hair short on your picture? You already knew. How?'

Oh, no. Aaaaak. She had homed in on the one question I had

promised not to answer. Recklessly I hedged, 'Detective Tadlock, do you know what brought about that psych hold?'

'No. Enlighten me.'

'A question of ghosts,' I intoned, lowering my chin to look at her mysteriously askance. 'Ghosts, or at least one ghost. And I swear I never used to believe in them. Before.'

She stared at me for what felt like a very long moment before she shrugged, then reached for a pen. 'OK, I'll take a report and we'll see whether it goes anywhere.'

'Spending the night at your desk, Tee Jay?' asked one of the other detectives on his way home.

She answered with a shrug and a wide, wry smile, feeling her heart warm; these guys were her family.

'Beer and pizza, Teej?' invited another colleague and buddy.

'Next time. Promise.'

Left alone, Detective Tadlock block-printed *BONNIE JO, BONNY JO* on a pad of scrap paper made of discarded office memos clipped together with their blank sides up – T.J.'s way of recycling. She hated waste.

BONNIE JO, BONNY JO were the only variants of the name she could think of. Next she wrote down *LEE VON, LEEVON, LEVON, LEE VAUGHN, LEIGH VON, LEIGH VAUGHN*, cripes. Those plus all the illiterate alternatives meant that any sort of attempt to put a last name together with that first name was not going to be easy. But what the hell; nothing was ever easy in old, cold cases.

If she ended up grappling with this one all night, no problem. No one was waiting for her to get home to her little apartment, her Betty Boop poster, her collection of novelty salt-and-pepper shakers. She had been married once when she was just a kid, before she went to the police academy, but she'd found the good sense not to waste her life. She'd cut her losses. Now she was married to the job, a much better option.

T.J. had run the license plate number of the vehicle Bonnie Jo had been driving, but it was registered to a deceased man. Inquiries related to him had yielded nothing, so he was a dead end, quite literally.

Next, hoping to trace the phone from which Bonnie Jo had

called Beverly, Detective Tadlock had begun the process of getting an administrative subpoena to access Mrs Vernon's phone records. But if Bonnie Jo had used a borrowed phone or a public one – for a few public phones did still exist in Cooter Spring – then this might lead nowhere.

Meanwhile, T.J. was contemplating the difficulties of doing a computer search of birth certificates in Skink County during . . . when? T.J. didn't know Bonnie/Bonny Jo's DOB and couldn't even guess her year of birth, not knowing whether she was an older sister or a younger sister relative to the boy's estimated birthdate. LeeVon's DOB was vaguely pegged by the coroner as sometime between 1949 and 1951, but his name was too damn mutable.

Little boy dressed as a girl. What the hell was that all about?

Physically abused – the coroner had reported finding several bone fractures in various stages of healing – and malnourished – whether because of poverty or deliberate starvation was yet to be determined. He had been young and weak and he had died, probably from neglect or outright murder, and he had been buried in an unmarked grave, wearing a dress. T.J. had done some internet research on that particular anomaly, and she had learned that, in previous centuries, very young boys had routinely been put in loose dresses for practical purposes of potty training, because it was a lot quicker and easier to lift a skirt than to undo pants. But so what? The practice had not extended into the twentieth century. And LeeVon was a six-year-old, not a toddler; wasn't that pushing it a bit?

T.J. had also found out that the roots of the practice went back to more primitive times and reasoning. Because young children often died, and boys were valued more than girls, they had been disguised as girls so that the gods might not snatch them away. Or, to put it another way, girls were less valued than boys.

That sort of thinking resonated bitterly with Detective T.J. Tadlock. It had taken her a long, long time to feel comfortable and respected as a female in her life, let alone her law enforcement career. T.J. felt one hundred percent certain that LeeVon's abuser had put him in a dress for no purpose other than to humiliate him.

She wished she had more aspects of this case to feel certain about.

She especially wished she could feel more certain about Beverly Vernon. Both cop sense and common sense made T.J. suspect that the little artist woman was fabricating one whopper of a story. But a different, opposing, very uncommon sense had made T.J. listen to Beverly Vernon's story with an inkling of truth that lay beneath and beyond. When the painter had held up the portrait, T.J. had seen beyond the artwork. She had seen, in Beverly Vernon's eyes, the knowledge that has no name. Not since she was a very young child had T.J. seen that wise, secret look – in the eyes of her great-grandmother, her beloved Nana.

The grownups had ignored Nana as much as they could, because Nana had said things that embarrassed them and sometimes frightened them. Nana had sometimes seen the future, had sometimes heard voices in the night. Only long after Nana was dead did T.J. realize her great-grandmother had possessed a gift or power that no one understood.

No one including T.J.

Sitting at her desk while the night shift cops came and went, T.J. blew out a puff of exasperation between her lips. More than once one of the guys had stopped to chat with her, but her investigation was taking a direction she couldn't share with her colleagues.

SEVENTEEN

The next morning, Friday, I woke up annoyingly early as usual, but got out of bed with some alacrity and went to see what LeeVon had left me during the night. First, of course, I checked the studio, but I found no new creations there, and nothing out of place. I headed on into the front room, but found no sign of my spirit child's activity there either. Increasingly alarmed, I searched throughout my little house, but there was no trace of anyone except me. Miffed, I flounced over to my Joseph chair, gave its colorful upholstery a punitive thump, then took stock of myself and had to smile. It had been barely a week since a paranormal presence had manifested in my home and made a babbling idiot out of me, I was so scared. But now look at me, acting like a child with no stocking on Christmas morning! If LeeVon had gone away, I should be relieved. Right?

Nope. I felt absurdly upset.

'Beverly,' I muttered to myself, 'it's not as if someone *died*.' Sheesh, he was already dead, so why had I come to care about him so much? Ridiculous.

I got myself moving, bathed, dressed, had breakfast and tackled item number one on the to-do list I had jotted courtesy of my erstwhile lawyer: line up character witnesses. I left a message for Marcia Wengleman and one for Dr Roach, then hesitated, beginning to feel keenly how small my circle of acquaintance in little ol' Skink County was; most people who lived here based their entire social lives on extended family and membership in a church, which were often the same thing. By comparison, I had no social life, but I did call the Skink County Public Library in search of someone who remembered me as a frequent reader. And I contacted a handyman who had done some work for me. Both said they would get back to me.

Feeling lonesome and discouraged, within an hour I found myself in the front room again, sitting on the sofa and contemplating LeeVon's portrait on the opposite wall.

'Where are you?' I grumbled. 'I miss you.'

Tears on his face.

That reminder made me set my own feelings aside. This wasn't about me. 'Kiddo,' I asked him gently, 'what's the matter?'

Of course, he didn't answer, but I managed a few empathic thoughts. I had put his portrait up on the wall. His sister had seen it. He had been so affected when she called his name that he had wept. Validated as a person, he had crayoned a triumphant aureole around himself.

Up until then, he had been most often an angry child.

Underlying great anger, always, was great sorrow.

And I had started to crowd him, knowing his name, seeing his tears, talking to him, trying to be his grandmother and savior. Realizing this, I felt a pretty clear intuition that he wasn't gone. He was just withdrawn. Keeping to himself, moping. Sad.

Heartbroken. Because children love their mothers, even when their mothers are abusive.

'I'm a mom, too,' I told him.

LeeVon gazed back at me.

'I'm not sure what I can actually do for you, to bring you peace,' I told him, 'but I'll keep trying.'

On Friday morning, Maurie phoned her sister. Again.

The previous day, after talking with Mom, Maurie had settled at her desk and tried to work on the essay she was currently writing: 'Inferences Regarding Mycenaean Civilization Prior to the Trojan War.' She had hoped that searching the *Iliad* for the references she needed would help her crowd all other thoughts out of her mind. But intrusive worries about Mom, her putative ghost and Aunt Gayle, whose name rhymed with 'betrayal,' had shredded Maurie's scholarly focus. Giving up, she had gone outside with a broom to attack the latest cobwebs festooning the gingerbread of her Victorian fixer-upper.

It was a beautiful, sunny day, warm but not hot; there were too few such summer days in Ithaca. Soothed despite herself, leaving the spiders alone and choosing instead to sweep the wrap-around porch, Maurie admired the planks she and Rob had recently painted. Instead of the customary gray, they had chosen a subtle lavender to complement the railings, for which they had chosen a creamy honeysuckle-blossom color hovering between white and yellow. But what color they would paint the peeling house itself, or how they would afford to get the job done, Maurie had no idea.

Still, she knew it would happen.

Finished sweeping, she went down the lavender plank steps to weed the pansies and impatiens she had planted. Pansies symbolized pensive cogitations; that worked for Maurie, but impatiens . . . She felt all too much impatience in herself as her thoughts, rather than remaining pensive, insisted on returning to her mother.

Stop footling around and own the situation, Maurie, she told herself; despite her doubts about Mom's ghost, still she felt responsible for enabling Aunt Gayle to interfere. She had to do something.

No. No, dammit, she didn't *have* to do anything.

And so on, back and forth in the brain. Maurie had resisted her uneasy conscience throughout Thursday's gluten-free dinner and evening of reading, but found herself unable to sleep. Consequently, first thing Friday morning, once more sitting in her favorite bay window, she phoned her sister.

'Berthe?' Cassie sounded drowsy yet wide-eyed with alarm. 'Is something wrong?'

'Probably, somewhere. Sorry to call so early, but I wanted to catch you before you went to work. Have you had your coffee?'

'Think, Berthe. For me, going to work and having my coffee are the same thing. So no, I haven't. I repeat: is something wrong?'

'More or less, depending on relativity. Make that sorority. Are we finished fighting? You and I?'

'Oh. That. Yeah, we're good. I apologize for thinking you were trying to have Mom put away.' A pause. 'But I don't understand. Why did Aunt Gayle do it?'

Feeling a bit better already, Maurie explained Gayle's motive, meaning the coveted house. She heard a clatter as Cassie evidently dropped her phone, then retrieved it.

Cassie exclaimed, 'I had no idea Aunt Gayle was like that!'

'Shallow, selfish and materialistic were the terms Mom used.'

'And here I always thought she was more normal than Mom.'

'Which says trenchant things about normalcy.' Maurie hesitated, then made herself ask, 'Sis, what do you hear from Mom?'

'You refer to the G-H-O-S-T?'

'Of whom we're trying not to speak? Yes.'

'In my grammar, you mean that thing we're trying not to talk about? No, I haven't heard a word.'

Silence. For a moment, Maurie listened to the phantom whispers in the darkness of cell phone cyberspace. Then something from her gut answered them with a burst of feeling. 'Damn it all to perdition! I don't grudge Mom her freaky ghost, but Aunt Gayle is insufferable. She's predatory. I would like to hang her by the ears right in front of Saks Fifth Avenue. I—'

'Berthe,' Cassie interrupted, sounding pleased yet puzzled, 'who are you and what have you done with my sister?'

Maurie took pause. 'Paraphrase?'

'What made you stop being all bent out of shape about Mom and start defending her?'

'Hello, she does happen to be my *mother*.' Maurie hesitated, then added wryly, 'OK, I confess, you know me. Mom's current activities give me the heebie-jeebies and I didn't want to get involved. But, empirically speaking, she's not doing any harm, and anyone with the brain of a crustacean should be able to see that, so Aunt Gayle's interference was totally uncalled-for. It was inexcusable; she needs to be dealt with, and I want you to know I plan to kick her fashionable ass.'

With no idea what else to do with myself, I selected a sheet of cold press paper, soaked it with water at the kitchen sink, then carried it dripping to my easel, where I stretched and taped it in place. Then I needed to wait until it dried, but so what? I hadn't the faintest notion what I wanted to paint next.

What I really wanted to do was to find Bonnie Jo and – from LeeVon's big drawing it looked as if he had at least one other sister – for whatever good it might accomplish, more than half a century late, I wanted to find his family. But I had not a clue how. That was the plain-Jane woman cop's job. T.J. Tadlock. I wondered what T.J. stood for, but it would have been rude to ask.

I phoned her.

'Tadlock.' She sounded curt.

'Good morning, Detective. This is Beverly—'

'I know, Mrs Vernon. Some of us have caller ID.'

'Who pissed on your Cheerios?' Aaak, it just slipped out, because she really sounded ready to morph into a junkyard dog.

But I startled her into a laugh, or at least a sort of bark. 'I've been up all night, Mrs Vernon, running the license plate and putting a BOLO out on the car and otherwise doing my job, and I am going home to sleep now.' She sounded quite decided. 'If there is any news, someone will contact you. Goodbye.'

She did not tell me to have a blessed day, as some folks around Cooter Spring were wont to do, and I appreciated that. She did not even tell me to have a *nice* day, which was fine; sometimes that annoyed me too. I preferred days with a broad spectrum of unpredictability, and I despised pseudo-comforting platitudes, especially the pious ones my husband had been forced to listen to while dying of cancer.

I missed him. But in a comfortable way. Jim had been pillowed in love when he died, and he was laid to rest, and I felt no sense that he would ever encounter LeeVon.

LeeVon had not died gently at all.

Somebody out there ought to miss LeeVon. Starting with his sisters. One of whom was Bonnie Jo.

Sitting down at the kitchen table with Skink County's thin phone book in hand, I began searching it, entry by entry, starting with Aaron, Abbott, Abrams, Ackerman, for anyone with the first name of Bonnie or Bonnie Jo. Common sense told me how futile this was. One look at Bonnie Jo's car had suggested to me that she couldn't afford a phone, probably not even a cell phone, which wouldn't have been listed anyway. Nevertheless, I stubbornly scanned each and every first name, feeling more stupid by the page because I couldn't come up with any better way to find her.

And I had barely reached Campbell, Canal, Cannon when I started to see double. Eye strain. Obstinacy could no longer prevail.

Mentally promising LeeVon I'd be back, I took a break and looked out the front picture window at the shaggy green yard I loved like a pet, at long-necked blue wildflowers that would close before noon, at crepe myrtle bushes in passionate pink sprawling bloom. Beautiful, but my yard couldn't talk with me. Wistfully, I thought of women I could phone for a chat, some of whom had been my friends for years, people I *should* call – but I couldn't, not without babbling about LeeVon and shocking the hell out of them. As if I had a skeleton in my closet, LeeVon was isolating me.

I wandered through the house (since it was now too hot to wander outside) and, of course, I ended up in the studio, musing over my paints, selecting colors to suit my hue of mind before I consciously realized I was going to use the still-damp paper on the easel just to goof off. OK, whatever. An artist learns to go with the internal flow. Right now, my conscious mind had crawled off someplace to take a nap. As for colors, I found myself mixing a fascinating range of warm, wet grays, letting rose madder, yellow and cerulean blue blend on the moist paper into a really lovely sunset shadow, while terracotta and jade made something more like Arizona stone, and indigo plus burnt ochre grayed into a swirl of twilight . . . the fuzzy curls of gray building on the paper made me think first of stylized clouds, then of mice at a committee meeting, then of some grandmother's poodle-permed hair, the grandmother being not me but maybe LeeVon's grandmother, and if she had ever existed, I hoped she had been sweet to him, making up a little for his awful mother. If she was still alive, she must be very old. Wrinkled like a dried apple under her poufed hairdo . . . with rudimentary brushstrokes of ivory yellow and muted magenta, I shaped a granny face of sorts, kind of a caricature. I gave her eyes like tiny nightfall-gray fish swimming deep in their sockets, a nose growing longer by the day, a mouth getting smaller between jowl furrows, and thin, shirred lips, puce colored. There she was, narrowly eyeing me, so ancient she had actually known LeeVon when he was a little boy . . .

I gasped, yipped and jumped back as if she was a rattlesnake, exclaiming, '*Wilma Lou?*'

I couldn't believe me. I mean, yes, it was sort of Wilma Lou, and no, it was sort of not her, but the point was that she had lived next door to my house for freaking ever, had probably been right there spying when LeeVon had died, and my muddling, doodling mind had broken through my stupidity, had come up with a possible way to find out about him, while—

At this point, my logical, sensible mind woke up from its nap and complained, 'Well, why didn't you think of that before?'

Because Wilma Lou was the last person in the world I wanted to deal with, that was why. But my dreaming mind and my crafty hands had put me face-to-face with her on my easel, leaving me no choice but to realize: I needed to coax the truth out of my damned interfering religious bigot of a neighbor. I needed to have a long talk with Wilma Lou, and it wasn't as if she would welcome me.

EIGHTEEN

I responded to this challenge in the only humanly possible way: I went back to bed. But not to hide my head under the pillows. I lay on my back in an orderly fashion, as if I were practicing being viewed in a casket, because I find it works better to think horizontally. The position seems to slosh my thoughts into flowing more helpfully. Examples: peace offering. I would need one to get past Wilma Lou's front door. Brownies? Custard pie? Nuh-uh;

anything I could cook, she could cook better. Fresh hand-painted picture? Definitely not the one I had just created; it was unflattering, all too clearly advertising that I didn't like Wilma Lou.

Why didn't I like Wilma Lou? Because she was narrow-minded and intolerant, that was why, whereas I was quite the opposite. I was broad-minded, tolerant, non-judgmental to the max.

So, being a broad-minded, tolerant, non-judgmental person, shouldn't I stop judging Wilma Lou?

Ouch.

Didn't tolerance mean I should be able to accept Wilma Lou as she was and find some common ground with her?

Sheeesh. While processing that, I stared at my ceiling. I had painted it as a velvety blue moonlit night sky with stars and comets and angels – not Christmas card angels, but beings made of energy and light, like the angels in some of Naomi Walker's paintings. As one of my Jewish friends had once told me approvingly, these were angels with no Christian iconography. They didn't even have wings, not exactly, but something more like auras of flight light, because, after all, they did have to fly. I knew that with great certainty, even though I did not know whether I believed in angels any more than I believed in ghosts . . . but what I believed did not seem to matter, did it?

Practically since the beginning of recorded time, I mused, people had made traditions including beings of brightness who were messengers of good. Eldolils, Tolkien called them, as far as I could remember. Fairies, peris, elves. Then to the Jews, then Christians, then Muslims, they were angels, some with eight pairs of wings. And now, arguably, they were the ETI, extra-terrestrial intelligence, of urban legend. I would love to see one sometime, some inexplicable manifestation of golden-white light, maybe, or a shadow moving against the wind, or woodland foliage forming a green face. But what Wilma Lou would think if she ever saw my kind of angel, I couldn't imagine—

Wait.

Yes . . . yes, maybe I could imagine.

I cradled a concept in my supine mind for several moments longer, trying not to jostle it until I felt sure of it. Then I sat up, shoved my feet into my sneakers and headed across the hallway to the office-cum-craft room for the shoebox in which I kept things such as my oyster shell and frothy deer moss and the wings off fallen butterflies, if they were not too battered, and dried teazel heads, and tiny seashells, and maple wings, and the burry balls that sycamore trees seem to specialize in. Sorting through my happenstance collection, I found almost everything I needed. On a crafty roll and feeling fairly well chuffed, I strode toward my car and drove away from my home to go get one thing I lacked.

Ten minutes later I was back with a bouquet of tiger lilies from near a neighbor's pond. Earlier in the year I would have used the rain lilies that sprang up in my yard or the Easter lilies that grew wild along the dirt roads. But tiger lilies would work nicely, and their color would complement the antique gold of the passionflower seed pod. I got out the hot glue gun and plugged it in.

I chose the largest tiger lily blossoms, trimmed their stems off, then slipped them into each other and glued them that way, staggering the petals, to form a kind of fantastic but fairly sturdy skirt atop which I glued the smooth egg-shaped seed pod for a torso, then a live oak acorn on top of that. On to this 'head' I layered pine cone scales to form shining brown hair extending halfway down the back. I hesitated over the wings, because butterfly wings seemed too easy, a cliché. I ended up feathering multiple translucent dragonfly wings together, and the way my little pantheistic angel's wings shimmered in the light made me start wanting to keep her for myself. But I knew she wouldn't last. The lilies would wither. My angel was ethereal, a gift to the Now.

Who would think I could ever offer such a heartfelt gift to Wilma Lou?

For the arms, I used maple wings. Their seeds formed shoulders, and then they hung like wide sleeves. After I was satisfied with the arms, I felt the need for a break. While not exactly tired, not physically, some inner oomph I depended on was about to rebel, and I knew from sad experience that, even though my peace offering needed only a few finishing touches, if I continued working on it, I would mess up. So I left it on the craft-room table and went to get myself something to eat, long overdue; I'd had no lunch and it was nearly suppertime.

But there was a lot of sunlight left in the long summer day. As it began to slant and glow more yellow toward sunset, bestowing cool shadows on my yard, I went outside and picked the tiny white four-petaled flowers that salted the grass, then sat on my back porch to make them into miniature daisy chains. This was twiddly work, but I managed to put together a flowery sort of sash for my angel to wear around her waist, and another by way of a necklace. Back in the craft room, after placing the flowers on my brain-baby, I painted a face on to her acorn head with my very smallest brush.

A lovely sunset was forming in the sky as I took my peace offering and walked across my yard toward Wilma Lou's lawn (much more respectable) to ring her doorbell.

Although Maurie fully intended to remain faithful to Rob until death did them part, she had not taken his last name but kept her own: Vernon. She and Rob had a marriage of love, yes, surely, but also of ambitions: theirs was a career-driven partnership with benefits. They conversed easily and passionately about financial planning, global crises, rising stars in the arts, trendy travel destinations, politics both national and workplace, networking, contacts and hipsters and frenemies. They had fun together, laughed often, cheered each other on. But Maurie had never asked for Rob's help with a family matter. In fact, they seldom talked about their families at all.

Well, there was a first time for everything. Maurie made sure she got home first and mixed drinks to serve as a conversational lubricant. When Rob let himself into their condo, and, as always, dropped his briefcase to the floor with a wham, she handed him a martini as she kissed him hello.

Rob ogled it and asked, 'What's the matter?'

'Relativity.' Maurie guided him toward a sofa and sat next to him.

'Which relatives?'

'My mother and Aunt Gayle.' Sipping from her own daiquiri during the several minutes it took to fill him in, Maurie told him all about it, from skeleton to portrait to psych ward.

'Usually,' ventured Rob, 'when you tell me crazy-making stories, you say you don't want me to do anything, just listen.'

'This time's an exception. I need your professional advice.'

'Regarding your mother?'

'No! Just leave my mother out of it!' The vehemence of her reaction caught her by surprise, and she saw that it flummoxed him as well. 'My mother is my mother,' she tried to explain in a more reasonable tone. 'She makes me nutsoid and I don't want to play her goofy game, but if she insists on pretending she has an imaginary spooky friend, if that makes her happy, then fine. I am not going to interfere and Aunt Gayle absolutely has no *right* to interfere. She is so far out of line she's practically in orbit.'

'I thought you liked your Aunt Gayle.'

'I did. Before. But now I'd like to smack her bony ass with a lawsuit.'

'Seriously?'

'Yes! For illegally trying to railroad Mom into psych-ward limbo.'

Rob frowned. This in no way detracted from his appearance; he was a good-looking man, and his frown conveyed deep thought and concern such as he was accustomed to display when addressing a jury. After a suitably timed silent moment he said, 'Illegal how?'

'Conniving with Mom's neighbor. Trying to put Mom away based on hearsay.'

'Although an argument could be made . . .' But Rob dropped that argument, in quite an atypical and unlawyerly manner, to ask a question instead. 'Maurie, what's your main intention? Are you mostly trying to punish your aunt, or are you mostly trying to protect your mother?'

'Some of both. I guess protecting Mom is more important.'

'Good. Because your aunt would probably win a lawsuit, given that you yourself said your mom was acting goofy.'

Maurie felt her blood pressure rise along with the hair on the back of her neck. 'But—'

Rob interrupted smoothly. 'But your Aunt Gayle doesn't know that. She would probably run away with her tail between her legs if you just *threatened* to sue.'

Trying to imagine what Aunt Gayle would choose to wear by way of a tail, Maurie began to smile.

Holding my peace offering delicately in both hands, I walked across my yard and on to Wilma Lou's lawn – quite a different, more meek and well-behaved sort of house frontage to mine – and across her boring homogeneous grass to her front door. Another ranch house structurally identical to my concrete bunker, hers had been upgraded with a veneer of brickwork, foundation plantings, window boxes, shutters and other extras such as a doorbell. I pressed it, then wished I hadn't, hearing chimes within the house play 'Jesus Loves Me.' This was so damn Wilma Lou that it nearly made me lose my carefully maintained smile.

When she opened the door and saw me with a friendly face and a gift in my hands, she gasped, staggered back and clutched at the gold cross she wore around her neck, holding it up as if to shield herself from a vampire. 'Git away, Devil worshipper!' she squeaked, sounding much more panicked than righteously wrathful.

Without even rolling my eyes, I said, 'I'm not a Devil worshipper, Wilma Lou, and I don't hold any grudge against you for trying to get me taken away and locked up.'

'Y'all ain't got no business messing around with dead people!'

'I don't mess around with dead people. Look, I brought you an angel.'

'That thing?'

'It's an angel made of examples of what I believe in – like maple seeds and wild lilies and dragonfly wings and Innocence—'

'Innocence?' Wilma Lou shrilled. This was the name of the tiny white flower from my yard, but why try to explain?

'Of course, Innocence,' I reassured my rigid neighbor. 'I believe in the goodness of nature, Wilma Lou.' Including snakes, although not necessarily poisonous ones. 'You see that beautiful sunset?' I tilted my head toward the sky behind me, where the play of light on clouds was quite a lovely sight. 'That's the kind of thing I believe in. Not dead bones or devils.'

'But she said—'

'The woman on the phone? She lied to you. She's not my sister. I don't even have a sister.'

I saw her lower her guard slightly, the hand holding her cross sagging, while her facial contortion eased from frenzy into its more normal obstinacy. 'Y'all sure y'all don't hold no grudge?'

'No, not at all. I just want to be a good neighbor. Why do you think I brought you an angel?' I lifted the gift in my hands, offering it again.

Eyeing it, she looked more than ever stubborn, doubtful. 'Y'all believe in angels?'

'Of course! Don't you?'

'That there don't look like no proper angel.'

'It's a pantheist angel. You don't like it? You want me to leave it here outside the door?'

She hesitated, the expression on her face teetering on some moral cusp, but finally her innate Southern hospitality trumped her dour religiosity. 'No, no,' she said, dropping her cross and lifting her hands as if in despair, 'y'all's a nice person to bring it to me. Come on in.'

NINETEEN

Finally done in the cafe for the day, snug in her cozy upstairs living quarters and just settling down in her secondhand La-Z-Boy to watch some TV, Cassie said 'Damn!' when her iPhone tootled into a jazz saxophone riff. Picking it up, she blinked in disbelief when she saw her sister's name on the caller ID. For Maurie to call her at all was rare; for Maurie to phone her twice in one day was unheard of. Thumbing the little green button, she demanded, 'Berthe, is something wrong?'

'Why should anything be wrong?' Cassie needed to hold the phone a few inches away from her ear as Maurie's voice rose, more excited than angry. 'Listen, Mary Cassatt Vernon, you and I are going to neutralize the hell out of Aunt Gayle, and Rob helped me brainstorm a plan. We . . .'

Maurie spoke on for a considerable length of time before Cassie could get a word in. 'A *lawsuit*?'

'You haven't been paying strict attention, sis. No, we don't want to actually file a docket under the circumstances, but to get Aunt Gayle to retract her claws, we want to convince her we might. However, we don't want to send her anything in writing because that would give her something to show a lawyer. So what we need to decide is how best to confront her. I could contact her by phone, but I think it would impact her more if you went to see her personally—'

'*Me?*' Most of Cassie's ire flipped to incredulity.

'Why not? You live close to her. All you have to do is fire a lot of legalese at her very sternly. Rob made me a list of buzzwords: civil litigation, punitive damages for mental anguish, wrongful detainment, religious discrimination, harassment, libel—'

'Then *you* go see Aunt Gayle,' said Cassie.

'But I'm trying to finish an article for the *Journal of Greek Prehistory*! I'd have to take time off, drive down there—'

'Excuses, excuses. You'd find time if you wanted to go shopping with her. What's the matter, Berthe? You having second thoughts?'

'What? No! I'm so pissed at Aunt Gayle I feel like an IED on feet. If I get in the same room with her, I might kill her.'

'Then I'll go with you, all right?' said Cassie. 'We'll both go. Period.'

I had never actually been inside Wilma Lou's house before, although she had barged into mine often enough. So, after handing her the angel-cum-Trojan-horse that had gotten me inside, I was able to establish myself as a nice visitor by looking around her living room and complimenting everything from her pseudo-crewel drapes to her waxed wooden coffee table with a piecrust edge, meaning a carved ruffle. I bet myself most of the furnishings had come from Ethan Allen, especially the severe brown sofa and its two repressively tall and dignified brass lamps on matching end tables.

'Such nice tables,' I said. 'Solid wood. They don't make tables like that anymore.'

'Ain't that the truth. I had 'em since I was married. Would y'all like a glass of sweet tea?'

'Yes, that would be lovely.' Good. I was going to be allowed to stay in her deadly dark parlor and – oh, Christ, there was a large picture of a blond Aryan Jesus on the wall, but also something even more incongruous: a smallish crucifix with a Jesus who looked like a clothespin?

As soon as Wilma Lou turned her back to go get the tea, I moved in for a closer look. Yeppers, mercifully blank-faced, Jesus was made of a clothespin, all right, split in half by removal of its wire spring, then reversed with its flat sides facing, ingeniously forming a bifurcated figure with round head, a torso of sorts and tapering legs. His arms were made of the narrow ends of another clothespin glued at the appropriate suffering angle on to – oh my

God in whom I did not believe, the cross was made of clothespins too, segments glued side by side and puzzled together with their narrow ends overlapping.

Bearing two tall glasses of tea, Wilma Lou returned from the kitchen to catch me peering at the grotesque thing.

'My daddy made that,' she said proudly. 'He was a real artist.'

Doubtful. But to be fair, the clothespin crucifix was arguably no tackier than my makeshift pantheist angel.

'Why don't you have a seat, Beverly.' Yet Wilma Lou regarded me doubtfully as I perched at one end of her sofa, and she blurted, 'I ain't never gived sweet tea to nobody who wasn't no Christian before.'

I said cheerfully, 'Well, there's a first time for everything. Thank you.' I sipped the tea. 'It's very good.' If you enjoyed drinking a big glass of candy. 'You mentioned your father, Wilma Lou. Was he from around here?'

I wanted to get her talking, which she did with gusto. Of course her father was from Skink County, as was her whole family, so during the next hour I heard a great deal about all of them, plus Wilma Lou's long-deceased husband. I kept her garrulously reminiscing until I hoped she'd more or less forgotten her reservations against me and until the right moment offered itself.

She was holding forth about how her father and her then-fiancé had built the house she still lived in, and I perked up. By now I had drunk enough sugar to make me manic, eyes wide open. With unfeigned interest, I prompted, 'So you moved in right after you were married?'

'Yeppers. Folks didn't need no honeymoons back then.'

'Weren't you lonely? My place wasn't built yet, was it?'

'No, Papa done that soon after. He said now he knew how to put up a house, he'd go ahead and make him an extra one to rent. I wish he wouldn't have done that.'

'Why not?'

'Them-all was ungodly people who moved in over there.' Yes, definitely she had forgotten what a heathen I was. 'A low-down, shiftless, white trash woman with three brats but not a husband in sight, nor a job. Furree, her name was.' She said it with the emphasis on the second syllable, so I pictured it with that spelling. 'You know what all them Furrees is like.'

All I knew was that the woman with three children was almost certain to be LeeVon's mother and I had to remember her name, which was a challenge, as I had readily forgotten the names of everyone else Wilma Lou had mentioned. Low-down woman named Furree; desperately my brain fished for a mnemonic. Ferry boat? Fairy princess? Furry animal? As a child, I'd had a cat named Purry Furry. Mentally, I added that cat's large fluffy image to the picture LeeVon had drawn of his family.

'. . . Disremember the mother's Christian name,' Wilma Lou was saying with some annoyance.

'How about the children?'

'Oh, them.' Wilma Lou elevated her gaze in a martyred way. 'Three little girls all acted like no-account boys. It must have been four years I put up with them, because the littlest one was just a baby when they come and she was running like a wild animal with the others by the time they went. Four years and I never saw one of them clean or decent or going to church or school, just making trouble. Stole every mortal one of my bricks.'

'Your *bricks*?' My interest was quite genuine.

'Left over from when Papa built my house. Them brats had no business taking them.'

'What did they do with them?'

'Piled them up and knocked them down and buried them in holes and suchlike nonsense. Their mother didn't give them no sensible toys.'

'I hope they didn't throw them.'

'They sure did. The oldest one was the wildest; she went and cut her hair off with a pair of scissors and got whupped for it. She threw bricks at her mother sometimes. But they was all bad children. Wet the bed. That woman didn't hardly never do no cooking or washing but there was always sheets drying on the line.' Wilma Lou shook her head, expressing a shocked and superior kind of pity.

I nodded vaguely, concealing anger for the sake of the girl/boy no one had loved. I wished he had thrown a brick or two at Wilma Lou. Struggling to compose my voice, I asked her, 'You sure you don't remember the children's names?'

'No, I don't. I ain't give them a thought for fifty years. It was a blessed relief when they moved away.'

'Moved away to where?'

'Don't nobody know. Now, that was peculiar.' Zest for the memory made Wilma Lou sit up straight and look almost pleasant. 'They went off in the middle of the night and didn't give no notice, and I ain't heard nothing about them since. Papa said they were skipping out on two months' rent they owed, but I had a feeling it was something more than that, because what little bit of furniture they had, they left it behind.'

Along with a freshly dug grave in the backyard, I hypothesized, and why had hawk-eyed Wilma Lou not spotted that? Duh, because it was covered with bricks, of course, as if the children had been playing.

'Now, once them no-accounts left, things got better,' Wilma Lou prattled on. 'The next people moved in was named—'

One more name would have endangered my precarious hold on Furree. (Furry Purry, Purry Furry, fluffy Payne's Grey cat in painting.) With no effort at a graceful transition, I stood up. 'Wilma Lou, I have to go now. Thank you so much for the iced tea and the company.' I waved away her startled protests with both arms. 'No, really, I must leave. I just remembered something. Thank you again. I'll see you some other time.' But not too soon, I hoped as I bolted out of her house.

The sun had set, and it was pretty dark out there. I wanted to run, but I didn't want to blunder into something, so I felt my way from her house to mine, all the time thinking, *Furree. Furree.*

I had just gotten back into my own house and turned some lights on when the phone rang. Damn! In imminent danger of losing my grip on the name in my head, I grabbed for something to write with and something to write on – what came to hand was an orange magic marker and a paper napkin with pink flowers printed on it – and I scrawled *FURREE* before I ran for the phone.

'Hi, Mom!' It was Maurie.

Instantly, I stopped cursing telephones. 'Sweetie! How *are* you?'

'Chuffed! I had a very good day, plus Cassie and I were talking about you. What's new with you and your ghost, Mom?'

That jarred me, partly with relief – Maurie, accepting after all – but partly with resistance to the term she had used. I answered slowly, 'I don't exactly think of him as a ghost.' Even though he was, of course. He had died a painful death, he was angry, he was haunting the place where he had been hurt – all classic ghost behavior—

Maurie yelped, '*Him?* Don't tell me you have another one!'

'Oh, shit.' I'd messed up. 'No, Maurie, it's the same one, but you're not supposed to know he was a boy. Please don't tell anyone, promise? The police are keeping it back that he was a boy and he wet the bed and that awful mother of his punished him by making him wear a dress—'

'*What?* I'm a girl, so is it a punishment for me to wear pants?'

'Honey, whatever happened here went way past sexism. LeeVon died.'

'LeeVon?'

'I think his mother killed him.'

'Your ghost's name is LeeVon?'

'According to his sister Bonnie Jo, yes.'

'Is she a ghost, too?' Maurie was beginning to sound a bit round-eyed, and I had to laugh, rueful.

I said, 'She might as well be a ghost unless I can manage to find her.'

TWENTY

Maurie and I talked for a long time, to my great satisfaction. Then, at the insistence of my body, I had supper – one of those Healthy Choice microwaved dinners. But while I was eating it, I looked in the Skink County phone book under F for Furree.

Damn. I found no Furrees, Furees, Furries or Furrys.

But finally, as if my brain functioned better after being fed, I had the sense to try Fe instead of Fu, and found nearly a whole page of Ferees.

You know what all them Furrees (make that Ferees) *is like*, Wilma Lou had said.

Actually, I didn't know. But the way that sounded, the local police might know. I phoned Detective T.J. Tadlock, not just out of civic duty but really wanting to talk with her. However, I got her voicemail. I supposed she had to go off-duty sometimes, but dammit, why right now? With what the shrinks call 'magical thinking,' I phoned again, but, of course, the same thing happened and I left a message: my elderly neighbor said the victim's family was named Feree.

Then, feeling obstinate but trying to sound as sweet and Southern as pecan pie, I started calling all the Ferees in the phone book, placing check marks next to the few who answered, to whom I said, 'Hi, y'all, I'm looking for Bonnie Jo. Y'all know where I can find her?'

They didn't. And they weren't very polite about it, either.

Partly because of this and partly because I had to stand in the kitchen to dial my old wall phone, I gave up for the night pretty soon. I felt tired and grumpy. LeeVon had kept me busy all day, so I had gotten nothing practical done. My laundry was piling up, as were dirty dishes in the sink. I was running out of everything and needed to go grocery shopping. I'd even forgotten to get the mail, and it could just damn wait until tomorrow. I watched some TV, attempted to solve a Sudoku at the same time, fouled it up and went to bed.

Dressing to go in to work the next morning, Saturday, for a moment Detective T.J. Tadlock wished she could just wear a uniform and not have to make tricky decisions. She had given her all to be a Smokey, and she didn't just mean hours of training at the gym to stay in shape; heck, she still did that. When it came to subduing a perp, she felt she could hold her own with any cop. But a plain-clothes detective, female, very plain indeed in the clothes she could afford, had to look professional.

Still, uniforms or no uniforms, being treated with respect was more attainable for her than it was for her young, pretty female colleagues.

The tricky decisions involved being dressy but conservative and never sexy. Sighing, T.J. selected a navy-blue top with a geometric print, matching navy knee-length skirt and navy cork-soled wedgies. The clothes fit her stocky body perfectly because she kept herself fit – no paunch, no flab and no damn cleavage. She took pride in that. Onward.

The uniform at the desk said, 'Morning, Detective,' and handed her two messages. Saying something to the effect that yeah, it certainly was morning, T.J. took the papers and headed toward the coffee machine to get a cup of caffeine, black. Sipping it, she looked at the first paper: Beverly Vernon said the last name of the long-dead kid was likely Feree. T.J. smiled to herself, admiring the persistence of the woman, but the information was not much help. There were whole trailer parks in Skink County that should have been surrounded with razor wire and turned into jails to simplify the legal process. Most of the people in them were named Feree.

The second message was a whole lot more interesting: a sheriff's deputy on patrol had stopped a car matching the BOLO and had brought in the driver, Bonnie Jo Slegg, who had shown a disinclination to cooperate and therefore was waiting in a closed room, Interview 3.

Immediately, T.J. went to have a look at her through the observation mirror and assessed her as a type she knew too well – no longer young but with no dignity of age, beaten up by life and poverty and probably boyfriends. Scraggly hair that had never known professional care. Probably snaggly teeth, ditto. Skinny with the emphasis on the skin, pallid, parched and hungry and not nearly as tough as it looked, psychologically speaking. Slumped at the table, Bonnie Jo looked sullen and vulnerable in the windowless room with handcuff bars and shackle rings mounted on the walls and floors.

T.J. walked in, and Bonnie Jo jerked to sit up steely straight, like a sprung trap. 'Hello, Bonnie Jo, I'm one of the detectives. Call me Tee Jay.' Bonnie Jo Slegg was a witness, not a suspect, and T.J. wanted her to relax. 'Can I get you a cup of coffee?'

The Slegg woman sat with her mouth open and her teeth – the yellow-brown remains of her teeth – on display, but she didn't answer.

'Bottle of Dr Pepper? Something to eat?'

No reaction.

So much for hospitality. T.J. tried again. 'Ma'am, you're not under arrest or any sort of suspicion. We just want to talk with you.'

Bonnie Jo Slegg got her mouth moving and spoke. 'But I told them when they brought me in, I gotta get back! There's groceries in my car and the milk and such is gonna spoil!'

T.J. noted that, while there was no doubt Bonnie Jo was upset, she was not shrill, not whining, not even very loud. This was a welcome change from the usual and she gave her points for it. 'You've been here for what, an hour?'

'And the day getting hotter every minute!'

'Where's your car?'

'Back on Gator Creek Road where they pulled me over, I guess.' Then she sounded even more distressed. 'Unless they towed it or something?'

'Let me see.' T.J. got up, went to the door and called the nearest rookie over, conveying directives for Bonnie Jo's car to be brought to the station and her perishable foods refrigerated. This took no more than the normal amount of back-and-forthing with the rookie's commanding officer, after which T.J. closed the door and returned to the table. 'Is that better, Mrs Slegg?'

'Don't call me missus,' she said, no longer upset but not happy either. 'That slimy Bernie Slegg took off years ago.'

T.J. sat down. 'Was your birth name Feree?'

Her eyes widened. 'How'd y'all know that?'

That clinched it for T.J.; she had felt pretty sure this was the right Bonnie Jo, and now she felt positive. But she didn't reveal the source of her information; it was her job to ask questions, not answer. 'And you had a brother named LeeVon?'

Bonnie Jo shrank as if something threatened to hit her, and her face huddled into a mute sort of compression, childish despite her papery, crinkled skin. Jaw clamped, she did not answer.

T.J. made sure to speak very softly, very gently. 'The skeleton that lady found a week, ten days ago – wasn't that your brother, LeeVon?'

No response.

'Just tell me one thing. Was he older than you?'

This seemed to startle her into a slight surrender. She made eye contact and nodded minimally.

This was good, because now that T.J. had Bonnie Jo's birth-date from her driver's license, it might help with finding her brother's birth certificate. 'Was he a year older than you? Two years?'

But T.J. could see she had pressed too much. Bonnie Jo looked away and shuttered her face, mulish.

'Nobody's blaming you for anything, Bonnie Jo. You were just a little kid. Whatever happened, it wasn't your fault.'

Nothing.

T.J. leaned toward her across the table. 'Don't you at least want to identify LeeVon and claim his remains so he can be buried in a proper grave with a marker?'

She didn't speak, but T.J. saw tears puddling in her stony eyes.

'Miss Bonnie Jo, don't you want your brother LeeVon put to rest with flowers and prayers?'

The tears overflowed her eyes, but her rainy face didn't move and she didn't make a sound.

T.J. passed the Kleenex. 'I can see you do. So why not help it happen? Talk to me.'

Silence.

'I guess it's a hard story to tell. Have you ever told anybody?'

Bonnie Jo took a Kleenex, wiped her eyes, then broke the silence – but only by blowing her nose.

'Have you ever told anybody in your whole life?'

The woman actually shook her head with emphasis. No.

'Are you afraid? I'm sure you were afraid when you were little, but you're a grown woman now, Bonnie Jo, and nobody can punish you, can they?'

Bonnie Jo just stared as if the question confused her.

'It's hard to tell a secret when you've been quiet for so long, isn't it?'

No response, not a flicker.

T.J. decided it was time to push a little. 'Bonnie Jo, why don't you just go ahead and tell me?'

It was as if she had stepped on a land mine. Bonnie Jo lunged to her feet, yelling, 'What the hell would I tell you for! I ain't telling nothing to you or nobody else, never! Ain't nobody got no right!'

T.J. asked without raising her voice, 'What do you mean, no right?'

'I mean what happened to LeeVon was a crying shame and ain't nobody entitled to tell stories or talk stupid about it. What's done is done and folks in this heartless world ain't fit to know.' But then she blinked and her voice, although still fierce, softened. 'Except maybe for one. She might understand. That woman who done his picture.'

TWENTY-ONE

For the first time since I don't know when, I slept late, waking up around nine a.m. I felt remarkably good, so refreshed that it was as if I had woken up young. As if I had become a child again, light-hearted, happy for no reason.

Maybe even LeeVon had felt that way sometimes. I hoped so.

The first thing I did when I got out of the bathroom was head for the studio, eager to see any sign of him, hoping he was back and that he was feeling better.

Eureka! When I saw my offhand rendition of an old woman on the easel, I convulsed like a girl into a giggle fit: LeeVon had embellished it with a walrus-worthy mustache, a shaggy beard and hair bristling out of the ears, all in black crayon.

'She looks more like Wilma Lou than ever,' I joked aloud, laughing harder. But then a thought made me stop laughing. 'LeeVon,' I asked, 'was this just for fun, or does she remind you of somebody?'

Standing there talking to the air, I felt a bit demented, but decided I was no more crazy than people who prayed out loud. I wasn't relaying a message to another world, either. LeeVon was right damn there, in my house, in my studio. I could feel him.

I could feel his mood, and it made me sigh. 'I can't blame you for holding a grudge against her, kiddo. I'd be angry, too. But isn't it about time you let it go?'

Yeah, right was the sarcastic sense I got. *Like that's ever going to happen. She killed me. My own mother killed me.*

'Half a century ago. Sweetie, what's it going to take for you to have some peace?'

The phone rang, and I almost didn't answer; it felt like such a rude interruption. But I did answer, and, weirdly enough, it was almost like a continuation of the same conversation. It was Detective T.J. Tadlock asking me to please come talk with Bonnie Jo about LeeVon.

* * *

I did not take the portrait, because it had scared her. Instead, I carefully rolled the first picture LeeVon had left me. I did not want to rubber-band it – that's a brutal way to treat art – so I reached up, yanked an origami butterfly down from the ceiling and tied its soft violet yarn around the tube of paper. Then, without even taking the time to eat breakfast, I went.

Detective Tadlock must have been waiting for me, because there she was the minute I walked into the State Police building. Print blouse, straight skirt, low heels; a no-frills-no-nonsense woman. She didn't thank me or waste time in small talk. She didn't ask me what I was carrying. She said without preamble, 'Nobody will be videotaping or recording. I will be the only one at the observation window. Bonnie Jo Slegg is here voluntarily and so are you. Neither of you is making a legal statement; since she is not talking to me directly, anything she says will just be hearsay. I hope she'll tell you what happened to LeeVon, but I promise you, if anything weird comes up, I will forget it instantly.' She glanced at my roll of paper, then lifted her heavy face to look me straight in the eye. 'Do you understand what I'm talking about?'

I hoped she could tell by my smile how much I approved of her. 'Yes.'

She led me to the interview room, opened the door for me and stepped aside. When I went in, Bonnie Jo's clay-brown gaze shot at once to the roll of paper I carried.

'Is LeeVon with you?' she demanded, halfway to her feet, sounding more frightened than hopeful.

'No, I don't think so.' I found that, with her, I could be matter-of-fact about LeeVon. 'I think he stays at the house.' I sat down, not across the table from her but just around the corner. 'That's where he died, isn't it?'

She nodded and settled back into her chair, seeming to understand that ghosts haunted the places where they suffered wrongful deaths. 'What's that?' She remained fixated on the rolled-up paper, so I slipped off the violet yarn, unrolled the picture and placed it between us so we could both look at it.

She stared for several moments before she said in a whisper, 'What *is* it?'

'The first drawing LeeVon did for me.'

She didn't look at me but her voice glared. 'What the hell you talking about? What you mean, he done this for you?'

'I mean, a few days after I found the skeleton, I put out paper at night and found pictures like this in the morning. I assume they're by LeeVon. Don't you think so?'

'Oh, yeah.' She sounded shaky and sardonic. 'That's Ma with her whupping strap.' Her thin forefinger with its frail, ragged nail hovered over the towering, shouting woman. 'That's my little sister, Sukie,' she continued, pointing to the smallest figure. Her hand trembled, but her voice did not, as she moved on. 'That's me in the middle; I was five years old. And that's LeeVon.'

'Why's he wearing a dress?'

'Ma made him. We all three wore dresses all the time so she could get to our hind ends easier to whup us. But she beat LeeVon the most. And mocked him.'

Bonnie Jo hadn't yet looked me in the eye, and now she turned her face away. I wanted to know what else Ma had done to LeeVon, but sensed I needed to back off. So I asked, 'Where was his father?'

She slewed around to look hard at me. 'We didn't have no fathers. Ma didn't do no marrying, just a lot of screwing around.'

'Was her name Feree?'

'Still is.'

'She's still *alive*?'

'Alive and mean as ever in some government project up in Alabama. Flat on her back and it's her turn to piss the bed. I hope she fries in hell.'

I heard something ready to either snap together or break apart in her low-spoken words. She was as open to me as she would ever be. Keeping my voice as quiet as hers, I said, 'Tell me what happened to LeeVon.'

Observing from just outside the interrogation room, T.J. was taking notes and passing them on to an officer at a computer: *search Feree, female, first name unknown, age approximately 85–95, check with Department of Indigent Elder Care in Alabama.* Hearing that the abusive mother was still alive startled and troubled T.J., raising as it did the question of prosecution, if it could be proved that she was indeed responsible for the death of her son. In order to do that, witnesses were needed. *Search local birth records approximately*

1951–1954 for Suky/Sukie Feree. T.J. based those dates on Bonnie Jo Slegg's age as recorded on her motor vehicle operator's license. If LeeVon, Levon, Lee Von, Lee Vaughn, Leigh Von et cetera Feree was older than Bonnie Jo, he should have been in school, so T.J. had expanded the search for him to include kindergarten and first-grade school records countywide, but so far it hadn't found him. If it wasn't for his skeleton, T.J. would have found it hard to believe the boy had existed. Finding out anything about him was like trying to track a ghost.

She had general ideas about his brief life, though, from observation of other dirt-poor families and, in fact, from growing up with them. She knew that his shoes had probably been a pair of secondhand or pass-me-down flip-flops, even in winter when the temperature dropped almost to freezing. His clothes – dresses – had probably come from thrift shop sales: stuff a grocery sack full for a dollar. He might not have gone hungry, but it was not likely he and his sisters often had a real cooked meal, unless it was maybe heated-up frozen pizza. More likely they had eaten canned ravioli, boxed macaroni and cheese, Ramen noodles, peanut butter, spongy white bread: the stuff the food pantries gave out free. T.J. pictured them snatching whatever was available, running off with it to eat outdoors, maybe getting a beating if they took something their ma wanted for herself. T.J. could not imagine there had been much dependable routine in the children's lives, not with men coming and going, their mother partying with them and taking them for every penny she could get. No doubt there were single mothers who did a good job of raising their children, but the Feree woman sure as hell wasn't one of them, making her son wear a dress and then mocking him, probably calling him a girl, putting down her own sex and despising men at the same time. T.J. had a pretty clear picture that LeeVon's mama was a sociopath.

By picture, she meant her own theories, not that weird painted paper lying on the table in the interrogation room. What that looked like, she didn't want to know, or where it came from either.

Almost whispering, keeping her gaze and her right hand on the crude picture of LeeVon in his triangle of a dress, Bonnie Jo said, 'Ma didn't want no boy child. She never called him LeeVon, just

Lee or Lee-Lee. I think she told people he was a girl since the
day she birthed him. She hated men, you know.'

'She did? Because of, um, her job?'

'Yeah, she said men only wanted one thing, and if she had her
way, she would cut all their pricks off – every man in the world.'

'Wow.' Then my feelings splashed up against a wall of horror.
'Oh, no, please don't tell me—'

'No. She didn't do nothing to LeeVon down there. But she still
messed him up pretty good.' Tracing the drawing with her fingertip,
Bonnie Jo spoke even more softly. 'He wasn't stupid. Since the
time I can remember, LeeVon knowed he wasn't no girl. I mean,
it wasn't hard for him to figure out once me and Sukie come along.
Plus in our house it was hard not to see men sometimes with their
pants down. So he knowed, but Ma kept on making him wear a
dress just to spite him. She wouldn't never get him no boy clothes,
so he had to dress like a girl or go naked.'

My emotions, in a whirlpool, spurted up an insight. LeeVon
had painted pictures for me but never written anything on them,
not a single word. 'Was she so crazy she kept him out of school?'

Bonnie Jo gave me a look of sour amusement. 'She was crazy,
all right. But none of us Ferees was ever much for school.
Nobody come looking for us.'

'Oh.' The implications made it difficult for me to speak. 'Nobody
interfered.'

Bonnie Jo heard what I wasn't quite saying. She nodded. 'It
was hell. There was never a day LeeVon didn't fight her back, and
when she whupped him, she wouldn't stop till he cried. She was
mean to us girls, too, but not that mean. I remember one time
LeeVon swore at her that he hated her. She said right back, calm
as a carcass, "I hate you, too," and I felt like it was true.'

Five years old and faced with such a truth, Bonnie Jo could not
have been much better off than LeeVon.

The silence that followed was so hard and dark I had to break
it. 'So is that why she killed him? Because she hated him?'

'No, it was because he wet the bed.'

But Wilma Lou had said there were sheets drying on the
clothesline all the time. 'Once too often?'

'No, it was usually me or Sukie that wet the bed. Us kids all
slept in one bed, and Ma was in the other bed with a boyfriend

or a bottle, and we was scared to get up in the dark and go to the bathroom when we didn't know what was going on.'

'But had she ever come close to killing you or Sukie?'

'No. I'm not sure she meant to kill LeeVon. She just put him in the bathtub full of hot water, like, to teach him to be clean. He screamed and screamed and never stopped screaming, it was so hot. And she kept running it hotter, and she kept pushing him back into the water, it seemed like forever.'

Perhaps I would not have realized how horrible this was had I not myself encountered the water in that house. I sat there in that police station interrogation room thinking about scalding burns, deep ones, second or third degree, over most of the little boy's body. And I couldn't say a word.

Bonnie Jo kept touching the figure of LeeVon in the picture he had made, stroking him. She kept her eyes on him. 'Me 'n' Sukie run and hid under the bed,' she said in a whispered monotone. 'We couldn't stand it. But once she finally let him out and the noise stopped, we thought it would be OK, maybe. We stayed where we was and I guess we went back to sleep. When we woke up in the morning, we seen LeeVon laying on the floor in the bedroom with us, with the bottom half of him all swole up and—' Bonnie Jo choked on what she was trying to say, but fought to say it anyway. 'And red and split open like a hot dog over a campfire, and his skin falling off.' She jerked her head around to look at me, eyes huge, words spilling like tears. 'His skin puffed up in white patches then just slid on to the floor and laid there like toilet paper.'

'Shhh,' I said, 'shhh. Oh, you poor thing—' Or something equally inane, reaching toward her but hesitating with my hands in midair, not sure whether she would accept my touch.

She kept staring at me. 'He was making noises like an animal.'

'He was still *alive*?' The instant I said it, I knew I sounded unforgivably stupid.

Bonnie Jo's eyes narrowed and she flared at me, 'Course he was still alive. It would've been too simple if he just died. Me and Sukie had to watch him and we didn't know what was going on. Ma heaved him back up on to the bed and sprinkled baby powder on him. She give us Pepsi to feed him but he wouldn't open his eyes or swallow or anything, just whimpered like a puppy.

He was sweating one minute, shivering the next. After a while he got stinky, and yellow stuff started to come out of him like slime.'

I could barely speak. 'How long?'

'How long this went on for? I don't remember. It's all a bad blur and I was too young – I didn't understand what it was about. One day we woke up and he wasn't there in the bed with us. Mom said he was gone and don't ask no questions, just go put our stuff in trash bags because we had to move to Alabama. So we got out of there but it was all mixed up in my mind, like Ma done it to punish Sukie and me for spilling Pepsi on LeeVon. I thought maybe she give LeeVon away to a circus or a zoo or something.'

I didn't know what to say. There were a lot of things that clamored to be said. But what I finally asked was, 'Where's your sister now?'

'Sukie? She come back here to Cooter Spring, same as me.'

TWENTY-TWO

Before going back into that interview room, T.J. had found out two things. One, that old lady Feree, Romaine Louise Feree, was eighty-three. She must have started having babies without the benefit of marriage pretty damn young. The other was that Sukie Feree had done the same thing. She had produced two baby Ferees, both now grown, the boy doing OK in the Air Force but the girl a crackhead and prostitute.

T.J. had to take a deep, steadying breath before walking into the room where Beverly Vernon and Bonnie Jo Slegg were talking. Both women hushed and looked up at her as if she was a stranger. Bonnie Jo seemed like the last leaf hanging on a tree, frail and shaky. Beverly Vernon seemed more like the tree, determined to support her.

T.J. said, 'Mrs Vernon, I need to speak with Miss Bonnie Jo privately.'

But Bonnie Jo grabbed for the other woman across the table, clutching her. 'No! She stays.'

'Of course I'll stay,' said the Vernon woman in soothing and motherly tones.

Restraining herself from letting go of a gusty sigh, T.J. sat down at the table with them rather than standing over them. 'Bonnie Jo, I need you alone to get your legal statement concerning your brother's death.'

'You already know what happened.' In her voice, T.J. could hear that she was choking back tears.

'I know what happened and I would like to see your mother charged with murder for what she did.'

'That's all right with me.' Bonnie Jo sounded pretty well used up. 'She's still mean as a snake.'

'She's competent to stand trial, then?'

'Huh?'

'You wouldn't consider her senile?'

'Not hardly. She remembers all her cuss words. But it ain't like I seed her lately. I can't stand to go visit her no more than once a year around Christmastime.'

T.J. confirmed the mother's full name and current residence with Bonnie Jo, then said, 'Sometime soon I need formal statements from both you and your sister, if possible. Does Sukie remember your brother's death?'

'We didn't neither of us understand what was going on at the time.'

'But she remembers.'

'You better ask her.'

Beverly Vernon butted in. 'Detective, aren't you getting a bit ahead of yourself? Doesn't the District Attorney have to decide whether to prosecute?'

'After I get the evidence together, yes.'

'And even though it's a murder charge, because the Feree woman is so old now, won't there be some question whether to proceed?'

'I'm sure there will be.'

'And what will settle that question?'

'You'd better ask the District Attorney,' retorted T.J., who did not like finding herself to be the one interrogated. Also, there were things she could not say in front of Bonnie Jo.

But Beverly Vernon seemed to know those things anyway.

Turning to Bonnie Jo, she said, 'It's really all up to you and Sukie, depending on whether you decide to cooperate. And it seems to me that the first thing you need to know is what LeeVon wants.'

Tough-minded, as was top priority for any detective, T.J. policed this statement. 'You mean what you believe LeeVon would have wanted if he had lived.'

Beverly turned her head with the patience of a kindergarten teacher. 'No, Detective Tadlock, that's not what I said. I mean what LeeVon wants right now.'

This was the sort of thing T.J. was afraid of, but a detective cannot show fear. T.J. hardened her face. 'What the hell are you talking about? You can't expect me to deal with crazy ideas of—'

The Vernon woman interrupted, steady-eyed and oak-solid. 'Detective, you know exactly what I mean, and we all have to deal. Now, it's not that I mind having LeeVon around the house. He's good company. But he's not a happy camper. He deserves to rest in peace, and we—'

'We nothing!'

'We need to do what would be best for him. He has victim's rights, doesn't he?'

T.J. took a deep breath, let it out through her sizeable nose, then said, 'You do what you need to do and I'll do what I need to do, OK, Mrs Vernon?'

Cassie had to admit that Maurie was redeeming herself from having fled when they were at Mom's. Now, this Saturday, Maurie had sneakily and mendaciously phoned Aunt Gayle to make sure she would be at home; Maurie had made the trek from Ithaca and picked Cassie up at Creative Java; with Cassie in the passenger seat, it was Maurie who quested through Montclair to confront the dragon, Gayle Vernon Perkins, aka Grendel, in her lair. Silently, Maurie spurred her mechanical steed onward, and Cassie noticed an adamantine glint in her sister's eye.

They hardly spoke a word. The matter was too serious for chit-chat.

Arriving at Aunt Gayle's condo, Cassie wondered not for the first time why in the world this fashionable woman wanted the old Montclair house. It was shabby Victorian, whereas Aunt Gayle's place was ultra-slick, ultra-chic, hard-edged modern, all chrome and glass, through which could be seen low-slung black leather furniture.

Aunt Gayle herself met them at the coffered metal door wearing a sleek black tunic and leggings, edgy steel jewelry, and her hair all but lacquered into its red wedge. 'Darlings!' she cried, her coolly arched brows at variance with the warmth in her voice. 'Cassie! Maurie didn't tell me she'd invited you.' Hence the raised eyebrows. 'Please, come in.'

'I think not, Ms Perkins,' said Maurie in a remarkably flat tone Cassie had never heard from her.

'Ms Perkins' froze, teetering on five-inch heels. 'I beg your pardon?'

Cassie fielded that like a pro, surprising herself. 'You *ought* to beg our pardon, after trying to have our mother put away.'

Maurie added, 'I am very glad indeed to inform you that your ploy has failed.'

With a hurtful pang, Cassie hoped this would become true. Mom still had her court hearing on Monday to get through.

Her indignant aunt was saying, 'Ploy? Just what are you accusing me of?'

'We're beyond "accusing." It's proven fact,' Maurie said in the same stony tone. 'What you did – having mom effectively kidnapped based on merest hearsay – was felonious, but it would be complicated to have you arrested by the authorities in Florida, so Cassie and I are more inclined to file a lawsuit.'

Cassie expected her aunt to keep on protesting innocence, but quite the opposite; Gayle Perkins stood rigid, righteous and reddening with outrage. 'I only did what I thought was best. You yourself said that your mother—'

'Is *my mother* and *you* need to *let her alone*,' Maurie flared with such heat that Gayle stepped back. 'If you do not cease and desist harassing Mom and causing her mental anguish, Cassie and I *will* file against you—'

'Oh, really?' interrupted Gayle in a sarcastic drawl.

'Quiet!' Maurie snapped, teacherish.

'Shut up and listen!' ordered Cassie at the same time.

'Listen? The coffee-brewer says listen? The P-H-whoopie-D says be quiet?' Gayle laughed, but not very convincingly. 'Who do you think you are? As far as I'm concerned, you're just a pair of brat kids! I happen to know powerful people, influential people, and—'

Cassie burst out, 'Bullshit, Aunt Gayle! You're just a poser, a snob and an aging hipster. Nobody gives a shit about you.'

This shocked Gayle silent for just enough time to give Maurie an opening.

Maurie went on, 'File against you for punitive damages on the basis of unlawful detainment and defamation of character. You are to cease and desist any machinations involving our mother or you will be sorry. Are we clear?'

Her face contorted and livid, Gayle screeched, 'You are the ones who are going to be sorry!'

'Are we clear?' Maurie repeated.

'I'm cutting both of you out of my will!'

'Just so long as you got the message.'

Turning to her sister, Cassie felt herself actually grinning; it had felt so good to call her aunt an aging hipster. 'Come on, Berthe. I think we're finished here.'

'You're finished, all right!' their aunt shouted at their backs as they turned away. 'You're disowned!' She continued yelling as they walked to the car and got in, but Cassie didn't particularly notice what she said. Once in the car, she and Maurie started laughing with relief as they drove away.

'Cross her off the Christmas list,' said Maurie.

The rest of that Saturday, I worried. I worried about Sukie Feree, how she would feel if Detective Tadlock found her and questioned her. I worried about Bonnie Jo, headed home with her groceries and her messed-up emotions and her bad memories. I worried about how to confer with LeeVon when he and I were communicating on such a primitive level. It wasn't as if I could leave him a note.

What I finally did was to sit down with his most telling picture and another piece of cheap sketch paper. Using black marker instead of paints, as simply and accurately as possible I copied the three skirted figures he had drawn, smallest to largest, and the towering mother – with a few important changes. In my version, Ma's whupping strap had dropped to the ground. I put a noose around her neck, yanked her off her big feet and hanged her from a primitive gibbet. Next to her, in red, I put a question mark.

I left this on the easel when I went to bed.

In the morning, there it still was. LeeVon had not done anything to it or to anything else that I could see.

Damn. Now what?

After breakfast, I phoned Bonnie Jo to see how she was. I felt pretty sure I wouldn't be interrupting any preparations to go to church on her part, but just in case, I asked, 'Do you have time to talk?'

'I ain't got nothing much but time.'

'Are you OK since talking to the cops yesterday?'

She snorted. 'No. They called about releasing "the remains" to me. That's what they call LeeVon's skeleton – "the remains." What the hell am I supposed to do with him? I ain't got no money for—'

Without consulting my brain, my mouth opened and said, 'Bring him to my house.'

'Really?' She sounded relieved. 'You sure?'

I wasn't at all sure, so I hedged, 'It's a thought. We should ask your sister. Are you and she close?'

'Sukie? Hell, yeah. We talk all the time.'

'Oh. Good. So you told her about—'

I was trying to ask whether Sukie knew about LeeVon's portrait, his active spirit or ghost or whatever, but Bonnie Jo interrupted. 'Sukie is all fussed up. The cops been to her place already. Her and the grands played bill collector and hid like there was nobody home. It ain't as if she don't got enough problems—'

'Excuse me,' I said, all my other concerns forgotten as my mind wrapped around a single word: grands. 'Grandchildren?'

'Yeah, she got stuck raising them. Their ma's a druggie.'

'Sukie's daughter is an addict?'

'Yeah. Sukie was a good ma, but you know how it is.'

I didn't know how it was. I couldn't imagine being a single mother raising children in poverty. And now grandchildren. Humbled, I asked, 'Is Sukie a good grandma, too?'

'She ain't got nothing to spare except hugs, but she does the best she can.'

Oh. Oh, for LeeVon's sake and my selfish own, I just had to do something. 'Bonnie Jo, could you take me to see her?'

Hesitation. Reluctance. After a moment I sensed why. Mix poverty with a little bit of pride and people don't want visitors.

'Or could you and she come to see me?'

'I think she'd like that better,' Bonnie Jo said.

Marcia Wengleman rarely got to spend a relaxed Sunday at home just lounging in her favorite butterfly chair, catching up on her reading. When her phone summoned her with 'Dem Bones Gonna Rise Again,' she rolled her eyes. But when she saw the name on her caller ID, she smacked herself on the forehead, remembering she had forgotten to return the little woman's call. Laying the journal she was reading in her lap, she thumbed the green button. 'Hello, Beverly.'

'Oh! You know it's me. I keep forgetting about smart phones. How are you?'

'No more ghoulish than usual, and I'm sorry I forgot to call back. Yes, I will be there for your date with Judge Simmons tomorrow.'

'Oh! Oh, that's great. Thank you. But that's not why I phoned.'

Marcia's jaw dropped. What could be more urgent than court?

But nattering on, Beverly was already answering that question. 'I'm sorry to bother you on a Sunday, but I'm very concerned to know what is going to happen to LeeVon. His skeleton, I mean.'

Marcia had to clear her throat before speaking. 'Detective Tadlock tells me you've found him a family?'

'Two sisters, yes.'

'Well, after the court releases his remains, they can claim him.'

'What if they can't afford a funeral or even a cremation? Will the county bury him?'

'No. We stopped using the potter's field years ago. Our John Does go into a freezer over in Tallahassee. Or if they're just bones like LeeVon, they're filed in a box on the shelf.'

Beverly Vernon said, 'Huh.' Then there was a considerable silence, during which Marcia imagined she could hear the grinding of mental molars as the other woman ruminated.

Marcia intervened. 'No, Beverly, you are not allowed to take him and put him back where you found him in your backyard.'

'I don't think that would be a good idea anyway. But I have to do *something*. The hell of it is he needs . . . I haven't talked with Bonnie Jo and Sukie yet, but it's absolutely crucial . . .'

After listening to fraught silence for a few moments, Marcia asked, 'What's so absolutely crucial?'

'To lay his spirit to rest, not just his bones.'

'*What?*' The journal Marcia was reading slid off her lap on to the floor, punctuating her startled reaction with a smack as if something had hit her.

'To get him back together.' Struggling with the words, sounding as if she might cry, the Vernon woman abruptly ended the call. Marcia sat staring at the blank face of her cell phone, wondering whether Beverly Vernon had really been saying what Marcia thought she had heard.

I met Sukie that same day. Bonnie Jo brought her and her grand-kids out to my place that afternoon, and I walked outside to meet their beater of a car as it sighed to a stop in my front yard. 'Is it OK we brought the kids along?' Bonnie Jo asked out of the driver's side window. 'There ain't nobody to watch them.'

'Of course it's OK!'

'This is Sukie,' Bonnie Jo informed me, gesturing toward her passengers, 'and Chloe and Emma and Liam.'

Sukie acted too shy to speak. Plumper and shorter than Bonnie Jo, she looked like LeeVon with a more rounded face. The children got out of the car and stood still, as silent as their mother. Chloe, the reed-thin oldest, I guessed at early grade-school age, and Emma, a curly-haired mocha-skinned charmer, a bit younger. Liam was a sturdy toddler in shorts and a well-worn T-shirt like his sisters.

Bonnie Jo asked, 'Miss Beverly, is it OK if I take these curtain climbers for a walk around your yard? Show them where Sukie and me used to play?'

'Of course it's OK!' I felt stupid, repeating myself that way, and followed up with something even more stupid. 'You can teach them how to throw bricks.'

Both women, to my relief, looked surprised but started laughing. Sukie even smiled at me, and the children came alive, yelling and running in circles. Bonnie Jo started grabbing them, and leaving her to it, I reached out for Sukie. 'Come on inside.'

The idea, I deduced, was for Sukie to have a look at LeeVon's portrait alone, without her grandchildren there to see her reaction.

She didn't say a single word until she stood face-to-face with the image of her dead brother, when she asked him softly, 'Please don't cry.'

I think both she and I held our breath for the next moment. We heard happy noises from the children out in the backyard. But inside my house nothing unreal happened, so I, for one, relaxed.

Sukie looked at her brother some more, and she was the one who started to cry, a little, silently. Tears on her face. She took in the oval aureole of pictures crayoned on the wall around the portrait, pointed at a bright red airplane and asked a bit unsteadily, 'Was it LeeVon done this?'

'Yes.'

'I thought so. He liked things that flew – but how did he reach so high?'

'He's a spirit,' I said, amazed to hear myself say it in such an ordinary way, as if I were talking about having my hair cut. 'He floats, kind of, I suppose. Would you like to see what he did in the other room?'

Sukie's eyes widened and, once again wordless, she nodded.

I led her into the studio and watched her gaze flash from the origami critters hanging on the ceiling to the rainbow handprints on the walls to the junk in baskets on the table to the pictures LeeVon had painted. Turning to me, she lifted her eyebrows, questioning.

'LeeVon did the handprints one night,' I said.

I was about to go on telling her about other gifts he had left me, but she brought me up short. 'But *how*? His hands is bones miles away from here.'

Such a practical-minded question I had never thought to ask – I stood there flabbergasted.

'You don't know how,' Sukie rightly observed after a while.

'I sure don't. I guess you have to believe in magic,' I admitted. 'But he did put those handprints on the wall. And I guess Bonnie Jo told you about the picture I showed her?'

'Yeah. Is that it?' She pointed.

'Yes.' I peeled it away from the Poster Putty holding it to the wall. We sat at the table and, as she looked at the childish depiction of three kids versus Ma, I told her about my experience of LeeVon, about how he had played with my toys one night, and trashed my place the next, and painted his pictures after that, then left his handprints and turned playful again, sorting my paints and arranging my flittercritters in circles by species. About how he had taken charge of the portrait I was trying to do, although I had not known for sure it was him until he replicated the dress he had been buried in.

'And I don't have a clue how he did it, any of it,' I admitted. 'It's not as if he took hold of my hand and guided the brush.'

'Do you think he's here all the time?'

'I don't know. But sometimes I talk to him like he is.'

Through the window we could see Bonnie Jo and the kids; they had gathered around the hole in the ground, and the little Ferees were indeed trying to throw bricks.

'Brats,' Sukie murmured, smiling.

'LeeVon is a brat,' I told her fondly. 'Look what he did to this. Not that I mind. I was just fooling around.' I got up and lifted my line drawing off the easel to show her the painting underneath. 'Look what he did. He put a beard and mustache on her.'

But Sukie was looking at the magic marker picture in my hand, the one with Ma hanging from a gibbet. She pointed at it. 'Did LeeVon do that?'

'No.' I returned the line drawing to the easel and went back to the table to sit with her. 'No, I did that, and I just put it out last night. So far LeeVon hasn't responded. I'm trying to ask him a question.'

'What question?'

But before I could answer, Sukie went stark still and her face went so pale that for the first time I noticed she had freckles. She was staring at the line drawing. I turned to look, and gasped.

The smallest black-and-white figure now wore a yellow-and-aqua striped dress.

'Oh,' Sukie wailed, 'I loved that dress,' and then she cried.

TWENTY-THREE

'**B**onnie Jo,' I called out the back door, 'bring the kids and come see this.'

She did, and I left Sukie to explain things to Bonnie Jo in the studio while I took Chloe, Emma and Liam, along with some of my junk, into the front room and got them settled playing there. Chloe all but worshipped the toy horses I brought down from my bookshelves for her, Emma dove right into the bowl of Mardi Gras beads and Liam was fascinated by a Rubik's cube.

'I love your grandkids,' I told Sukie, returning to the studio where she and Bonnie Jo stood in front of LeeVon's latest artwork, whispering.

Before Sukie had a chance to respond, Bonnie Jo demanded, 'How'd he do that?' Her attenuated finger trembled as she pointed at the yellow-and-aqua striped dress.

I touched it. Not pastel, not crayon or colored pencil, not paint, my fingertips told me. It just *was*, as if the paper itself had changed colors.

'I have no idea.' Admitting this was not difficult, as the past couple of weeks had included so much new experience I did not understand. 'He's never done anything like that in the daytime before. He must be really happy to see you, Sukie.'

The dress of the second figure on the picture began to glow, then flushed, then focused to become maraschino cherry red with white polka dots.

'And you too, Bonnie Jo,' I added, unable at first to take my eyes off the picture. A couple of moments passed before I checked on Bonnie Jo; tears ran down her face and she was trembling as if she wanted to run away, but she didn't – not this time. Mentally, I chalked up points for Bonnie Jo. I wondered whether the polka-dot dress had been her favorite, but didn't ask.

'So I guess we can all agree your brother is here, in this house, in some weird way,' I said.

Perhaps unable to speak, they nodded.

'Which is why I want his bones brought back here,' I said, 'before burial.'

'Burial? What burial?' Bonnie Jo sounded harsh and hurting. 'We can't afford no burial.'

'How do you get by, Bonnie Jo? Financially, I mean.'

'Cleaning rich people's houses for them and a little bit of this and that. *Not* what Ma done.'

'I never would have thought so,' I said very gently, turning to her sister. 'Sukie, you have the kids, so I'm guessing government money?'

She nodded. 'But it ain't never nearly enough.'

'I'm not rich either, but give me a few days and I think there's a way I can finagle a funeral for LeeVon. Is it OK with you if I do that?'

Silence. Intuiting that they weren't the sort of people I could push to accept help, I waited.

Bonnie Jo spoke first, her voice rasping very low. 'I guess so. Since he sort of done adopted you.'

Sukie nodded.

I said, 'Thank you.'

Sukie found her voice. 'Thank *us*? You're the one giving us charity. Not that most Ferees ain't too proud to accept it,' she added wryly.

'It's not charity. It's me worrying about LeeVon.' I took a deep breath; giving LeeVon's spirit rest was more important than I could say. 'So, if I can get the money to pay for a burial plot and a casket, can we have the funeral from here, from this house?' They were his family. I needed their permission.

Sukie and Bonnie Jo eyed each other, and then they both nodded. 'This here house is where he is,' Sukie said. 'That's why me and Bonnie Joe come back to Cooter Spring. To find it. Where LeeVon was.'

Detective T.J. Tadlock drove an hour and a half to get to Delaine, Alabama, and was halfway there before she realized it was Sunday. Not that it mattered; almost certainly it made no difference to the perp, and all days of the week were workdays to T.J.

Once she reached her destination, Sunset Haven Assisted Living Home, she had ironic thoughts about its name as she parked in its gravel lot. Haven? More like a sharecropper's shack, super-sized. The moment she walked into its shabby, narrow, dimly lit front hallway, she smelled the reek of cheap food, talcum powder, irregular bowel movements and old bodies going rotten from the inside out. There was no one at – sheesh, there wasn't even a front desk. With her Naturalizers clopping on the linoleum, T.J. walked back the dark hallway, past several rooms with open doorways from which she averted her eyes, until she found a woman in a uniform of sorts. Nurse? Maid? Both?

T.J. wore a mauve blazer today so she could display her shield on her lapel. She asked in friendly cop tones, 'Hi, how y'all doing? I'm here to see Romaine Louise Feree.'

The woman frowned at her over an armload of laundry. 'I don't know no Romaine, but there's an old lady Feree last room in the back.' She pointed the direction with her chin.

T.J. walked on. Sunset Haven (so called) was depressingly, even deathly, silent, but as T.J. neared the far end, she heard a raspy voice holler, 'Where the smelly bumfuck in this hell hole is the party? I wanna party!'

It came from the room to which T.J. had been directed. She stepped in and asked, 'Romaine Feree?'

The old woman swung around, her mouth a toothless rictus that might have been a grin or a leer. Not in bed like most of the others, she stumped toward T.J. on bare, knobby feet the same dried-urine color as her formerly white nightgown. She yelped, 'Romaine, go get fucked! Don't nobody call me Romaine!'

'I beg your pardon. What do they call you?'

'My ma so stupid she named me after a lettuce, fucking whore! So I go by Lettie. Lettie Lou Feree, that's me!' She stood aggressively close in front of T.J., malodorous, thin and saggy, with skin that looked a lot like the inside of a banana peel.

T.J. managed not to step back, and forced herself to smile, to sound friendly. 'OK, Lettie Lou. I'm a police officer, Detective—'

Trying to introduce herself, she got no farther. Lettie shrilled, 'What the fuck? You a cop? Well, no wonder, you so ugly.' She pronounced it 'ooo-gly,' with emphasis.

Still mean as a snake, the way her daughter had said. *Insult to snakes*, T.J. thought, but she replied only, 'Never said I was a beauty.'

'Fucking bitch cop, if y'all was a man I'd bite your pecker off and shove it up your ass! I hate cops. And mans.'

'Charmed to meet you too,' responded T.J. quite evenly. 'I came to ask about your son, LeeVon.'

'Son! I ain't got no son! I don't do no man kids. Just girls.'

'How many girls?'

'Three.'

'What are their names?'

'Lee-Lee, Bonnie Jo and Sukie.'

'By Lee, don't you mean LeeVon?'

Thus challenged, Lettie Lou gave her snarl of a toothless grin and, by way of response, she let loose with a stream of urine. T.J. smelled it, heard it, felt it splash on to her shoes and the legs of her slacks. Reflexively, she stepped back, exclaiming, 'Aren't you housebroken? Why don't they put you in a diaper!'

Lettie Lou Feree crowed, 'They can't keep no fucking diaper on me!'

T.J. knew when she was defeated. She retreated to a bathroom – *not* the Feree woman's bathroom – and washed away the outrage as best she could with hand soap and paper towels, cursing under her breath, although she used the F-word far less frequently than that virago Lettie Lou did. When she had cleaned up and calmed down, she sallied forth to look for the manager or the head nurse or some such person.

She discovered a small office behind the deserted area where there should have been a front desk, and in the office she found an administrator, a fashionable woman whose gray hair seemed premature, perhaps due to excessive paperwork.

Noticing T.J. from behind the avalanche of documents on her desk, the fashionable administrator said, 'Detective.' Obviously, news had gotten around Sunset Haven. 'How did it go with Ms Feree?'

'She pissed me off. Literally.'

The woman didn't even blink. 'Yes, she pisses people off in quite a variety of ways. Thankfully, she won't be here much longer,' she added, motioning T.J. toward a solitary faux-leather chair.

Taking a seat, T.J. asked, 'Why is that, Ms, um . . .' The name plate on the desk was mostly hidden beneath its paperlanche.

'Oh, I'm sorry. I'm Alison Banks, buck stopper. Please consider yourself shaken hands with. As for Ms Feree, a bed was open, but she doesn't really belong here. Medicaid is having trouble placing her.'

'Why?'

'The official reason is because the experts can't decide on a diagnosis.'

'Might the unofficial reason have to do with her filthy personality?'

'Certainly there's that,' said Alison Banks dryly. 'But even more regrettable is the fact that she has no filthy lucre, not even social security.'

T.J. smiled in appreciation of the buck stopper's honesty, but she hadn't driven to Alabama to talk about the Feree woman's lack of a pension as a retired prostitute. 'Why can't she just be institutionalized?'

'Because she doesn't meet the criteria for true insanity. But in my opinion, she has one mother of an extreme personality disorder.'

'A personality disorder?'

'I would vote for antisocial, although she could also be described as narcissistic, histrionic, borderline . . . but I'm not even a doctor, so what do I know?'

'I think you've nailed it. How about all of the above?'

Alison Banks had a charming smile, but she was still a bureaucrat, and she was done kidding around. 'Detective, may I ask, what is your objective in visiting Ms Feree?'

'I'm sorry, I can't divulge that.' To soften her refusal to answer, T.J. added, 'And I can't say I've learned much from her.' She stood up, thanked Alison Banks for her time, reached across the desk to shake her hand, then left.

Once she stepped outside the front door of Sunset Haven, she breathed deeply, trying to purge the smell of decaying people out of her lungs.

Actually, she had learned a great deal from Lettie Lou Feree, most of it disturbing enough to haunt her thoughts as she drove back to Cooter Spring. But she had not learned what she most wanted to know: whether the woman was legally competent to stand trial. Admittedly, it was hard to imagine her sitting in a witness box. Perhaps with duct tape over her mouth? Secured into a diaper, perhaps one made of Kevlar? Even when Lettie Lou was younger, she must have been an extremely crappy person. Not the sort of person to have for a mother.

Unexpectedly, T.J. found herself thinking that it was high time she stopped avoiding her own mother, who still called her Shannon Marie and had no idea what T.J. stood for. Heck, T.J. herself hadn't known until way too late. But since becoming a cop, she didn't mind the initials. She enjoyed invulnerability and a kind of defiance, especially when she had occasion to arrest one of the lowlife guys who had nicknamed her.

Poor, blissfully ignorant Mom; she had been so proud that her only daughter, Shannon Marie, was popular in high school, with the boys flocking around her even though she was a funnyface. And to this day, Mom remained proud of her and had never stopped caring about her, even when bewildered by her choices: divorcing what appeared to be a perfectly OK husband, then throwing away the gift God gave her by insisting on breast reduction surgery, and then deciding to become a *cop* of all things? Carrying a gun? Dealing with criminals who might try to hurt her or even kill her?

Mom worried. And Mom wondered all too vocally whether her daughter would ever find love, settle down and give her grandchildren. Mostly, Mom just didn't understand how messed up life had been for Shannon Marie as a girl whose only distinction had been size quadruple-D breasts.

Tremendous Jugs.

'T.J.,' the high school boys had snickered behind her back. 'Tee Jay!' they had called her blithely to her face, all innocent and ignorant. 'Jugs,' her husband had taunted when, after the honeymoon, he decided to hurt her. 'Tremendous Jugs. You're nothing but a huge pair of boobs.'

Mom had no clue that not one of Shannon Marie's beaux, including the one she married, had given a hoot about anything except those honkin' huge hooters.

But T.J. realized with a sigh that, compared with the Feree woman, her own well-meaning mother was a saint. So far, no one except her mother had ever loved her for herself.

Visit. Soon, T.J. told herself as she got into her unmarked car and headed back toward Cooter Spring. In the meantime, to hell with sympathy for the devil; Lettie Lou might be ancient and warped, but she did not appear to be criminally insane. And the law was still the law. It was T.J.'s job to collect evidence against that nasty old woman and make a case strong enough so that she could be tried for the murder of her son.

TWENTY-FOUR

Bonnie Jo said, 'We wasn't even certain sure he was dead till you found him.'

Bonnie Jo, Sukie and I sat around the table with glasses of pepsi and a box of oatmeal-raisin cookies. I'd given the kids popsicles, and because of the mess the popsicles were likely to make, Sukie had sent her grandchildren outside with orders to stay in the backyard, away from the road.

Bonnie Jo continued, 'I guess we didn't want to be sure, and maybe that's why we didn't look harder.'

Stuffing a cookie into my mouth, I nodded.

Sukie asked Bonnie Jo, 'Sis, now you know what happened, how do you feel?'

'How do *you* feel?'

'I asked first.'

Bonnie Jo said, 'Weird. Like, what are we going to do?'

'About the funeral or about Ma?'

'Mostly Ma. She done murder. Do we want her to go to jail?'

'I do.'

'I'm not sure—'

What I had to say was so important that I interrupted. 'Feel however you feel, but it has to be up to LeeVon whether he wants your mother to be punished.'

Understandably, they both gawked at me, so I tried to explain. 'LeeVon is an angry spirit. I don't mind having him around, but it would be better for him if he could rest. I think he needs to either forgive your mother or have his revenge before he's able to rest. That's why I put up that picture, for him to make a decision on. And that's why I want his bones brought here. I hope the part of him that's here in the house might choose to go to rest with them.'

Sukie whispered, 'Jesus,' which I did not hold against her, and then we all sat wordless, looking out the back door, watching her grandkids climbing my mimosa tree. Mimosas are good for that. Even little Liam managed to scramble up to sit, crowing, on a low branch.

I said, 'I bet you two climbed on that tree.'

'Not that one,' Bonnie Jo said. 'Them kind of tree comes and goes even quicker than humans.' I heard a shadow in her voice.

'I wish Ma was dead,' Sukie said. 'Ain't it up to the cops whether they arrest her?'

'Yes and no,' I said. 'It's kind of up to you and your sister. How much you care to remember.'

'Oh, I remember about LeeVon. Just I was too young to understand.'

'But have the police questioned you yet?'

'No.'

'And Bonnie Jo, you haven't signed a statement yet, have you?'

'Nope.'

'So if you could both please stall a few days, until, um . . .'

Not sure how to explain any more than I already had, I turned around to look at the picture I had copied for LeeVon, the one I had drawn so austerely on white paper with black marker.

The other two women must have looked also, because I heard them both gasp.

In the otherwise colorless picture, little Sukie had her yellow-and-aqua striped dress, little Bonnie Jo had her favorite red polka-dot one, and now little LeeVon had a plaid shirt with a collar, a red jacket, blue trousers and running shoes. The outline of his dress remained, but the revised LeeVon overrode it.

None of us spoke for several moments. Then Bonnie Jo said in a low, strained voice, 'I'm sorry, but I gotta get out of here.'

'Understandable.' I went to the back door and called the kids.

Staring at the picture, Sukie whispered, 'What does it *mean*?'

'I'm no damn expert, but I think it means he's feeling better. Will you wait before you tell the police anything?'

They had gotten very quiet, but they both nodded.

*   *   *

After they had left, I finished off the whole box of cookies as I sat looking at the picture. The colorful clothing warmed my heart, but the children were still without hands, and their faces without any expression, lacking a mouth to smile with. I got up and paced around the front room and my studio, then inevitably found myself standing in front of the picture again.

'I know, kiddo,' I muttered.

I knew we had more to do before it could be all right.

I needed to make a long-distance phone call.

On a Sunday afternoon there was no reason she shouldn't be home; I had no excuses.

It took me a while to find the number, as I so seldom used it. First I tried dialing 411 for information, but the number, although a landline almost as archaic as mine, was unlisted. Eventually, I located it in an old address book I had apparently stored in my underwear drawer, perhaps because I no longer used the underwear just as I no longer used the book. Sometimes my own logic is inscrutable to me.

Having found the number, I stalled. I spent quite a while on the toilet, extended my stay in the bathroom by standing at the mirror studying the rosacea pimples on my face, and then it suddenly seemed imperative to clean out the refrigerator right that moment – but damn, I knew myself. I had to do this thing. I had to call her.

'Her' being Gayle Perkins née Vernon, my sister-out-law.

Sighing, I dragged a kitchen-table chair over to the wall phone so that I could sit down during the ordeal. I dialed, then perched on the chair and braced myself.

She was home. 'Hello?'

I said, 'Gayle, it's all right, don't drop the phone. I can't crawl through the line and smack you.'

I heard what sounded like hyperventilation, and then she squeaked, 'Beverly?'

'That's right. Listen,' I said quickly in case she was thinking of hanging up, 'do you still want my house?'

'*Your* house?' Good, she had regained her snooty attitude already.

'The Montclair house. Do you still want it?'

'Do you realize I shouldn't even be speaking to you? Your

daughters came to my home and confronted me in an outrageously disrespectful manner.' This was news to me, very good news; it made me smile. But Gayle railed on. 'They called me names—'

'*I'm* the one who shouldn't be speaking to *you*,' I interrupted with all due force, 'and you know damn well why. Do you want the Montclair house or don't you?'

Silence.

Taking her wordlessness for *yes*, knowing that her bruised pride made it nearly impossible for her to tell me so out loud, I softened my voice to continue.

'I won't outright give it to you, Gayle, but I will sell it to you for way below market price, because I need money right now.'

I quoted her a ridiculously low price. Back to being herself, she haggled, offering even less. I countered, telling her that I would finance her purchase myself charging zero percent interest, with low monthly payments. Her voice sounded prim and cool as we reached an agreement, but I felt sure I could hear her salivating. 'Furniture included?' she demanded.

'Whatever doesn't belong to the current tenants, of course. And their lease expires at the end of the year, which gives you plenty of time to prepare.' Smoothly, as if this were an afterthought, I continued, 'I do, of course, require a down payment as a gesture of good faith.'

'Money upfront?' Her voice immediately grew fangs. 'How much?'

'Say ten thousand. If you will send a cashier's check tomorrow by overnight express mail, I will get the paperwork started.'

'Ten thousand!'

I estimated this was about as much as she spent most years on clothes alone. 'Any less and I would have to increase the amount of your monthly payments.'

Protracted negotiations ensued, and I was glad I had a sturdy chair to lean back in. But when the phone call finally concluded, I was smiling. Despite all of Gayle's protestations that Legalities Should Be Worked Out First, within a couple of days I could expect to have the money for LeeVon's funeral.

I spent a large part of that evening exploring the mysteries of the Yellow Pages. I found no mention or acknowledgement of Burial, Interment, Cemeteries, Graveyards or Undertakers.

Instead, I found Funeral Homes and Funeral Directors. I did not want LeeVon's funeral to be at any other home but mine, and I did not want it to be directed; this was going to be a peculiarly DIY send-off. But, damn the long arms of bureaucracy reaching even to the dead, I needed an officially sanctioned location for his grave.

I needed to consult someone, and I knew who, but it was too late to call her.

At bedtime, I took the old lady with the beard and mustache off my easel and stuck her up on the wall with Poster Putty so LeeVon could admire her if he felt like it, but I left the line drawing on the easel. Also, after hiding my good brushes, I lavished the studio with several more large sheets of paper for LeeVon to use if he felt like it.

On Monday, LeeVon left several colorful but enigmatic pictures of what might have been a dragon, a pterodactyl or maybe even Two-Toed Tom with wings. It did not eat cows or breathe fire, but it had red eyes and it appeared to fly, although LeeVon outlined the blue sky rather than filling it in. Still, his brushstrokes seemed smoother and less scrubby than before – maybe less angry? The variable winged creature did not look unhappy, either flying or standing or sprawled on the ground (a green horizontal line), perhaps sleeping, perhaps dead.

But LeeVon did nothing to the drawing with his mother, quite surely dead, hanging on a gibbet.

Not knowing whether he thought she should be punished was worrisome, but my more immediate problem was not knowing what to wear to court for my hearing, given that I no longer owned any apparel with a skirt. The last time I had worn a dress, panty-hose and heels had been years ago at Maurie's wedding. The inch-and-a-half heels in particular, by making me walk like a duck on tiptoe, had caused me so much unrelenting pain for so many hours that I had thrown them away the minute I took them off, along with any pretensions of ever again being less than comfortable.

So I knew damn well I had gotten rid of all my dressy clothes. Just the same, I pawed through my closet for half an hour trying to find some forgotten garment suitable for a judge to look at.

Dammit that I hadn't thought of this last week; I could have bought something . . . but no, I knew I wouldn't have, not really. Rolling my eyes at myself, I found my one pair of slacks that did not have paint on them, and yes, a T-shirt – but over the T-shirt I put on a blouse with buttons, to signal respect. And I wore my newest, least-worn Skechers. Nervous, yet weirdly confident – dealing with the paranormal on a daily basis apparently will do that to a person – off I went, cleverly disguised as myself.

TWENTY-FIVE

The first thing I saw when I walked into the courtroom was Wilma Lou in what had to be her very best Sunday-go-to-church dress: a shiny black poplin floral print with a full skirt and a fitted shirtwaist to show that she still had a figure, at least when she wore a girdle. And hose. And old-fashioned patent leather heels shiny enough to reflect her underwear if she had been standing up. Which she wasn't. Sitting down beside a business-suited young woman behind the table on the prosecution side, she gave a wince and a grimace when she saw me.

For some reason, I felt surprised to see her, too. Hadn't realized she might be there. Naturally, I said the first dumb thing that came into my mind, which was, 'Wilma Lou, I could have given you a lift!' I knew she didn't drive.

Her beady eyes shifted in evident discomfort. 'This here young lady come and fetched me, Beverly.'

By then I was standing right across the table from the young lady in question, a robot-like creature with hair like a teakwood helmet and face completely masked with makeup. Without stirring from her seat or offering me a hand to shake, she announced herself. 'Jill Spintaro, DCF.'

'DCF?'

'Department of Children and Families, Health Services Division. We handle Baker Acts. I take it you are Beverly Vernon?' Without waiting for a response, she pointed a long crimson fingernail at the table on the opposite side of the courtroom. 'Sit over there.'

Keeping my mouth firmly closed so as not to express any of my uncomplimentary thoughts about her, I obeyed. I sat. I heard a couple of other people slip in and sit to the back of me, in the chairs behind the railing, but before I could turn around to see who they were, a weary-sounding old man in a brown uniform not unlike that of a UPS driver bawled, 'All rise!' and as we did so, Judge Simmons made his entrance.

I have a bad habit of picturing people in my mind before I even meet them, and I had pictured Judge Simmons as a middle-aged, overweight, balding man in a black robe. For once, I was right, except regarding the robe. Sweating, he wore lightweight slacks and a short-sleeved shirt with a tie – but he had loosened the tie. Once in his big chair flanked by the state and national flags, he rapped his gavel and said, 'Be seated.'

I sat, studying him rather more anxiously than I studied most people. He had remarkably large earlobes, capacious enough to accommodate multiple piercings had he so desired. His nose, bulbous, complemented his earlobes, and his eyebrows, scanty and graying, complemented his hair. His eyes and nose were neither smiling nor petulant; like a good poker player, he showed no expression. I supposed neutral effect was appropriate for a judge. And a neutral accent. He had none that I could discern.

Leaning back in his chair, he scanned the courtroom and said, 'If I had known there were gonna be so few of us, we could have held this hearing in chambers. Heck, we could all sit in the jury box.'

Realizing how very much there was no jury, no court stenographer and no black robe helped me relax a little – those things and the judge's casual tone. Directing his bland gaze to me, he said, 'Are you Mrs Vernon?'

I stood up, as I had failed to remember to stand up at my own daughter's wedding when she was here-coming-the-bride. 'Yes, Your Honor.'

'Where's your lawyer?'

'I fired him, Your Honor.'

'Why?' Still poker-faced.

'I didn't like him. He's an ambulance chaser. And I didn't see any need for him to complicate what seems to be a simple matter, Your Honor. You just have to decide whether I qualify to be Baker Act-ed, correct?'

His gaze a little less bland, although maybe no more friendly, he responded, 'Concisely put. Please be seated. Mrs Ledbetter?' He turned his attention to the other table. 'You filed this action?'

Wilma Lou did not stand; she looked shaky, bleating, 'Her sister tole me to.'

'Your Honor!' Jill Spintaro shot up to stand far taller than seemed possible, until I saw her shoes, elevated soles, eight-inch heels. 'The charges here specified are of a serious nature notwithstanding their origin, and—'

'And you're out of order,' interrupted Judge Simmons with a rap of his gavel. 'Sit down. I want to hear what Mrs Ledbetter has to say. Mrs Ledbetter?'

Wilma Lou clawed at the table edge in an attempt to stand.

'Please remain seated, Mrs Ledbetter, and explain to me what happened.'

From her chair, Jill Spintaro glared at Wilma Lou, looking flinty enough to spit fire. Obviously uncomfortable, Wilma Lou faltered, 'I got this phone call, see, tole me things, but I'd already seed some myself. I just wanted to be a good neighbor, but she tole me she weren't Christian and when I wanted to know what-all she meant, she said she worshipped animals, which I took to mean goats and bats and such, minions of Satan . . .'

I had great difficulty keeping my mouth shut, waiting for my turn.

'Go back to the phone call,' Judge Simmons prompted Wilma Lou.

'It was some woman, said she was Beverly's sister, and she tole me them other things, about the ghost and suchlike craziness, and she said it was up to me to stop it because I was the next-door neighbor but she didn't live no place near.'

'And this person's name was?'

'I disremember. I ain't sure she ever rightly tole me.'

Jill Spintaro rose to her feet again. 'Your Honor, no matter what the source of these allegations, they are of serious concern to the Department of Children and Families, Health Services Division, concerning the public well-being of—'

'Sit down, Miss Spintaro. I think I know how to do my job. Mrs Vernon.' He turned to me and, as I began to rise, he said, 'Please remain seated. This is an informal hearing, not a trial. Still,

I expect you to tell the truth as if you were under oath. Did you tell Mrs Ledbetter you worshipped animals?'

'Does what I worship determine my sanity?' In this part of the country, such an approach seemed frighteningly possible.

'Please just answer the question.'

'Yes, I told her that I was not a Christian and that I worshipped animals, in the context that I wanted her to get out of my house and stop shoving tracts at me.'

I hoped to see the corners of his mouth twitch, repressing a smile, but they did not. 'So do you worship animals?'

'I do not formally worship anything, and my feelings of awe and wonder are not limited to animals. I have a spiritual sense about nature in general. I guess you could call me a pantheist.'

'She brung me this to show me about that there pancreasm!' shrilled Wilma Lou, surprising both me and, apparently, the judge. We looked over to see her holding up the tiger-lily-seed-pod-etc. angel, surprisingly recognizable considering the time that had passed.

'Wilma Lou,' I exclaimed, 'how did you keep that from wilting?'

She flashed a triumphant grin at me. 'Spray starch all over.'

'All over *what*?' snapped Judge Simmons.

'It's an angel. See? Made out of all them things she believes in, like acorns and sunsets and such.'

I sat, touched to the heart and speechless. His Honor peered at Wilma Lou as if she, not I, were the candidate for the psych ward.

'She can't be no Satan worshipper and believe in angels,' Wilma Lou said, so earnest she looked as if she might levitate. 'I was mistook—'

Before she could say any more, Jill Spintaro sprang up to control the damage. 'Your Honor, no matter what doubt the complainant may now be experiencing, she did file this action, and it is now a matter of public record—'

'Sit *down*, Ms Spintaro.' That order from the judge evidently included a tacit *shut up*. Welcome silence followed, and Judge Simmons turned to me.

'Mrs Vernon, I have just a few questions for you.' He opened a manila folder and consulted something inside it, presumably his copy of my own personal Baker Act file. 'Did you ever vandalize your own home, then state that a ghost did it?'

I answered quite truthfully, 'No.' I hadn't messed up my house.

'Have you ever produced paintings which you then declared to have been done by a ghost?'

'No, not at all.' I hadn't painted those pictures.

'Your neighbor stated that you believe your house is visited by a ghost. Do you?'

'Wilma Lou has no personal reason to say that, Your Honor. I have learned she was told to say it by my sister-in-law, my deceased husband's sister, who cannot possibly know what goes on in my home. She hasn't visited in two years, for the simple reason that she dislikes me.'

'Duly noted,' the judge said dryly, 'but you have not answered the question. Do you believe your house is visited by a ghost?'

Confound that word 'ghost,' which had always seemed utterly the wrong moniker to me, connoting something that went bump in the night, wore a white burka, rattled bones or chains and said, 'Boo.' The visitor in my house wasn't like that; it was a spirit, a revenant child. Yet 'ghost' supplied me with a comeback. I took a deep breath and said, 'Your Honor, there are a lot of people around here who swear every Sunday that they believe in a holy ghost.'

Maybe he was one of those people. He frowned. 'Mrs Vernon, are you refusing to answer?'

A voice I should have recognized came from right behind me. 'Your Honor, may I speak?'

Judge Simmons addressed his frown to her. 'Coroner.'

Marcia! All of a sudden I could have cried just because she was there for me. But I hope that feeling didn't show in my face.

'I believe I can assist the court in this matter,' Marcia was saying.

'By all means, please do so.' Judge Simmons sounded a bit owlish.

'Thank you.' I heard her stand up. 'I want to say, as one who deals with dead people, that it makes a difference. I am not sure whether you know that quite recently Beverly Vernon happened to find a skeleton buried in her backyard . . .'

The judge's eyes widened. He hadn't made the connection.

'A young child about six years old at the time of death,' Marcia was saying. 'A very disturbing discovery, suggestive as it is of

abuse, neglect or murderous brutality. Beverly Vernon was appro-
priately affected by those implications, and due to her concern for
the dead child, she and I have become acquainted. I would like
to say that she is one of the most big-hearted and sensitive yet
courageous persons I have ever known. And I think it quite possible
that, like me, she has a problem with the word "ghost." Beverly?'

'You think right.' As I spoke, I turned around to smile up at
her and received another surprise: standing next to her was
Detective Tadlock.

Marcia told the judge, 'Spending a lot of time with dead bodies
as I do, I have sometimes experienced a sense of the deceased
person's presence, and I refuse to ascribe this feeling to imagination, because my mind is totally occupied with my work at such
times. Nevertheless, I feel an inkling or an intimation of the
deceased person's essence, or soul, or spirit, call it what you will,
there in the room with me, quite benign, not at all frightening,
just patiently waiting. I would never say I have seen or heard a
ghost, because I have seen or heard nothing, and of course people
would think I was bonkers if I believed in ghosts. Anyway, it's
not a matter of believing anything. It's just a sixth sense. Is that
the way it's been for you, Beverly?'

By way of answering truthfully, I beamed at her. 'Thank you
so much for explaining! Yes, "ghost" is utterly the wrong word,
isn't it?'

Hearing Judge Simmons clear his throat, I turned around like
a pupil facing the teacher. But T.J. Tadlock spoke up first. 'Your
Honor, may I say something?'

'Detective Tadlock?' Judge Simmons frowned at her. 'You've
had dealings with Beverly Vernon?'

'Yes, as I am investigating the circumstances relevant to the
skeleton found on her property.' Hearing T.J. take a deep breath,
amazed she was there to speak for me, I wished I knew her first
name, could thank her that way. Teresa Joy? Tammy Jo?

She spoke on. 'Your Honor, although I have known Mrs
Vernon only a short time, I can testify that she is coping with
a difficult situation at a very high level, not at all like a person
who requires psychiatric intervention. Mrs Vernon has answered
questions that defeated me, found witnesses I could not locate;
she has been exceptionally helpful to the cold case investigation.

In my experience, she is an intelligent, resourceful person of notable integrity.'

'Dumbfounded' means to be unable to speak (dumb) because of astonishment, so I suppose that's what I was. The 'founded' part may have something to do with foundering, like a lame horse. Anyway, I sat there with my mouth open but unable to utter a word.

'Thank you, Detective Tadlock. Please be seated.' Judge Simmons turned his unreadable scrutiny to me. 'Mrs Vernon, in your folder I also have a letter from Doctor Roach on your behalf, stating in his usual forceful tone that as your personal physician he considers you perfectly sane, he considers this action a mockery of the Baker Act, et cetera.'

Quite agreeing with Dr Roach, I managed to blurt, 'That's nice.'

Judge Simmons nodded, looking bemused. 'Three professionals have offered expert testimony on your behalf, Mrs Vernon. But I am wondering: where are the throngs of indignant family members who usually fill my courtroom on occasions such as these?'

I had to smile. 'I have a very small family, Your Honor, indignant or otherwise, and they live rather far away from here.'

'Then I must call on one more expert witness.' He slewed his gaze to Wilma Lou. 'Mrs Ledbetter. Placing this document entirely aside' – he demonstrated, shuffling all the papers together in the folder and shoving it to a dramatic distance – 'with no reference to any previous statements, would you please tell me about Mrs Vernon.'

Jill Spintaro rose to protest. 'Your Honor—'

'Be seated and be silent, young lady. This is my courtroom, and I'm curious. Mrs Ledbetter?'

Wilma Lou faltered. 'I don't hardly know what to think about her. She says she ain't no Christian, but she's a real nice person, anybody can see that, and she don't seem like one of the lost – not when she believes in sunsets the way she told me.'

'In your opinion, is she likely to hurt herself or anybody else?'

'You mean like hit a person with a brick or something?'

'That's exactly what I mean.'

'No, sir. She'd never do that, Yer Honor.'

'Thank you. I believe Dr Wengleman and Detective Tadlock agree, and so do I. Therefore, I am upholding Mrs Vernon's appeal.'

For the first time, he smiled at me, and he seemed quite amused. 'Mrs Vernon, you are free to go.' Gavel thump. 'This hearing is adjourned.'

TWENTY-SIX

I spent the rest of that day in kind of a fugue state of exaltation and, I suppose, some exultation too. I remember things only vaguely, through a kind of golden haze. That's the way I recall turning around to thank Marcia – and I would have thanked T.J. also, most sincerely, but she was already heading toward the nearest courtroom exit. Avoiding me?

'I hope y'all ain't got no hard feelings,' shrilled Wilma Lou, sudden as an apparition under my chin, shoving an Avon catalog at me. Maybe my empathy for T.J. was wasted; maybe she was just ducking Wilma Lou, who had already served the judge, the DCF and the coroner with Avon papers.

No hard feelings, no, indeed. In my beatific mood, I may actually have thanked Wilma for the catalog, which may be why Marcia took me in hand as if I were mildly drunk, leading me off to lunch with her someplace that was definitely not Waffle House. I retain only a dreamy impression of excellent seafood and high-caliber conversation, and I don't remember driving home at all, but that's not unusual. I do remember emailing my daughters with the good news that I was deemed sane, feeling a bit guilty for not phoning each of them but too damn tired. Then I suppose I headed straight to the sofa for what I call a happy nappy. I know that's where I was when the phone rang – not an electronic warble, not from my old rotary, but an honest-to-noisy metallic clangor – waking me up.

'Mom!' It was Cassie. 'So they let you go home!'

'Yes, I was deemed unworthy to be a psychiatric case, thank God.'

'Mom, you don't believe in God.'

'I keep forgetting.'

She laughed at me and teased, 'Should I start worrying about Alzheimer's again?' But before I could answer, she suddenly became serious. 'Mom, why didn't you phone me? Why haven't you *been* phoning me? You promised me you'd call every day. Is something going on that you don't want me to know about?'

Conditioned by my morning in front of the judge, I answered with reflexive truth. 'Um, yes.'

'Mom!' Cassie sounded simultaneously outraged and intrigued. 'What is it? What's going on?'

I wasn't supposed to let her know that LeeVon had an unexpected gender, let alone a name and a family. And then there were my hopes for him, too tentative to bear the scrutiny of my clear-eyed daughter. I bleated, 'Didn't we just concur that I don't want you to know?'

'Mother, that's unfairly logical!'

'I can't argue with you, sweetie. I'm falling-down tired.' I really was exhausted; I guess reaction was taking over as my adrenaline flow slowed down. 'I love you.'

As if I could hear them, I knew her eyes were rolling. 'What*ever*, Mom. Love you too.'

The next morning I felt quite restored, or, as Wilma Lou would have said, full of piss and vinegar. First thing after brushing my teeth, I scanned the studio for anything new from LeeVon, but found nothing. Next to my big question mark, his mother still hung from the gibbet; he wasn't ready to give me an answer. Disappointed, I reminded myself that I could hardly understand what he was going through. Communicating with his sisters had probably taken a lot out of him.

After breakfast, I phoned Marcia Wengleman.

'Beverly!' She sounded actually pleased to hear from me. 'How arc you?'

I chuckled. 'Better than yesterday, for sure.'

'Silly question. I can't imagine. But I thank you again for being so discreet.' At lunch the day before, she had complimented me for managing to tread a narrow path between perjury and revealing the whole truth about LeeVon. 'As far as I can tell, there still haven't been any leaks.'

'Good. I don't want a publicity circus any more than you do.'

'Amen to that. But,' she added with good humor, 'I'm guessing you haven't called me at work just to chat?'

'Good guess. I'm hoping maybe, because your specialty is dead people, you might be able to help me find a place to bury LeeVon.' I went on to explain that I was trying for the most informal of all possible funerals in my home. Nothing churchy, no preacher or undertaker, just a small coffin LeeVon's family and I could take all by ourselves to a gravesite.

'For LeeVon, since he's just bones, you won't need a vault or anything. No sanitation precautions. I think you can get away with just a coffin.' Marcia sounded thoroughly intrigued.

'Good. The problem is what gravesite, where?'

'Is there any huge hurry?'

'No, just to get it done before the ground freezes.'

She chuckled; where we lived the ground didn't freeze. 'Let me ask around and get back to you.'

Reassured and relaxed, I spent the next couple of hours with a soft pencil and recycled paper doing sketch after sketch of Chloe, Emma and Liam from memory. I drew them playing with bricks and climbing the mimosa tree, but mostly I drew their heads from different angles, planning a portrait of Chloe which would be the first of three, the other two being, of course, Emma and Liam. I yearned to start Chloe's portrait right away but knew damn well I was not yet ready; I had only met the girl once. I needed to sketch Chloe from life, take photos, spend more time with her and her family—

Wait a minute. I knew myself; I was using art as a sneaky way to do something. What was it?

It would seem I had forgotten all about painting myself a bunch of *imaginary* grandchildren.

Hmmm.

Introspection can be scary. Blessedly, it was interrupted; the phone rang.

'Beverly,' said a quick-stepping New York voice, 'I'm just calling to touch base.'

Oh, crap. It was Kim, my agent.

'How are you doing?' She tap-danced onward without missing a beat. 'I hope you've come up with something exciting to work on?'

Another children's book, Kim meant. Blowing sunshine up

my ass on the off-chance that, painting my heart out one more time, I might happen to accomplish parturition of something marketable.

I said with no elaboration, 'No.'

'No?' Kim's voice slid up an octave.

'No.'

'Beverly, what do you mean? Aren't you painting at all?'

From where I stood by the phone, I could see LeeVon's portrait on the wall in the front room, and a nearly tangible lifeline passed from it to me. My heart surged. I stood tall.

'I'm not doing any more picture books,' I said, sounding perfectly cool but feeling fiery with exultation. My masterpiece of a portrait, once I entrusted it to my daughter, was going to make the New York art community take me seriously (about time) instead of dismissing me as a kiddie-lit illustrator. No more velveteen bunnies for me; I would be a real artist, a critically acclaimed artist, and anyone who had ever condescended to me could go bugger themselves.

I told Kim, 'I'm taking time to enjoy my grandchildren. Excuse me, I have to go now. Have a *fabulous* day. Bye bye.' I hung up.

LeeVon's portrait was going to show them.

For the next half hour I just zoned out on the sofa in the front room, entranced by LeeVon's painted face. I might have lingered there in a heady haze of self-congratulation for even longer if I hadn't been disturbed by the sound of a Jeep driving into my yard.

By the sound of the engine, I knew it was rural delivery accessing my mailbox. When I had first moved here, it had amused me that the mailboxes faced away from the road, but now it seemed merest common sense to have mail carriers get out of traffic and deliver from the driver's side window. I ran outside; the woman behind the wheel saw me coming and stopped trying to wrestle with my rusty mailbox. We both said, 'How y'all doing?' and she handed me one of those overnight express envelopes, cardboard.

O frabjous day!

I scuttled back into the house and opened it to be sure. Yes, it was the check from dearest darling Gayle, together with a minatory letter about forthcoming paperwork I would have to sign. Fine. Whatever. It wasn't as if I had sold my body. Just my old house.

And if I'd let it go for less than market value, so what? I was going to be able to take care of LeeVon.

I hoped. Very much hoped I could really and truly help him.

The phone rang, and in a few minutes I had more reason for hope. The call was from Marcia, and she had good news.

So that afternoon we all met – Bonnie Jo, Sukie, her three grand-kids, Coroner Wengleman and me – in the Piggly Wiggly parking lot, and after I had finished introducing Marcia to everyone and telling them how wonderful she was, she headed up a small caravan – her van, my Vo, Bonnie Jo's junker – and led the way to the fringes of town and Potter's Field Road, which dead-ended (how preciously appropriate) at a small cemetery without a fence or fancy gates but not without the dignity of age. That, and a view! By Florida standards, the graveyard was on a hill, perhaps eighty feet above sea level. We could see to all sides: cow pasture, distant ponds, pine woods.

'Don't you go running around over the top of no dead people,' Sukie admonished the children as we got out of our vehicles. We had tried not to park on top of any dead people, either.

'I ain't never been here. I never knowed this was here.' Bonnie Jo stood studying the old burial place, some graves marked with stone slabs rounded by the winds and rains of time, some with wooden crosses that had maybe once been painted, some evidently unmarked. 'Who-all are these people?'

Abandoned babies, I thought, *drifters, unidentified murder victims, poor souls unclaimed by any family, each with a story untold.* But Marcia said, 'Unfortunate folks who needed a place to rest.'

'It's nice up here.'

'Peaceful,' Marcia agreed, beckoning. She led the way, and the rest of us – except the children, who were running around the cemetery's irregular edges – followed her between the graves. Potter's field, a place tottering on the brink as regards official recognition, felt deserted but not neglected; the grass was mowed, which was more than I could say for my yard.

Near the back edge of the potter's field, Marcia stopped beside a plot marked off by rough wooden stakes at the corners, each with a bright plastic ribbon stapled to the top and waving like an oriflamme in the breeze.

We stood looking down as if we had never seen a rectangle of land before, and for quite a long moment none of us said a word.

Finally, I asked, 'Sukie? Bonnie Jo? What do you think?'

Bonnie Jo made a dry sound in her throat, then nodded.

Sukie said, 'We can bring flowers to him here.'

Although I didn't say so, I felt as if LeeVon might like it here. Relieved, I turned to Marcia. 'So how do we do this?'

'It's already done. You are all taxpayers; in a sense, this is already your land. But, Beverly, the borough is going to want you to pay if you decide to use county maintenance workers for the labor.'

'No problem. The check that's earmarked to cover the funeral just arrived.' I turned to Sukie and Bonnie Jo. 'Are you sure you're both satisfied so far?'

Sukie nodded. Bonnie Jo seemed to have regained her voice. 'We're more than satisfied. We're grateful.' She extended a leathery hand toward Marcia. 'Thank you, Doc.'

Somehow handshakes turned into hugs. I love to give hugs, but being on the receiving end of gratitude embarrasses me, so I took evasive action, going to gather the kids, who had strayed a small distance into the woods to inspect a gopher turtle burrow. 'Chloe! Emma! Liam!'

As they ran toward me, I memorized their happy, upturned faces, all so different. Chloe, rose-petal-skinned and sharp-boned. Emma, golden brown and round. Liam, still half a baby with a flat nose and a soft triangular mouth. Each of them individually alive and lovely. Such beautiful grandchildren.

Sukie's grandchildren, I reminded myself.

That evening, following Marcia Wengleman's directions, I drove quite a convoluted dirt-road distance into the swamplands south of Cooter Spring to see Nick Crickens, of all people.

'Of all people' because I knew him only as the one who had twice visited me during unfortunate circumstances, the youngest deputy of the Skink County Sheriff's Department. But Marcia had explained that Nick Crickens, like his father and grandfather before him, had a passion for making wooden furnishings with hand tools. 'Don't even go near a funeral home,' Marcia had advised Bonnie Jo, Sukie and me. 'They'll soak the life out of you for a custom coffin that's really nothing more than a nice wood box. Try Crickens.' Then, after Marcia had gone back to work, Sukie and Bonnie Jo and I had taken the kids to Cooter Spring's public playground. While Chloe, Emma and Liam wore themselves out on the colorful plastic equipment, we women sat in the shade talking about LeeVon's funeral, coming up with a consensus about some basics.

It took me only a few wrong turns to find 'Crickens's Fine Cabinetry'. But then my Vo punched through the wilderness into the clearing occupied by three generations of the family, each with its own . . . shack? Not really. These small, colorfully painted homes did look a lot like most of the housing around here, but nothing was slouching, shambling, rotting or falling apart. The lemon, persimmon and pistachio cottages stood proud beneath the shade of their live oak trees. I glimpsed porch swings, a plethora of lawn ornaments, a decorative windmill, playhouses and tree houses, and a Victorian-style martin house atop a towering pole. But at the heart of the place, and dwarfing all else, stood a big metal pole building. Light shone out of its large open bay, and Nick Crickens stepped out to meet me.

'Hello, Deputy Crickens!' I greeted him as I got out of the Vo.

'I'm off-duty.' His baseball cap and faded jeans certainly attested to this. 'Just call me Nick, ma'am, please.' He shook my hand. 'Mrs Vernon, I hope y'all don't hold it against me none that I hauled y'all off to the hospital that one time.'

'Not a bit. I'd be crazy if I did.' I waggled my eyebrows at him. He gawked, then burst out laughing.

'Y'all got me!' He sounded delighted. 'Come on in! Doc Wengleman said y'all need something by way of a casket for the little girl?'

I opened my mouth, closed it again and nodded. I'd nearly blabbed, forgetting that LeeVon's gender was still the closely guarded secret of an ongoing murder investigation.

'It's real good of y'all to be taking care of her remains,' Nick added as we walked into the pole barn. I didn't reply because I was too busy staring at hand-crafted rocking chairs, whatnot shelves and pretty damn fancy baby cribs; at big wooden-shingled doll houses, and old-fashioned cradles, and all sizes and shapes of lathe-turned bowls polished to show off the woodgrain; at carved horses and birds and Madonnas and crosses and bunnies, oh my. Nick stood watching, utterly in no hurry, until my wandering gaze settled on a huge pile of wood, specifically chunks of tree trunk, in a back corner.

'Cherry, apple, black walnut, tupelo, white pine and this and that,' he said. 'We grab up good wood wherever we find it and let it age while it's waiting to tell us what it wants to be made into.'

I felt an exceptionally wide smile take over my face, because I recognized the mentality of a fellow artist. 'Do you have anything that wants to be made into a small coffin?'

'Sure, but that would take a long time. Here's what I'm thinking.' He led me toward an area dominated by towers of nesting bowls atop what my mother used to call 'cedar chests,' some of them big enough to double as sofas, for storage of blankets. Around a corner, though, Nick kneeled on the dirt floor beside a smaller one made of wood polished to a honey gold sheen. 'I was making this for a hope chest for my daughter,' he said, 'and I was going to carve something pretty on the lid, but I can make her another.'

'Oh, Nick—'

'She ain't but six months old.' Interrupting my protest, he looked up to grin at me. 'I'd be glad for your poor orphan remains to be buried in this. It's about the right size, ain't it?'

'Doc Wengleman said four feet to lay out the bones with respect.'

'Well, it's four foot six. Now see here. All's I got to do is take the legs off, trim the depth some so she won't feel lonesome in there, and – dang, I forgot about that there padded silk they always put in these things.'

'Just keep forgetting about it. We're using crib blankets.' 'We' meant Sukie and Bonnie Jo and me. 'The softest, prettiest ones we can find.'

'Y'all got it all planned out, then.'

'Yeppers.' No way could he imagine how much we-all sure all did.

Nick stood up, smiling down on me like the tall, friendly young man he was. 'When y'all want it for?'

'How long do you need—'

'Heck fire, I could have it done tomorrow.'

'Well, then, we'll go ahead and set a date! I'll get back to you on that. And Nick, how much do I owe you?'

'Just whatever y'all care to give, Mrs Vernon. This here is for the child, y'all know what I mean.'

I drove home, and oddly, in some subliminal way, I felt as if Chloe, Emma, Liam, Bonnie Jo and Sukie were with me, but not just them; I felt the presence of Cassie and Maurie and Marcia Wengleman, T.J. Tadlock, Dr Roach and Judge Simmons and the janitor in the hospital and the woman who delivered my mail and all three generations of Crickenses and, yes, even pissy old Wilma Lou . . . I felt comforted by the number of people whose lives continued to brush like angel's wings against my life because of LeeVon.

But LeeVon wasn't among them. He was trapped in my house.

As soon as I got back home, I turned on all the lights and looked around for LeeVon even though I knew I couldn't see him – but at times I could kind of feel him. So I sat down at the table and started messing with my bottle caps – you know, the bright-colored plastic ones off milk cartons and such – sorting them into white, yellow, pale blue, purple, pink, orange and red. This is not abnormal behavior for me. It's just one of my ways of thinking without words. After a while I felt a clear sense of what to do next, so I supplied the studio with plenty of paper, and on the top sheet I drew a big red heart like an empty Valentine. My hands twitched with wanting to decorate it, but it was not for me. It was for LeeVon. I left it there and exiled myself to the back of the house. I looked up Crickens' Fine Cabinetry on the internet to get a clue how much to pay for the coffin, checked Facebook, then gave up on the computer, watched a little bit of TV and went to bed.

The next day would be Wednesday – two weeks since I had found a little boy's remains weighted down beneath layers of bricks as if somebody was afraid he might get out of his grave and come looking for them.

TWENTY-SEVEN

S huffling to my studio in bedroom slippers first thing next morning, I smiled because LeeVon had been there, but then I looked at his art and sighed. The heart I'd given him he had ripped in two. On another sheet he had painted a smaller heart weeping red tears. And on another, a heart afire, with ragged orange flames devouring it.

'LeeVon,' I said quite tenderly in case he might be listening, 'I know most of what your mother did to you, and it was so cruel it makes me sick. I can see you're heartbroken and crying and afire with rage. What can I do to help you leave the pain behind? Do you want your mother punished? If she was put in jail, would that help? Or would it just keep you stuck the way you are?'

I stood there in my sleep shirt waiting as if for a still small voice to speak, but none did. However, as I left the studio to go shower and get dressed, my own loud, large voice began singing a variation on a Beatles song: 'Ob-la-di ob-la-da, life goes on, LeeVon! La la, how the life goes on.'

I spent the day on funeral arrangements, which came together quickly, maybe because people in Cooter Spring don't have constipated schedules. The Skink County maintenance guys got the grave dug that same day. Nick Crickens said the coffin would be ready the next day, Thursday. Marcia said she'd bring the bones to my house and lay them out after Nick brought the coffin. Around lunchtime, when I knew the cafe would be busy, keeping her from asking me too many questions, I called Cassie with a quick request.

And that afternoon, as prearranged, the Ferees and I went shopping for everything else we'd need. I had offered to take all of us in the Vo, and the Ferees had pleasantly surprised me by accepting. Moreover, rather than meeting me in the Piggly Wiggly parking lot, they had told me how to get to their homes! By letting me give them a ride and see where they lived, they were honoring me with their acceptance.

Driving to pick them up, following their directions, I could not help thinking *on the wrong side of the tracks*, even though Cooter Spring had no railway. But on one side of town were pillared plantation-style homes, stately and historic mansions, Victorian monstrosities and the like, while on the other side the houses diminished in size almost to the point of invisibility, because who looks at shacks?

Or trailers. Bonnie Jo's trailer was in no worse repair than most, and it had flowerbeds in front, complete with some plywood art, including brightly painted cutouts of rudimentary birds, butter-flies and flowers on dowels stuck into the sand. Imagining how Nick Crickens would have cringed at this display of woodcraft, I grinned.

Sukie's rental house had flaking paint, some wood rot around the edges and screen doors patched with duct tape, but she had put sunny print curtains in every window, dollar-store wind chimes hung from the eaves, and bright plastic toys occupied the yard. No bricks for children in Sukie's care.

'She ain't got no car,' Bonnie Jo told me as Sukie and the kids headed out to join us. 'Social Services, the post office, the thrift shop, the Mini Mart, the kids' schools, most places in town she can walk to.'

'Other places, you're the chauffeur.'

'She don't ask me no oftener than she got to. Takes an umbrella in the rain. Hey, sis.' Sukie and her grandchildren loaded in. The Vo's occupancy was maxed, but Sukie sat in back and held Liam on her lap. In Skink County this was not a problem. Police turned a blind eye to scofflaw motorists; kids and adults alike rode the streets in golf carts, ATVs, motorized wheelchairs, farm tractors and in the ass end of pickup trucks.

'We're off to see the wizard,' I sang, as we three women and three kids headed out for our grave and glorious shopping spree.

Cassie found herself clenching her cell phone a lot harder than was necessary as she talked to Maurie, but she managed to keep her voice relaxed. 'You call me and I put you on speakerphone,' she said, explaining her mother's request, 'and I call Mom on my old phone, put it on speaker and set it next to you so we can all three talk, sort of.'

'Has neither of you ever heard of a conference call?' Maurie retorted, waspish as always when her academic routine was interrupted.

'Berthe, if you want to try contacting the phone company to set up a conference call, go right ahead.'

'All right, all right.' Maurie relented. 'It's exactly two weeks since Mom disemboweled the darkest secret of her backyard. I suppose she has something momentous and weird to share with us. Did she ever tell you her skeleton was actually a boy?'

'What? No!'

'Oh, yes. A boy buried in a dress, a boy named LeeVon, with a sister named Bonnie Jo.'

'Why didn't she tell me!'

'The police put a gag order on her. But she slipped up, talking to me, and I don't see why you shouldn't know. The sister, Bonnie Jo, came to the house, saw the portrait and recognized her dead brother.'

Berthe, Cassie noted to her astonishment, actually sounded more whimsical than sardonic. But she let that go, saying, 'I suppose that was in response to her ad.'

'*What* ad?' Whimsy had fled.

'She took a photo of the portrait and put it in the local paper, along with her phone number—'

'You cannot be serious!'

'Calm down, Berthe. Of course I'm serious. I am talking about our mother. What did you think she would do? Like, keep out of trouble?'

'Simplistic of me,' Maurie admitted. 'OK, call me tonight and we'll find out what *else* is new.' She clicked off.

Maurie's moment of nonchalance was feigned. Her apprehensions – what *else* was new? What had Mom done now? – piled into an unstable frame of mind, a tottering mental structure ready to topple under the weight of a single incautious word. Luckily for Maurie's marriage, Rob had to work late and was spared an unwary encounter with his wife.

By the time the phone rang, Maurie might as well have been a gorgon: coiling snakes for hair, bronze claws for fingernails, bronze fangs for teeth.

'How are you both, sweeties?' Mom said that evening, her voice wafting in a sort of speakerphone wind as if from a wilderness.

'Fine, Mom,' said Cassie.

'Medusa mode,' said Maurie between clenched jaws.

'Oh dear, honey. Why?'

As was to be expected, Maurie's tower of concerns tumbled out, squashing courtesy flat. 'Mom,' she demanded, 'what do you *want*?'

'Nothing!' Mom sounded only a bit surprised, not miffed. 'I'm not asking a thing from you two except the use of your ears, dears. I thought it would be easier to fill you in on the funeral and everything both at the same time.'

'Funeral?' asked Cassie.

'Everything?' barked Maurie. She had tried to make herself comfortable in her favorite window seat but could not seem to stay there. Phone to ear, she paced the perimeter of her living room.

Mom said, 'I suppose "everything" would include my selling the Montclair house to your Aunt Gayle after all.'

There ensued momentary hubbub. Maurie said pejorative things that she knew she would regret later, Cassie said plaintive things Maurie didn't hear, and as they were both talking at once, their mother paid no attention to either of them.

'Shush,' she told them. 'Relax. I needed money to give LeeVon a funeral, and I need to give him a funeral because I can't have him hanging around the house indefinitely. Well, I suppose I could, but it wouldn't be good for him.'

Maurie did not believe in the afterlife and knew her mother didn't either, yet realized that the situation Mom was describing implied the opposite, and a sort of mental gridlock prevented her from speaking. Cassie was quiet, too, maybe for the same reason, as Mom went on to explain how the coroner had arranged for a plot in the potter's field. 'I looked up why they call it a potter's field. It's because in old times, once potters dug the clay out of a field, it was useless for anything else, so that's where they buried the stray bodies.' She told them about the beautiful handmade coffin and how Nick – 'the deputy who hauled me in to the psych ward!' – would bring it over in his pickup truck and it could sit on the coffee table in the front room, and Marcia was coming to the house with the bones to arrange them in the coffin, and she, Mom, had taken the Ferees shopping for some things and expected to provide pizza. 'Tomorrow,' Mom said, then added in a low, maybe awed tone, 'I feel like I'm in a Broadway musical or something. All sorts of people just coming together, even the children. Their names are Chloe, Emma and Liam, and they are very different and just beautiful. I'm wondering whether we should have a wake.'

'Wake?' asked Cassie in a small, stunned voice.

'Yes. Then the funeral and the burial will be the next day. Well, you know, LeeVon's pretty much nocturnal, so . . .' A lot of the joy leached out of Mom's voice and anxiety crept in. 'So I figured, give him a chance. It's up to him. But what I'm hoping for is so – so apocalyptic – I can't talk about it.'

Maurie broke through her mental gridlock rather explosively. 'What the crazy are you trying to do, Mom? Morph the kid from a ghost into an angel?'

'No!' Then more quietly, 'Not at all, honey. I think he's made it pretty clear that the afterlife is hell for him, but as regards any kind of heaven . . . No, I just hope that death ultimately can bring him peace. That I can help his spirit to rest.'

Much more gently, with all traces of gorgon gone at least temporarily, Maurie asked, 'What do you want us to do, Mom?'

'Nothing! Maurie, Cassie, I don't want you to do anything. I just thought you'd want to know how things stand. This burial – I hope it settles something. The police haven't decided what to do about his mother yet and neither . . . neither has he.'

Implications stunned Maurie once again speechless. And maybe Cassie felt the same way. There was an awkward silence before she said, 'Mom, please let us know how it goes, OK?'

'Of course. But either way, I think I can handle it and it won't be necessary for you to come kiting down here, OK? I'll call you in a couple of days.'

I didn't sleep very well, and got up quite early the next morning, walking into my studio by the pearly pink light of dawn to see whether LeeVon had left any enigmas for me.

He most certainly had. Instead of a weeping heart, a broken heart or a heart afire, he had depicted a heart that was full. He had drawn, with paint, a big horizontal heart loaded like a popcorn bowl with colorful contents, but I couldn't tell what they were. Either the paint had run, or LeeVon had become an impressionist, or he was channeling Klimt. I thought I could distinguish compact human and animal figures, and round bright things that might have been fruit or flowers or, who knew, marbles? Mushrooms? Eyeballs? And why was the heart lying down like a cornucopia? LeeVon intended it that way; I could tell by the direction the paint had dripped.

I had no idea what it meant. But luckily it was so early in the morning and I was sleepy enough, so I easily turned off my analytical mind and, relaxing deep in my Joseph chair, I thought without words and began to feel hopeful that a full heart, especially a heart full of such color, was turned sideways maybe because it was ready to launch. Take off. Set sail. Something like that.

TWENTY-EIGHT

I dressed in mom jeans, a pink T-shirt with a pony on the front and pink Skechers: comfort clothes. I wanted to make the next couple of days comfortable for everyone involved, especially LeeVon.

After breakfast I cleared the front-room coffee table, removing stacks of huge books about art plus my Hoberman ball and Russian nesting dolls and ornamental Slinkies and my geodesic art-glass fishbowl full of Beanie Baby horses. But I didn't put the toys away. I distributed them around the room, on the floor when necessary. Because of rearranging things, I even dusted, which to me is a nonsensical activity, moving perfectly normal and righteous housedirt from one place to another. Luckily, Nick Crickens put a quick stop to this by driving his Ford pickup to my front door. In the truck bed, all swaddled in blankets and strapped in place like a papoose, was the coffin.

Nick unloaded it and carried it into my house on one shoulder. Following my cues, ever so gently he set it on the coffee table.

'It's just beautiful,' I said, which was true. Handmade of plain wood polished to a golden shine, the casket could not have been more lovely.

Bashful, Nick just smiled. He showed me how to work the hasps on each side of the lid, then took it off and leaned it against the coffee table. 'See y'all in the morning then,' he said, tugging at the bill of his camouflage cap, and he headed out the driveway at the same time as Bonnie Jo's old clunker of a car headed in.

I walked out to meet her and help her carry several armloads of stuff into my house. 'How are you, Bonnie Jo? I mean, how are y'all?'

This got a small smile out of her. 'All of me is all right all right except what ain't.'

'Well, that's as good as can be expected, I guess. Would you like a cup of coffee?'

'Let's do this first,' she said, standing beside the coffin and stroking it very softly with one hand as if it might be frightened of her. What we intended was to blanket it with softness. The previous day, shopping, we (meaning mostly me) had not been content just with what we found at Wal-Mart. So we had discovered a consignment store with handmade crib quilts and baby afghans. I had bought oodles, because we wouldn't really know what we needed until we saw how they fit in the coffin, and I looked forward to giving the leftovers to Sukie for her grandchildren.

'Let's put the plain fleeces underneath and the pretty things on top of them,' Bonnie Jo said, and for the next hour or so that was what we did, arranging in the coffin a nest for LeeVon. Both Bonnie Jo and I adored some pastel crib blankets crocheted in shell stitch, but we put them aside and finished instead with what we thought LeeVon would like: a bright quilt made of cowboy-print squares of flannel.

Finally satisfied, we were sitting in the kitchen sipping coffee and eating blueberry muffins when Marcia showed up carrying LeeVon in a box on one shoulder, just the way Nick had effortlessly carried the coffin.

I ran to open the front door for her. But rather than set her burden down, she stood gazing at the coffin. 'It's just perfect,' she murmured.

I stood with my hands upstretched. 'Please, let me help you with that.'

'He's not heavy.' She set the box sideways on top of the coffin. 'Coffee?'

'Later. Let me do this first.'

Sometimes, not nearly often enough, I feel an actual physical reaction, a special sort of frisson, just from watching a person do something with great and consummately skilled concentration. I felt it that day as Bonnie Jo and I stood by, both of us barely breathing as Marcia took LeeVon's bones one by one and arranged them in his coffin with perfect symmetry and meticulous respect. Skull, neck bones and backbones, collarbone and ribs, shoulder blades, arms . . . When she got past the pelvis to the legs, I held the box out of the way for her.

At the very end, she arranged wisps of tan hair around the skull. I saw tears seep on to Bonnie Jo's face, although she did not make a sound except to murmur, 'He still has his fingernails and toenails. Some of them, anyways.'

Marcia gave her a wordless hug, then asked me, 'Are you going to cover him with something?'

Still staring, intent on seeing her brother again, Bonnie Jo barely nodded. I led Marcia away toward the kitchen. 'Coffee? Pepsi? Iced tea? Heck, while I'm at it, I might as well fix lunch.' Which I did, making tuna salad. After a while, Bonnie Jo came in, sat with us and drank Pepsi but shook her head to food.

'Thank you for lunch,' Marcia said when she was finished. 'I guess I should be going.'

'Hold on just a minute till you see what I got in the car.' Bonnie Jo headed out and came back in carrying Wal-Mart bags from which she pulled a brand-new pair of boys' blue jeans, which she laid on top of LeeVon's legs as if he were wearing them. Then she pulled out a bright plaid shirt, western-style with collar, unmistakably meant for a boy.

'Oh my God,' murmured Marcia to me, 'please tell me the media aren't coming.'

'The media are *so* not coming. I so did not announce this in the newspaper or anywhere else. I haven't ordered flowers or a memorial – not yet – or anything that could spread the news. Stop worrying.'

Bonnie Jo placed the shirt on LeeVon, and white tube socks covering his feet, and Nike running shoes beside them. She glanced up at Marcia. 'I ain't going to try to cover his face. We got to look at him honest. But these here was the clothes he showed us he wanted.'

'Showed you?'

I said, 'Yeppers,' and trotted into the back room, the studio, to bring my line drawing that he had altered to depict himself, a boy.

But when I saw it, my eyes widened, and I had a speechless moment before I called, 'Marcia, never mind.' I returned empty-handed to the front room, ready for her to leave. 'Thank you so much for everything you've done. Not just releasing the remains to us, but coming here to lay them out. I can't thank you enough.'

Bonnie Jo said thank you too, and both of us hugged Marcia on her way out. As soon as my front door closed behind her, Bonnie Jo shot me a saucer-eyed look. I put a finger to my lips, waiting until Marcia was in her car and driving away before I told Bonnie, 'Come see.'

She was already on her way into the studio, and her long legs got her there ahead of me. I heard her exclaim, 'Oh!'

'Yes,' I said, walking in to find her hovering over the line drawing. Sukie still wore her yellow-and-aqua striped dress, Bonnie Jo still wore her polka-dot one, LeeVon stood there in his plaid shirt, blue jeans and running shoes, but the figure of Ma on a gibbet had been negated, crossed out, X-ed out heavily with black marker.

'What's that mean?' Bonnie Jo asked.

'I guess he doesn't want . . .'

Not sure of anything, I looked at a picture stuck to the wall, the original depiction LeeVon had done of him and Bonnie Jo and Sukie, with their mother towering over them, lashing a belt, raging, her mouth wide open with shouting, looking as if she might eat them.

Only she wasn't there anymore.

She was just not there. Not in the picture. Gone as if she had never been.

Momentarily unable to speak, I pointed.

Bonnie Jo saw, made an inchoate sound and stepped back. 'Oh my God, let me out of here,' she whispered. 'I gotta go get Sukie and the kids.' She bolted.

I could not stop gazing at the picture, and even though Bonnie

Jo was gone, I blurted, 'The children all have hands now. And they have mouths. And they're *smiling*.'

Cassie would be so glad. I thought of phoning her to tell her, but at the notion of mother speaking to child, unaccountably I started raining tears.

I didn't phone Cassie. Sometime I would tell her what had happened, but not yet; it still made me too shivery. I didn't want to talk to anyone for a little while. Lucky for me, then, that Bonnie Jo had left me alone in the house when she fled.

Without conscious decision, acting in a kind of LeeVon-induced trance, I went to the craft room for scissors and gluestick. I pulled the picture off the wall, the one in which the children, newly empowered, were smiling, and I trimmed it to eliminate the space where Ma had been. Then I carefully glued it without a single wrinkle to the inside of LeeVon's coffin lid where his skull could look up at it. Who says those without eyes cannot see? Then I just sat on the front-room sofa to keep LeeVon company until I heard the sound of Bonnie Jo's asthmatic junker coming down my yard. I turned to look and yes, she had Sukie and the kids with her.

Sukie walked into my house carrying Liam, supporting his butt with both arms while his head lay on her shoulder, moist and heavy in sleep. Without a word, she gazed down at LeeVon in his coffin while Chloe and Emma peeked in. I stood across from them and saw the tops of their faces, their wide eyes framed by their fingers curling like pale, exotic flowers over the coffin's edge.

'Careful, girls, don't joggle him,' Bonnie Jo said, standing behind Sukie with a couple of plastic shopping bags dangling from her hands.

Sukie, still intent on LeeVon, didn't turn around but said, 'He looks real nice, sis.'

Emma asked, 'What is it?'

Chloe retorted, 'A skeleton, silly, like at Halloween.'

'But today's not Halloween. Is tomorrow Halloween?'

'No, no! Skeletons aren't just for Halloween. Remember we ate the chicken and it had a skeleton?'

Emma pointed at the one in the coffin. 'Who ate him?'

'Nobody ate him. Somebody boiled him, that's all, like Gramma boiled the chicken for soup.'

This was so awfully close to the truth that I winced; Bonnie Jo turned so pale that age spots made her face look pinto, and Sukie said not very steadily, 'Shush, girls. You'll wake Liam.'

Detecting untruth, both girls turned to peer up at Sukie.

To distract them – heck to distract all of us – I picked up the coffin lid and displayed the artwork I had applied to the inside. 'That's your grandma's brother LeeVon in the coffin,' I told the girls, 'and he did these pictures.'

'They're nice,' Chloe said doubtfully.

'Bonnie Jo, Sukie, is what I did here OK with you?'

Sukie said firmly, 'It's way better than OK.' Bonnie Jo gave me a thumbs up. Little Emma piped up, 'I can paint a heart!'

'That, young lady, is a wonderful idea.' I guided the girls to the table and provided them up with paper, paints and LeeVon's much-abused brushes, then sat down along with them to make hearts and flowers. Soon Liam joined us and created less identifiable representations. I hovered, making sure everybody let Bonnie Jo and Sukie alone. When the three children got tired of painting, I cleaned them up, took them back to my bedroom, ensconced them on the bed and electronically anesthetized them by means of a *Muppet Show* video on the TV.

Walking back to the front room, I saw Sukie and Bonnie Jo, each with an arm around the other, standing by LeeVon's coffin. Both turned to smile at me. Sukie said, 'I put a few more things in.'

I looked. There was a bright yellow Florida Gators T-shirt, LeeVon's size, folded over one of his shoulders, and an equally bright sky-blue Cooter Springs Snappers T-shirt on the other. Underwear still in plastic packets had been tucked discreetly into the blankets, and the rest of the available space was lavished with toys and candies: matchbox cars, licorice sticks, a brand-new baseball, Snickers bars, a child-sized bow and rubber-tipped arrows, bubble gum balls, a hefty metal Slinky, a big Tootsie Roll, a chuffy red dump truck.

Things he would have liked. Things he probably never had.

Sukie said, 'Too bad they don't sell candy cigarettes no more.'

Bonnie Jo said, 'Liam lays eyes on that stuff, he's gonna want it.'

I said, 'I already have a bunch of presents for him and the girls.' I blushed, and had to force myself to meet Sukie's questioning eyes. 'They are your grandchildren, Sukie, I know that, and I know . . .' I knew I ran a risk of offending their pride, both sisters, by helping with expenses, giving them money. But I also knew better than to talk about it. I had other, better communication skills. 'Hold on a minute,' I said, and I hurried into the studio and headed back to them with a pile of sketches. 'Please have a seat.' Once the sisters had settled side by side on the sofa, I handed them the evidence and let them judge. I retreated into the kitchen, where I could hear only murmurs of their conversation, and busied myself excavating things from the freezer to make a dinner of sorts. Pizza rolls, chicken nuggets, garlic bread . . .

'These drawings, can I keep them?' came Sukie's small voice from behind me as I was trying to figure out how to work the oven, as not everything would fit in the microwave.

'Um, sure.' I could make more.

'They're *good*. How did you do them?'

'From memory, she means.' Bonnie Jo, older sister, took charge.

I turned around to face both of them. 'Since the first day I met Chloe and Emma and Liam, I've kind of imprinted on them like a big goose, that's all.'

It was Bonnie Jo who had the perception to demand, 'Why?'

'Because I don't have any grandchildren.' Both serious and smiling, I looked at Sukie. 'I know they're yours, and I will always remember they're yours, but please, could I borrow them and spoil them a little bit occasionally?'

Sukie apparently saw no harm in me, because she said without much hesitation, 'Um, OK.'

Poker-faced, Bonnie Jo added, 'Only if you spoil me, too.'

After supper, I took a sketchbook and some crayons, sat on the sofa and called the children to me, Chloe on one side, Emma on the other and Liam on my lap sucking at the red plastic truck I had given him. (As predicted, he had required pacification after seeing the one in the coffin.) 'I'm going to read you a story that's invisible,' I told them, 'but we'll fix that as we go along.'

Sitting nearby, Sukie and Bonnie Jo looked at each other, their glances like fingers crossing.

'A long time ago, before you were born,' I told the children, 'there was a messed-up monster sort of mama.' As best I could with my arms around Liam, I drew Monster Ma on page one; she looked kind of like one of the Wild Things from the Maurice Sendak book, only in a skirt. 'Messy Monster Ma was sad because nobody loved her. And being sad made her mean.' Quickly, I sketched her on page two trampling flowers and flattening bunnies with her oversized feet. 'She was so mean she didn't think and she made mistakes.' Page three, I drew her trying to pour milk on to her cereal and missing the bowl entirely; the children giggled. 'There was something wrong with her. She wasn't like normal people. Instead of thinking butterflies were pretty, she *ate* them,' I improvised, sketching more pages at top speed, 'and in her house, instead of putting pictures on the wall, she put *road kill*.'

'Ew!' chorused not only the children, but Bonnie Jo and Sukie.

'That was a big mistake, don't you think?'

'Yes!'

'But it wasn't her biggest mistake.' I flipped a page and started drawing Mean Mad Messy Ma cooking at a stove. 'She should have been thinking about what she was doing, but she wasn't, so *totally by mistake* she made three babies!' They looked kind of like Cabbage Patch dolls. I drew them popping up from the cooking pots, comically astonished. The children laughed; good. They knew that the babies in the story had nothing to do with them and the way they had come to be living with their grandmother.

Of the make-believe babies, I said, 'Two of them were girls and one was a boy. Messed-up Ma did not know what to do with them.' I cartooned her juggling three diapered, flying blurs. 'So she gave them pillowcases to wear and she fed them buzzard gizzards and lizard juice—'

'Ewww!'

'Wait a minute.' I flipped back to the page of Monster Ma spilling milk and I lettered *Lizard Juice* on the carton. 'There. See? Lizard Juice.' Returning to the narrative, I drew three round-headed tots in shapeless smocks while I continued, 'And sometimes she sat on them by mistake or dropped them on their heads, and sometimes she just plain forgot about them. She was a Messed-up Monster Ma and she just didn't know how to take care of children. It was sad,' I added, giving the children tearful eyes and tiny drooping mouths. Distancing was one thing; sugar-coating was another. 'But remember, this was a long, long, very long time ago.

And the two girls took care of each other and they're OK.' As I spoke, I drew two taller children hugging each other. 'But the Monster Ma was so mean to the boy that . . . he . . . died.'

There was a shocked silence, and although the scurrying of my crayons across the paper sounded very loud, I did not speak, only drew a sort of sideward cutaway view of a hole in the ground, and in it a stick figure of a body. As I was thinking what to say next, to my surprise Bonnie Jo spoke. 'Ma didn't care much.'

'It was like she broke a doll,' Sukie said.

'But she knew she done wrong, so she took and hid it.'

Nodding agreement, with a maroon crayon I drew rectangles into my diagram, bricks upon bricks, layers of bricks, covering the boy who had died.

Little Emma exclaimed, 'That's the hole in your backyard!'

Liam sucked both his thumb and his red toy truck.

Chloe, with tears in her small voice, said, 'That's LeeVon.'

I said, 'Yes. The bricks made kind of a roof over him, and he lay in the soft dirt for a long, long time. The gentle earth hugged his skin and muscle away so nobody could hurt him anymore. He still had bones left, but bones don't feel pain.'

'And then you found him,' Chloe said. 'And there he is in the box.'

'Yes. All comfy.' I stopped drawing.

'But that's him, too.' Emma pointed a chubby brown finger toward the wall, the portrait, the crayoned aureole of scribble-pictures surrounding it.

'Yes,' I agreed.

'And in the other room and all around here.'

'Yes. Which is why he needs us to give him a funeral tomorrow.'

Chloe sat up straight and demanded, 'What happened to the mean mama?'

I shook my head, smiling down on her ruefully. 'That's another story.'

Late that evening, after Bonnie Jo had taken Sukie and her grandchildren home, I stood beside the coffin looking into wells of indigo shadow, the eyeless orbs of the skull. The day felt satisfactory and complete; no need for a wake. I said, 'Good night, LeeVon. I love you.' Then I went to bed.

*   *   *

My sleep that night felt thin as gauze, stitched with butterfly dreams I could never catch. I was up with the dawn as usual and at once I went looking for LeeVon's presence in my home. Three weeks ago, when I had first known him, he would have trashed the coffin, but I sensed, I believed, I trusted – yes, the casket and its contents were just as I had left them late the night before. Hoping with all my heart for some subtle thing more – a hint, an intimation – I studied the bones, the blankets, the clothing, the candy and toys – but I saw nothing transformed in the slightest.

I found no sign of any overnight activity of LeeVon's in the studio, either, or in any of his usual places. I sighed, and probably would have started worrying about him, but just then somebody knocked at the front door.

What the fandango?

Dressed only in a butt-length sleep shirt, I yelled, 'Just a minute!' and snatched one of my husband's big old cardigans out of the coat closet. Wrapped around my waist, it overlapped, sleeves tied, to cover the more embarrassing parts of me. 'Who is it?'

A rather muffled voice, female, responded with something about delivery.

Delivery? I couldn't remember having ordered anything, yet as always, because I am too short to use a peephole, I opened the door with what I suppose must be called faith.

And I gasped. With delight.

'Flowers!'

The delivery woman's arms were loaded with arrangements in papier-mâché pots, her face obscured by Shasta daisies and larkspur and . . . hollyhocks? I grabbed the nearest bouquet and set it on the floor where I was, and she set three other pots of flowers down beside it. 'There's more,' she said over her shoulder as she headed back out the door.

'From *where*?' I yelped, but she didn't answer. I crouched to hunt the bouquets for a card or message, already beginning to notice how remarkable they were; these were not typical funeral offerings. No big solemn wreaths of lilies or carnations or chrysanthemums. These were . . .

'This is it,' said the delivery woman as she set three more bouquets with the others, making a total of seven.

'Who are they *from*?'

She glanced at her clipboard. 'Berthe Morisot and Mary Cassatt,' she reported. 'No message.' With a perfunctory smile and no apparent curiosity at all, she shut the front door behind her.

I collapsed from my crouch to a seat on the floor, clutching my own chest as if I needed to restrain a swollen heart from busting me wide open. My girls had sent flowers, so many flowers – why so very, overwhelmingly many? Not just roses from the two of them, or, if they couldn't agree, a bouquet apiece, but seven beautiful bouquets?

Seven different arrangements. One was mostly colorful daisies, another was a rainbow of miniature irises, then tiny tea roses mixed with cornflowers, and mini tulips striped like peppermint sticks – my eyes were starting to blur but I saw pompons, buttonflowers, snapdragons, bluebells, even buttercups . . .

Why seven?

Lucky number?

Nothing traditional, nothing big and white. All bright and small. Flowers for a child.

Oh, Cassie. Oh, Maurie. Oh, LeeVon.

'LeeVon, can you see these?' I asked as I carried daisies and irises into the front room and set them down by his coffin. 'Can you smell these?' as I brought in the roses and the bluebells. I felt no sense of his presence, but had I ever, really? Still, placing the plethora of flowers, I decided to keep my irrational and heathenish faith that he was there with me somehow.

I thought of phoning Cassie and Maurie to thank them, but there were other things I more urgently needed to do, such as get dressed. I put on green jeans and my favorite tie-dyed T-shirt. But I hadn't yet managed to choose the perfect pair of novelty socks or get my shoes on when somebody knocked at the door again – a brittle knock I thought I recognized.

I murmured in disbelief, 'Wilma Lou?'

Sure enough, when I answered the door barefooted, there she stood, a faded green housedress draping her desiccated body. That plus the way she cocked her head to ogle me brought to mind a giant preying (praying?) mantis standing on my doorstep clutching a fuchsia armload of crepe myrtle.

'I seed a flower delivery truck,' she chirped, 'and I figured might be you needed some more.'

In other words, she was hawk-eyed curious to know what was going on. But for some reason I didn't mind. It was about time I forgave Wilma Lou for being Wilma Lou. And this was LeeVon's special day; I couldn't be petty. 'Wilma Lou, such beautiful flowers, and they smell so *good*!' I gathered the mass of crepe myrtle from the twiggy woman's arms. 'We're giving my skeleton a funeral today, and I'll make sure to lay your flowers on the grave. Would you like to come in?'

She hesitated. 'Y'all giving the child a Christian burial?'

'Now, Wilma Lou,' I teased with a warm smile, 'what do you think?'

She teetered on my doorstep as if on the cusp of suspicion versus curiosity. Peering past me, she said hopefully, 'You took them animals down off your wall.'

'I'll put them back up afterwards. Or maybe I'll just paint some right on to the wall.'

With no ill will, I hoped she would retreat. I didn't want her to see the skeleton dressed as a boy. If she did, there would be no hope of keeping LeeVon's secret.

'It'll be just a few of us, all barefoot,' I fibbed, flexing my exposed toes, 'for a pantheist funeral.'

It worked; she backed off. 'Y'all have a real blessed day,' she quavered. Then added in a stronger tone, 'I'll pray for you. I been praying for you, anyways. I pray for you all the time.'

'I appreciate that, Wilma Lou. Thank you. And you have a good day too,' I called after her as she scuttled like a hunchbacked insect back toward her own lair.

I chose socks with butterflies on them, and my newest Skechers, which were cerulean blue. There: all set. Back in the front room, I put Wilma Lou's crepe myrtle into a big Pyrex bowl of water and set it with the other flowers, so many, so sweet, filling my heart with motherly warmth, my breathing with fragrance and my mind with an uplifted sensation that is hard to describe, a kind of beatitude. When I heard the first arrival knocking, I all but floated to the door, opened it without a thought and smiled with monk-like serenity into the unexpected face of Detective T.J. Tadlock.

'Good morning!' I sang at her. 'Come in!'

Just by what she wore – a flowing crinkle-cotton Indian-print caftan – I knew that she was here as a person, not a cop. 'This way.' I led her into the front room. 'Have a seat if you like, but we're all going to be standing around the coffin soon.'

I'm not sure she even heard me. She was already standing beside the open coffin with her head bowed, her homely face very still.

Wondering what she was thinking, I watched her until someone else knocked at the door. I should have known Coroner Wengleman would show up. 'Marcia!' Impulsively, I hugged her, and she hugged me back.

'I wanted to bring you a sympathy card,' she told me, 'but I couldn't find one that was even remotely appropriate.'

Bonnie Jo and Sukie arrived with the kids, bringing me more hugs, even from little Liam. I herded everybody inside, and without prompting they all gathered around LeeVon, sharing space as best they could, the kids in front with their hands on the coffin rim and their solemn little faces looking over.

'Since there's nobody else who could possibly show up,' I said, 'I guess it's time.'

Detective T.J. Tadlock and Dr Marcia Wengleman glanced questions at me, so I explained, 'There's no ceremony planned. We're just here to, um, talk to LeeVon.'

'I'll start,' Bonnie Jo said in the strongest voice I had ever heard from her. 'LeeVon,' she told him to his skullbone face, 'it's OK to hate Ma's guts. What she done to you was just plain mean low-down evil and don't nobody expect you to forgive her. I hate her too.'

'So do I,' said Sukie. 'I hate her more for what she done to you than for anything she ever done to me or Bonnie Jo.'

'I wish we could have done something . . .'

Bonnie Jo's voice faltered but Marcia spoke up. 'You were all just babies. None of you deserved for such an awful thing to happen. None of you could have changed anything and none of you is to blame.' She spoke quite naturally to the boy in the coffin; I wondered whether she often talked to the dead people she encountered. 'But, LeeVon, that was all a long time ago. Even when a person can't forgive, they can still move on.'

'You was the best big brother I ever had.' Sukie spoke with a quirk in her voice. 'I don't care how much you pulled my hair.'

All three children swiveled to look up at her. Emma squeaked, 'He pulled your hair?'

'Of course he did. But he could throw a brick farther than any of us.'

'Throw a *brick*?'

Chloe said to the bones in the coffin, 'Never mind, LeeVon. I bet if you'd growed up, you'd have been as nice as my gramma.'

'LeeVon,' said the voice I least expected – T.J.'s. 'It really was a long time ago. Now your ma is so old, she's the one who wets the bed. And people get mad at her. And she's so nasty that nobody loves her. And maybe nobody ever did. So what goes around comes around. The important thing is your sisters love you.'

'And you know I do too, LeeVon,' I told him. 'And as much as I'd miss you, I have a big, halacious, ginormous hope for you. I hope that right here, now, today, you'll be able to leave. I don't know whether you're still hanging around my house or whether you've already gotten back together with your bones, but that's what I want you to do. Because I love you, I want you to let go of the bad memories and just have some peace.'

Bonnie Jo said, 'That's what I want too, LeeVon.'

'Me, too, LeeVon,' said Sukie.

'We're all praying for you, LeeVon,' said Marcia.

Chloe and Emma both said at the same time, 'Amen.'

So I was a heathen – so what? I almost felt as if I might conceivably pray, what with the aroma of flowers like a magic carpet of scent uplifting me, caressing my mind; how I loved my daughters, and how good of them to send flowers, not just token flowers but so many so perfect all the way, not holding back. This was no time for holding back. LeeVon needed us.

Except for the children, we all looked at each other, forming a silent consensus: yes, we had done our best.

I glanced out the window. I thought I had heard Nick drive in, and yes, there he was, sitting in his truck. I said, 'Excuse me,' went and hailed him from the front door, and in he came, solemn in his best blue jeans, reverent in work boots. I noticed he avoided looking into the coffin as he passed it to where the lid awaited him.

Liam wailed, 'Don't put away the candy! I want the candy!' and started to bawl.

T.J. scooped him up, said, 'Hey, you can play with my badge,' and carried him outside. The rest of us stood taking a last teary-eyed look at LeeVon as Nick lifted the coffin lid so that he could fit it in place and fasten the hasps.

Absently, almost unconsciously, like a mother checking on a child, I glanced up at LeeVon's portrait on the wall to see how he was doing.

His painted, tearful eyes met mine – no, far more: they looked at me and into me, trying to tell me something. And I gasped, because again I felt a nearly tangible connection between us, as if one of us had thrown a lifeline.

Rescue . . .

So that he could save my measly career?

Really?

Such bullshit, and I yawped, 'Wait!' to stop Nick before he could close the casket. Dear earth-water airy deity of us all, I had almost blown it. LeeVon was the child, I was the mother. It wasn't his job to save me, my pride, my pitiful ego; it was my job to save *him*.

Turning so abruptly I almost stumbled, I reached up, lifted LeeVon's portrait down from the wall, took it gently in both hands like an offering, and laid it in the casket, face up, on top of his chest.

There were murmurs, and someone started to say, 'Beverly, you don't have to—'

I stopped hearing; I only gazed, and I gasped, because I saw that the tears were gone from those eyes I had painted. And I wasn't the only one gasping, because all the colorful, waxy airplanes, tractors, firecrackers, pickup trucks, watermelons, speed-boats, frogs, ice-cream yellow dogs and everything else LeeVon had crayoned around himself – all of those bright wax pictures peeled their filmy selves off the wall and lilted through the air; they flitted over to him like the most delicate of lacewings or falling leaves, wafting down to settle on him. Some landed as random and lovely as butterflies on his skull, softening its harsh bones into . . . transcendence.

LeeVon. LeeVon!

No more tears.

I stood gazing, so transfixed I could scarcely move or breathe, but I urgently needed to speak, because I thought I had heard a scream. 'Bonnie Jo, don't you dare run away.'

'I'm right here.' Her voice sounded as choked as mine.

'Ooooh, *pretty*,' breathed one of the little girls.

'He done it,' whispered Sukie. 'Looks like he gone and done it.'

And I, of all people, said, 'Amen.'

TWENTY-NINE

After that, the burial felt like no big deal, just comfortable, as if we were tucking LeeVon into bed. The only one of us who couldn't quite deal was Nick Crickens. He loaded the coffin and the flowers into his pickup in a rush and was already leaving the potter's field by the time the rest of us got there.

We circled around silently, watched the county maintenance men lower the coffin into the grave with a hoist. Then they stood back, waiting.

I stepped forward, took a handful of earth and tossed it down on to the coffin. People say that makes the saddest sound, but I felt as if I'd thrown a coin into a wishing well. I blurted, 'Please be at peace, LeeVon.'

Bonnie Jo went next, and then Sukie and the kids. Silently, she watched the maintenance men lower the coffin into the grave with a hoist, watched as each of the women and children in turn took a handful of earth and tossed it down on to the coffin as if throwing a coin into a wishing well, and their wishes were 'Peace, LeeVon' and 'Love always, LeeVon' and 'Bye, LeeVon!' But no one wanted to leave. We all waited as the county workers filled the grave and mounded the earth over it. Then we arranged the flowers on top of it, so many flowers that they completely blanketed it like a colorful quilt, a puffy comforter made of blossoms.

*   *   *

T.J. found herself hanging around by the graveside even though
Marcia hugged everyone and left. The kids zoomed away and ran
circles around the graveyard. But Beverly, Sukie and Bonnie walked
up to T.J. as if they thought she was hanging around for a reason.

'I have no agenda,' she told them. 'More than anything, I'm
just remembering my Nana.'

Bonnie Jo asked, 'Could you please forget what you know about
my brother and my mother?'

T.J. hesitated. She was a cop.

A homicide detective. It was her job to close cold cases.

And closing one this cold would sure look good on her stats.

But . . .

But she hesitated only for a heartbeat. 'No worries,' T.J. said.
'You didn't give me a statement.' The time spent on the case had
not been wasted, not when it had brought her here to this place,
these people. 'Anyhow, your mother is unfit to be interrogated.'

'I'll say,' Bonnie Jo agreed.

Sukie asked, 'You won't be bothering me none?'

'Nope. This case is going nowhere.'

Beverly said nothing at all, just gave T.J. a massive hug.

I invited the Ferees back to my house afterward, for cookies and
coffee and strudel cake and peach cobbler. And I was glad to have
their company. The moment I walked inside, I felt as if I had
stepped into an echo chamber of what was gone, an absence
extending far beyond the house.

Listening to a silence I'd never noticed before, I stopped just
inside the kitchen door. Bonnie Jo and Sukie stood there with me,
but the kids darted between our legs and ran on in to where they
knew cookies and cake awaited them at the table right next to the
studio.

'Hey!' Chloe exclaimed, her voice carrying to us clearly
although we could not see her, 'there ain't no handprints on the
wall no more!'

'They all gone!' called Emma.

I gasped, inhaling the implications, then hurried in to see for
myself. I blinked almost as if I were viewing a catastrophe. The
walls of my studio stood as virginally beige as when I had first
seen them, the ceiling was equally pristine eggshell white, and not

only were the handprints gone – all of LeeVon's art had vanished also. His angry flaming bathtubs, his stormy soaked beds, his broken, weeping, fiery hearts – all gone except that, oddly, the blank sheets of paper remained behind, good as new.

Behind me, Bonnie Jo and Sukie stood staring, like me, at what wasn't there. I turned to them, babbling, 'Paint doesn't just come off walls without leaving a mess. Paint doesn't just lift itself out of the fibers of paper. It's impossible. It's transcendence.'

Bonnie Jo nodded slowly. 'He really done it.'

Sukie said, 'He's all the way gone.'

'He's not hurting anymore,' I said. 'He's totally at peace now. I'm so – so proud of him, and—' And I meant to say I was happy for him, which I was. Very. Yet what I actually said was 'I miss him.' Silly tears escaped from my eyes.

Bonnie Jo hugged me, and Sukie, both of them. I hugged back, wiped the tears away, and said, 'I'm all right.'

'Damn straight,' said Bonnie Jo, and Sukie said, 'Beverly, don't you never even think of being lonely. You call me or come see the brats any time, night or day, you hear me? My grandkids are your grandkids too, from here on out.'

Cassie picked up her phone to hear her sister demand without even a hi-how-are-you, 'Did you hear from Mom?'

'Hello to you, too, Berthe. How's the pedagogy going?'

'Fine, and how are the gluten-free boysenberry muffins? Did you *hear* from her?'

'About ten minutes ago. She sounded completely normal—'

'*Normal?* She told me the crayon drawings flew off the wall and joined the picture in the casket!'

'Yeah, what a bummer,' Cassie said with feeling. 'I really wanted to exhibit that portrait for her.'

Maurie all but screamed, 'Sis, are you purposely being obtuse? I'm worried about Mom! This whole thing sounds insane!'

'It is insane, but Mom's not. Listen, Maurie' – her saying 'Maurie' instead of 'Berthe' conveyed her compassion – 'Mom sounds totally sure of herself, in control, satisfied she has handled whatever this weirdness was all about. And it's over. Her ghost is gone. And I've never heard her sound more . . .' Cassie hesitated, trying to come up with the right word: not just calm, serene, tranquil, but something with a quiet joy in it that went above and beyond most people's experience.

Maurie didn't wait for the transcendent word Cassie was seeking. 'Yes, she's completely cogent and coherent,' Maurie admitted. 'I'm the one who's freaking out.'

'Noooo. Really?'

'Oh, give me a break.' In her crabby way, Maurie sounded better. 'Did Mom tell you about the tree?'

'Yes, she—'

'Never mind,' Maurie interrupted; she was indeed freaking out. 'I don't want to talk about it; I'm out of here. Take care of yourself, sis. Bye.'

Cassie smiled at the phone and put it away. It would take Berthe a few days to assimilate Mom's news; so what was new? Relatively speaking, things were copacetic. Alone but far from lonely in her matronly fieldstone house-cum-cafe, Cassie reclined to the max in her venerable La-Z-Boy, closed her eyes and replayed Mom's phone call once more in her mind.

Mom was going to do a portrait of Chloe next, then one of Emma, and Liam when he was a bit older. Whether the artwork would come to the cafe, stay with Mom or go to the children's grandmother was irrelevant to Cassie. Mom had found herself a life.

Mom was going to buy *Harold and the Purple Crayon* to read aloud to the children, and *Goodnight Moon* and *Where the Wild Things Are*, and all the best books for kids to fall in love with. And she was going to play Chutes and Ladders with them on rainy days and plant a garden with them on sunny ones, and they were going to spray each other with the water hose and get soaking wet and climb trees.

Editing that thought, Cassie removed her mother from The Tree and placed the children in it instead, with Mom watching them climb.

Mom had told Cassie about The Capital-T Tree with such awe in her voice that Cassie wondered whether Mom was beginning to believe in miracles or deity or something of the sort after all. The Tree had appeared in Mom's backyard on the day of LeeVon's farewell, a magnolia that looked as if it could have been there for fifty years or so, standing where the 'duck pond' had been – no trace of bricks or excavation remained – spreading its glossy leaves in the slanting late-day light. On the day of the funeral, Mom had walked out there and discovered it after everybody else was gone, around sunset. She had stood a long time looking up at it – a big, buxom magnolia in full bloom – noticing that its pearlescent white blossoms did not nestle the way most other blossoms did. Mom had said the flowers perched on the branches, big and bold, looking like cream-colored birds in sunset's aureate light. Looking like milk-white doves, ready to fly away.